STEF

CU00867302

Stephen Edger was born in Darlington and raised in London but has lived in Southampton since studying law at University over a decade ago. He is one of the most exciting thriller writers to emerge in the UK and his debut novel *Integration* was met with acclaim on its release in June 2011.

Stephen and his wife Hannah celebrated the birth of their first daughter in November 2010 and it was the early morning wake up calls that enabled him to find the time to write. Stephen has worked in financial services for a decade and it is his detailed understanding of this industry that adds authenticity to his work.

Snatched is the latest work to leave his pen and looks set to reach similar heights to *Integration*, *Remorse*, and *Redemption*. Stephen regularly tweets about his work on Twitter.com and can be followed as @StephenEdger

Learn more by visiting www.stephenedger.com

STEPHEN EDGER

Snatched

Copyright © 2011 Stephen Edger

ISBN-13: 978-1480065550
ISBN-10: 1480065552

THANK YOU

This is my opportunity to say a big 'Thank You' to those who have helped / inspired me to write and have given helpful ideas and feedback on this story. You know who you are.

But special thanks this time around needs to go to Marina Dear, Hannah Edger, Jo Taylor and Tim Ford for proof reading my final draft, reminding me not to use hyphens and semicolons so frequently and for pointing out when I just don't make sense.

I would also like to recognise Alan Brindley and Fran Burke for recommending the title 'Snatched' at a time when I was considering several possibilities.

Final thanks should go to everyone who downloaded or purchased a paperback copy of *Integration*, *Redemption* or *Remorse*. It has truly inspired me to continue writing and to tell the stories that run through my imagination every day.

Until the next time, keep reading!

Prologue

'Where's mummy?' thought the little girl in the red coat, as she stood quietly next to the railings; her hood pulled up over her shoulder-length blonde hair to keep her dry from the intrusive and cold, wet raindrops. It had been raining most of the day, which had meant the class had not been allowed outside at break-time. She didn't like the rain as it stopped her from playing and having fun with her best friends. 'Stupid rain,' she thought to herself.

The little girl's name was Natalie Barrett and she had been stood in the same spot for the last twenty minutes, waiting for one of her parents to arrive and take her home. It would probably be her mummy, as it was rare that her daddy came and collected her, and it wasn't the first time she had been left, waiting to be collected. She knew she should probably go and wait inside the door of the school, so that her teacher knew she was still there, but then mummy would get into trouble and Natalie would be told off for getting mummy into trouble with the school again. Natalie didn't like it when daddy shouted at her. 'No,' she resolved; she would stay where she was and wait for mummy's white car to pull up.

Natalie looked back over her shoulder, towards the window of her classroom. She could see Miss Jenson stood, pinning some pictures to a large notice board at the far side of the room. Natalie liked Miss Jenson. She was a really lovely teacher, never really got cross and started every day with a smile. Natalie hoped she would grow up to be as friendly as Miss Jenson. Natalie wondered why Miss Jenson wasn't married yet as she would be a great wife and mummy. That's what Natalie thought anyway. Miss Jenson was much nicer than Natalie's mummy.

Natalie liked coming to school every day. She was friends with almost every girl in her class and some of the boys as well. She always tried to be good and worked hard on every piece of work she was given. Earlier that day, Miss Jenson had read them a story and had then asked them to all write a story of their own. Natalie had thought hard about it and had chosen to write about a brave knight who fought a dragon, so that he could rescue a princess in her castle. Miss Jenson had collected all the children's stories, so that she could read them, and had then asked them to all paint a picture of the story that they had written. Natalie liked it when they painted. Miss Jenson always told her she painted good pictures.

Natalie had painted a large grey tower in the middle of her page and a big green dragon, with fire coming out of his nose, to the left. She had then tried to paint a knight on a horse to the right of the tower but it had looked more like a man on a dog, than a knight on a horse. When everyone had finished their painting Miss Jenson made each of the class come to the front and read out their story while she held the paintings up. Miss Jenson had said that Natalie's story was very good and she had given Natalie a gold star to stick to the painting. Natalie smiled as she thought about that gold star. It was the fourth gold star she had received this term, which was more than any other child in the class. Natalie had asked if she could take her painting home to show her mummy, but Miss Jenson had said she wanted to stick it on the wall of the classroom but that it could be taken home at the end of term.

Natalie didn't know what time it was, but she knew that mummy was very late today, as the lady in the yellow coat with the 'STOP' sign was packing up to go home. Natalie looked to her left and then to her right, to check if mummy's car was anywhere nearby but she could not see it. She wondered why mummy was late again. She hoped it wasn't because mummy and daddy had been fighting. They had been arguing a lot recently, ever since Uncle Jimmy had come to stay with them. She wished her mummy and daddy would stop fighting. Natalie looked to her left again and tried to picture in her mind where her house was. She knew that when mummy collected her, they drove down the road and turned left at the end. Then there was a long road with shops on the right-hand side and houses on the left that went on and on. About halfway up the road, they turned right and drove down a road, past the secondary school, until they reached the leisure centre, where she sometimes went swimming. Her house was on the road to the right of the leisure centre and she knew her house was number 46.

Natalie knew she was supposed to wait for her mummy to come and collect her, but if daddy found out that mummy had forgotten to pick her up, he would be angry and would probably shout at mummy again. Natalie didn't want daddy to be cross with mummy, so she decided she would walk home. She knew she would have to be careful, and would have to wait for the green man before crossing the road, but she was confident she could find her way. Mummy and daddy would be so pleased to see that she had managed to walk home by herself.

Natalie looked around for Miss Jenson once more but could not see her through the classroom window. She could just about see the picture of her tower and dragon hung to the notice board where Miss Jenson had been stood, moments earlier. She smiled, as she thought about that gold star again, before turning and walking up the road. She started to hum to herself as she walked.

She had only made it a hundred yards when a car, as red as her coat, pulled up and the man behind the wheel opened his window and called out to her. The sudden noise made Natalie jump, but as she turned, she recognised the face of the man behind the open window. He asked her where she was going and she told him she was walking home. He asked her where her mummy and daddy were and she lied, saying they were at home and knew she was walking. She felt bad about lying to the man, but then she didn't want to get mummy and daddy into trouble with the school or the police.

The man asked if she lived nearby and she said she lived near the leisure centre. He said he knew where that was and asked if she would like a lift home in his car. She told him that she was not supposed to accept lifts from strangers. He smiled nicely at her and told her that her mummy had asked him to drive her home. The man said she should get in the car, as she was getting wet in the rain. He opened the door for her and she got in.

She noticed that the seat was very soft and comfortable and the car was quite warm inside. The car was much bigger than mummy's car and she wondered why daddy didn't have a car like this. The man asked her to fasten her seat belt and pulled away from the kerb. She wasn't allowed to sit in the front seat of mummy's car, so this was quite a treat. The man asked her if she wanted to listen to the radio and she said she did, so he turned it on and she began to hum along to the song that was playing.

Natalie checked that he knew where the leisure centre was, and he said that he did and smiled warmly again. She smiled back and he told her that she looked very pretty when she smiled. He was such a nice man. He told her that she could probably become a model when she was older. She told him she wanted to become a teacher like Miss Jenson, or maybe a writer. He smiled again and said they were also good jobs and that she would probably make a very good teacher. This pleased Natalie and she smiled again.

Natalie saw through the man's window that he had driven past the road with the secondary school on it and she told him he had missed the road. He said, 'Whoops,' but that he knew a different road that would bring them back around to the leisure centre. She said, 'Phew,' and began to hum along to the music again. The man pulled a white paper bag out of his coat pocket and passed it to her. She opened the bag and saw that it was full of brown toffees, like her grandpa used to give to her. The man told her she could have a toffee, for being such a good girl. She told him mummy didn't let her eat sweets before dinner, but he said one toffee wouldn't hurt, and they could keep it a secret between them; mummy didn't need to know.

Natalie removed a toffee and handed the bag back to the nice man. She placed it in her mouth and began to suck it. It tasted sweet, but was too hard to chew and she knew she would need to keep sucking it until it softened. She did like toffees.

As Natalie continued to look out of the window, at the stupid rain, falling against the glass, she suddenly felt very tired and covered her mouth, to hide her yawn from the man. She didn't want him to think she might fall asleep before she got home. She continued to look at the rain drops and could feel her eyelids starting to close. She tried to fight the wave of fatigue, as it enveloped her, but it was a fight she wasn't going to win. The last thing she remembered was the man telling her it was okay if she wanted a quick nap before they reached their destination.

And then she was asleep, away in a world full of fairies, dragons, knights and princesses, where good always overcomes evil; the lost innocence of a child's imagination. She didn't see the man behind the steering wheel turn off the road and head in the opposite direction to her house.

MONDAY

1

Sarah Jenson slumped into her chair and let out a sigh of satisfaction: it was lunchtime! The children would be out in the playground for the next hour, and although she still had a hundred and one things to do, she would at least have twenty minutes when she could eat her lunch and have a well-deserved sit down. It had been a hectic morning, but then every day, teaching Year 2 primary school children, was hectic!

So far today, they had spent an hour looking at and learning to say the numbers twenty-one to thirty, and this had been followed by an hour of learning and singing a song for a forthcoming assembly. The assembly was themed as 'springtime', and the Headteacher had tasked the Year 2s with performing "Morning has broken" to start the assembly. Sarah had been teaching the children a verse per week, for the last month, by making them sing the verse every other day, while she played the background music through her MP3 player. They had already mastered the first verse and could sing this without reading the words, but the second verse was proving trickier, and several of the less-bright children were muddling the lines of the verses. But Sarah had always been a fighter and she would persevere with it until they could all sing, without reading the words.

The final half an hour of the class had been spent looking at different foods and identifying them, using

French names. Teaching modern languages was not a mandatory part of Key Stage 1 Learning, but the school preferred the children to receive an insight into other languages, even in Year 2. It was part of the reason Sarah had opted to join St Monica's Primary School in Southampton. Sarah, herself, had a degree in Modern Languages and was semi-fluent in both French and Spanish, and she believed that the sooner a child grasps an acceptance of alternative languages and cultures, the better. It had been an interactive lesson. Sarah had instructed the children to bring in one item of food from home each. Most had brought in a tin of something their mother's had found at the back of the cupboard that they were never likely to eat in the future. The class would then learn the name of each food item. Sarah had brought in a large baguette and a selection of French cheeses and had shared the food out with the children. Most had said they did not like the smell of the Camembert or the Roquefort, but the Roulé had gone down a treat.

Sarah stood, from her slouched position, and surveyed the battle-site that was her classroom. There were chairs left pushed out during the mad rush to the door, when the bell had sounded. There were also cheese and bread crumbs on the tables, as well as various pieces of stationery; scattered on the floor, including pencils and erasers. The official school cleaners would not be around until four o'clock when all the children had left for the day, so Sarah knew that if she didn't attempt to get things straight now, it would only get worse. She quickly collected up the stationery items and wiped the tables down with a damp cloth, systematically pushing in the wayward chairs as she went. Within five minutes the place was looking in a much more reasonable state.

Sarah returned to the chair she had been sitting in earlier, behind her large teacher's desk, and fished out a plastic tub of pasta from her handbag. It was the previous night's left-over Lasagne, but Sarah didn't mind as she quite enjoyed cold pasta. Besides, she would need the carbohydrates as the next class was P.E. This afternoon, they were scheduled to be in the main assembly hall, which doubled as a gymnasium with various climbing and vaulting apparatus hinged to the walls. It would take about ten minutes to set it up so she would have to start preparing, before the school bell sounded again, to indicate the return of the class.

Sarah happily munched on her pasta and allowed her mind to wander, but a thought kept niggling at her brain. Natalie Barrett had not come to school this morning and no phone call had been received from the parents to indicate why. Natalie was such a bright girl and something of a star pupil for Sarah. It didn't matter what task Natalie was given to do, she always managed to deliver, at a standard higher than her peers. She had a particular talent for creative writing and art, and Sarah had very high hopes for her going on to become something great in the world. It wasn't unusual for Natalie to be absent from school as there had been a couple of times already this year when her parents had excluded her from school, because of some kind of domestic dispute. It amazed Sarah how such a smart young girl could ever have come from two such parents. Sarah wasn't a snob but she definitely considered herself higher up in the evolutionary food-chain than Mr and Mrs Barrett.

It was a shame that Natalie had missed the French

class, as in previous lessons she had shown she had a real aptitude for modern languages and was already demonstrating ability with pronunciation. The lesson probably would have gone much smoother, as well, as some of the other children seemed to look up to Natalie and performed better in lessons when Natalie was on-form. She was such a sweet girl, kind to all her classmates and even at this age it was clear she was going to be popular with the boys when she reached secondary school. She was a pleasure to teach and subconsciously Sarah hoped that if she were to become a mother herself, one day, she would have a child as advanced and well-adjusted as Natalie Barrett.

Sarah's eyes wandered to the large notice-board, which was currently displaying the children's stories and paintings from Friday afternoon. Most had written stories about talking animals; such was the current cinema-craze to produce computer-animated films about fluffy, talking creatures. One boy, Anthony, had pretty much plagiarised the plot to *Monsters Inc.* for his story, and his painting of a large, turquoise coloured blob was clearly his interpretation of Sulley from the film.

The painting that stood out so vividly now was of a princess trapped in a grey tower by a fire-breathing dragon. It was the picture that Natalie had painted to accompany her story. It wasn't uncommon for little girls to write stories about princesses, but something in the story had struck a chord with Sarah, and it had her wondering if there was anything more to it than just a child's vivid imagination. Sarah had taken a psychology course as an element of her teaching degree, and was aware of studies that explained how children would often associate scary episodes of their lives as evil creatures in stories and it had made Sarah wonder just who the dragon in Natalie's story could be. Clearly it was something or somebody that scared Natalie, as indicated by the flames protruding from the dragon's nose. Sarah remembered common experiences that traumatised children, included abusive parents, fears of family separation and dangerous animals. Sarah had no idea which of these possible scenarios, if indeed any, applied to Natalie. Sarah determined at that point that she would raise her concerns at the next parents' evening, due in a fortnight.

Sarah glanced up at the clock above the noticeboard and saw that it was nearly time for the children to return from their break, so she quickly put her empty plastic lunch tub back in her handbag and threw away the disposable, plastic fork she had been using. She glanced down at her phone and saw that she had missed a call from her partner Erin, a detective in the local police force. Erin had not left a voice message, so Sarah figured it probably hadn't been an important call. She considered whether she should phone her back, but decided she needed to start setting up the apparatus in the assembly hall, so she put the mobile back in her handbag and grabbed her gym clothes, which consisted of a pair of pink jogging bottoms and a white t-shirt. Sarah was only thirty and had worked hard, to keep her body in a slim and reasonable shape, with a carefully balanced diet and regular evening trips to the gym. Her latest buzz was for *Zumba* and she had been attending a weekly class for the past three months. She was due to be attending a class that evening, but had already made plans to spend the evening with Erin instead, so she would have to book in an extra exercise session later in the week. Sarah quickly changed into her clothes and headed for the hall.

2

A large group of about fifteen men in creased shirts, with their sleeves rolled up, stood in an office that was twice as long as it was wide. It was lined with wooden desks, each topped with a computer. Damp patches beneath the men's armpits revealed the extent of their perspiration and also explained the whiff of BO circling the room at nose-level. Amidst the testosterone-fuelled creatures were the occasional, soft features of a woman.

At the front of the throng, stood an average-sized man; he was in a white shirt, the sleeves rolled up to his elbows, with a dark blue tie, loosened to accentuate his masculinity. His hairy forearms made him look only one evolutionary step ahead of Neanderthal man. He was pacing backwards and forwards, with the occasional wave of an arm and raised inflection in his voice. He had jet black hair but only at the sides. A few stray hairs remained to cover his otherwise, bald head. To make up for the lack of hair on his head, he had a full, bushy, black moustache. He was a man's man, or at least, that's what he told himself. His seniority in the room ensured nobody else disagreed.

Behind the pacing man were three dry-wipe boards. On the first was scrawled in big black letters, 'What happened?' On the second board was scrawled, 'What we know?' and on the final board was the word, 'Theories?' This was one of several Major Incident rooms at the recently-opened Police Headquarters in the centre of Southampton. The name of the man addressing the sweaty crowd was Detective Inspector Jack Vincent, though he pronounced it 'Vin-sent' with the emphasis on the second syllable.

The wooden desks formed an unconventional frame to the room but the layout was perfect for briefing sessions like this one, allowing the officers to perch on each other's desks and face the speaker. The office had been set up this way at Vincent's request as he liked to have everybody's attention when he was leading a briefing. He had his own personal office, the entrance to which was just over his left shoulder, and from there he had a window into the Major Incident room where the rest of his team worked. He liked to be able to watch them work. It was why he made sure he was the first to arrive every morning and almost always the last one to leave every night. He felt he had a duty to lead by example and that meant putting more hours into his daily toil than his colleagues.

The Police Headquarters were on the edge of the city centre and from the room they were stood in, they had a perfect view of the Southampton docks, where trade boats and cruise ships would arrive and depart daily. The view served as a reminder that there was a big world of crime out there and they, as a team, were an integral cog in the justice-delivering machine and was duty-bound to provide protection to the residents of Southampton. To most of the men stood before him now, it was just a nicely-spaced office with a sea-view. That's why he was the boss and they were his officers, Vincent told himself: they couldn't see the bigger picture like him.

The windows to the office were flanked by

wooden-slatted Venetian blinds and due to how new all the furniture and machinery was, from certain angles, the office could have been straight out of an IKEA catalogue. This was even truer, given that the local Swedish furniture store was under five minutes' drive from where they were based and had, indeed, been the first port of call for most of the items in the room. There had been a budget to spend and Vincent had made sure it was fully spent.

On the dry-wipe board labelled, 'What we know' were several A4-sized photographs; some of the photos were in colour but a couple were black and white. The black and white photographs revealed the face of a man in his late thirties with dark, wispy hair and a hang-dog expression synonymous with mug-shots. Below the photograph was written the name, 'Neil Barrett' in the same black ink as the board's title. Beneath these two photographs were two colour photographs of a young, smiling face with long, flowing, blond hair. The smile was etched from cheek to cheek and had been taken on the child's seventh birthday, just a couple of months earlier. The name under this image was 'Natalie Barrett.' The innocence of the shot was in stark contrast to the furrowed brow of Vincent as he continued to address the listening army before him. The final photograph was of a school building with large blue gates protecting the building behind them.

'So as I have said, this is a really important case for us,' continued Vincent, making eye contact with a select few individuals to show he was speaking directly to each of them. 'There is going to be a lot of pressure on us from the local media and inevitably the national press within days if we don't make a break quickly. You are here because you have the best detective-brains in Hampshire, and because I have chosen you to solve this case. Are you with me?'

There were a few positive murmurs from the group.

'I said are you with me?' repeated Vincent, louder this time.

'Yes,' was the group's harmonious response.

'Good,' said Vincent, pleased that his little pep talk had done its job. 'Now, D.C. Cooke was the first on scene when the call was made early on Saturday morning. Cookie, if you'd like to tell everyone what we know so far?' said Vincent taking a couple of steps to the side so that he was stood next to the first board.

A woman in a grey trouser suit with a white blouse shuffled off the desk she had been perched on. She was, by no means a large-framed woman, but she was certainly no push-over either. She emitted the air that you wouldn't want to get on the wrong side of her in the wrong place but her soft face and striking cheek bones were not in keeping with her muscular arms and betrayed her feminine wiles. D.C. Erin Cooke, or 'Cookie', to her friends, and colleagues, moved to the front of the office where Vincent had been stood moments earlier, in preparation to address the crowd.

'Okay,' she said smiling, and taking a breath, 'The little girl in the photograph behind me is Natalie Barrett. She is the seven year-old daughter of Neil and Melanie Barrett of Sholing. She was due to be collected from school on Friday afternoon but when her mother arrived at the school there was no sign of Natalie. The Barretts checked with neighbours and Natalie's friends but none could confirm that they had seen or heard from Natalie. The Barretts went out walking the streets on Friday night to no avail and contacted us in the early hours of Saturday morning, when she still had not arrived home. As per standard policy, a statement was taken from the Barretts by the local uniforms and the case was then passed to the weekend duty C.I.D. I met and spoke with Mr and Mrs Barrett to confirm some details about Natalie.'

Erin paused and swivelled her hips so that she was half-looking at the whiteboard with the photographs.

'We know she was wearing a bright red coat, probably with the hood pulled up, as it was raining on Friday afternoon. Now, her mother was due to collect her at three p.m., when the school day ended, but was stuck in an appointment and did not arrive at the school until nearly four. Mrs Barrett is a self-employed nail technician and was at one of her client's houses in Lordshill and was late arriving because of heavy traffic. Uniforms have verified, with the client, that Mrs Barrett left Lordshill at two fifty-five on Friday.'

Cookie leaned closer to the board and pointed at the mug shot of Neil Barrett.

'Neil Barrett was arrested for possession of marijuana five years ago, and spent three months inside for intent to deal, but from what we know has otherwise been clean ever since. Local uniform have been called to the Barrett residence, by neighbours, a couple of times in the last three months to break up some arguments. No violence has been recorded in any of the reports but this is an angle we should probably take a look at.'

'Where was the father at the time?' asked one of the group, before blowing his nose on a stale and used handkerchief from his pocket.

'Neil Barrett is a mechanic and claims he was on a call-out at the time,' replied Erin. 'We are waiting to get hold of the garage's records to locate the name of the person whose car broke down. We should be able to confirm one way or another in a couple of hours.'

'What's the kid like?' came the voice of another sweaty shirt.

'She's very bright from what the Barretts have told us. She doesn't get into trouble, has never run away from home before and is a regular at St. Monica's Primary, where she was last seen.' Cookie paused for breath to ensure there were no other immediate questions. 'Mrs Barrett has admitted she has been late collecting Natalie in the past, but that her daughter knows not to walk home or to talk to strangers, so her disappearance is very out of character. Sir?' said Erin to indicate that Vincent would now continue the briefing.

'Thank you Cookie,' he said, as she returned to where she had been stood earlier, and he moved back to the front of the group. 'Uniforms will be doing door-to-door enquiries of the houses and shops between the school and the Barrett's house today to see if anyone saw her walking or being approached by anyone out of the ordinary. I want half of you to join them.'

There was a large groan let out from the crowd.

'Look,' continued Vincent, growing impatient, 'I know none of us like knocking on doors, but we need everyone to put personal taste to one side and get involved. The other half of you are to go and interview all known sex offenders in Southampton. The register is in my office and I will speak further with those after the briefing. I want you to also make contact with your snitches and ruffle some feathers. Somebody knows what has happened to this little girl and I want you to find out.'

'Are we certain it's not the parents?' asked the man who had blown his nose earlier. 'You know like that family up north a couple of years ago, doing it for the publicity and the money?'

'We cannot be certain of anything at the moment, and we shouldn't rule anything out. Cookie will go and interview the Barretts again with me today and we'll explore that avenue. In child abduction cases, the first seventy two hours are the most critical.'

Vincent glanced up at the wall clock to his right before continuing, 'Because of the weekend, we are already in the sixty-ninth hour and have no clues as to what has happened to this little girl. Now, get out there and let's crack this case. You're dismissed.'

The crowd hopped up off the desks and started milling around. Some headed for the door, in need of an urgent nicotine and caffeine burst, others moved to their desks and started placing calls, whilst a couple went to the boards to take a closer look at the photographs.

'Cookie?' said Vincent, calling her over. I'm meeting with the Headteacher at the school in twenty minutes and then I'll be speaking to Natalie's teacher. You should come with me. It's going to come as a shock and hopefully your relationship with the school will help smooth things out and help us get to the facts sooner.'

'My relationship with the school?' she questioned.

'That's right,' said Vincent, smiling reassuringly. 'Natalie was in Sarah's class. Your girlfriend may have been the last person to see her.'

<u>3</u>

The school bell sounded and was followed by the inevitable scraping of chair legs on the tiled floor as twenty-three children simultaneously stood up. They grabbed at the school bags that had been sitting in front of them for the last ten minutes, whilst Sarah had read them a story.

'Okay, that's today complete,' she told them, shouting over the din. 'Well done for all your hard work today. Have a good night and I will see you all in the morning.'

The children all made their way towards the single door that led out to where their coats were hanging up and then out of the exit door. In all, it took under three minutes for there to be complete silence and Sarah found herself stood alone, surveying the mess before her. In fairness, it didn't look as bad as it had done at lunchtime, but there were still a few stray chairs that had failed to find themselves back under the table. Not that it mattered, as Sarah was going to have to pick them all up off the floor and stand them on the tables to allow the cleaners to come in and sweep and mop the floors. In truth, it was Sarah's least favourite part of the day, as she genuinely loved each of the children in the class as if they were her own and she would have to wait another eighteen hours until she would see them again.

The P.E. class in the hall had gone relatively well. She had made them do warm-up stretching exercises to begin with. Technically, they were doing very basic yoga but Sarah didn't want to admit this as the school would be expected to notify all the children's parents that they were being taught yoga by an unqualified instructor: it was just easier to maintain the white-lie. Sarah found that the class, in particular some of the troublesome boys, were much better behaved following yoga, and this is why she practised it.

The yoga session had been followed by rope-climbing, jumping and basketball dribbling skills. The class had finished at two thirty, and once the children had changed back in to their uniforms, she had read them a story before the bell had sounded. It was a nice way to end the day, and ensured that there was less mess to clear up afterwards. Sarah had planned the class for today to be fun but relaxing and she was pleased that she didn't feel as exhausted as she usually did after class. The reason for today's approach was the evening she had planned for Erin later.

Today was Erin's thirty-first birthday and Sarah had planned to recreate the atmosphere of their first date. It had been seven years ago and they had met through an online dating website that had deemed them compatible. They had sent emails back and forth for a few days before Erin had plucked up the courage to phone Sarah and talk. They had chatted about their interests and hobbies, where they had grown up and that kind of small talk. The conversation had been a little stilted, with neither quite able to ask the other on a date. Sarah was the one who had decided to bite the bullet and had suggested they go out for a meal together. Erin had just moved to Winchester, since completing her Police Constable training, and didn't have a car. Sarah had been living in Southampton for a little over a year and had volunteered to drive to Winchester. Erin had accepted the offer and had suggested a new Italian restaurant in the city that had recently opened.

Sarah had been so excited that Erin had agreed to the date that she had failed to ask what dress-code was appropriate. On the day of the date, she had tried on nearly twenty outfits before opting for an elegant black, sequined dress with thin shoulder straps. She thought she was probably hideously over-dressed but preferred that possibility to being embarrassed for being too informal. They had agreed to meet at Erin's flat first, as there was free parking available and the restaurant was just around the corner anyway. When Erin had opened the door, Sarah had been blown away by how beautiful she looked, with straightened, black hair down to her shoulders and a figure-hugging crimson, maxi-dress. Erin would later reveal that she had fallen in love with Sarah at that same moment.

They had walked casually from the flat to the restaurant in an awkward silence. It was only Sarah's second date with a woman, and she was still coming to terms with her sexuality. Erin had just come out of a two year relationship and was just reacquainting herself with single-life again. The Italian restaurant was beautifully decorated inside and, although small, it had a real Renaissance-feel that made them both imagine they were, in fact, in Rome, rather than Winchester.

They had ordered a garlic ciabatta as a starter, to share as neither had particularly large appetites and still the awkward, stilted conversation had continued. It felt like a real God-send when the clumsy waiter inadvertently dropped their main courses, as he approached from the kitchen. Sarah had burst into a fit of giggles and soon Erin had been in tears, as she tried to contain her laughter. Erin then admitted that the restaurant wasn't her usual style and had suggested they make their excuses and head for a *McDonald's*. Sarah agreed that she would feel more comfortable in less-frivolous surroundings, paid the bill and they walked five minutes into the city until they saw the famous golden arches. They knew they looked ridiculous in their luxurious gowns, chomping on fries and drinking milkshakes but they didn't care and it made it feel like they were sharing a private joke that nobody else in the world was in on. Conversation had flowed from that moment and they only stopped talking, when the spotty duty manager had told them they needed to leave, as he had to close up.

The conversation had continued until they arrived back at Erin's doorstep, where they had said their goodbyes for the night. Erin had leaned in and tenderly kissed Sarah on the lips. An electricity had flowed through Sarah, and she had just known that Erin was the one for her. Erin had blamed an early shift the next day for not inviting Sarah up for a nightcap, but, in truth, Sarah had been relieved that she would not need to allow her clumsy awkwardness ruin what had been a thoroughly enjoyable evening. They had agreed, instead, to meet again at the weekend for a coffee.

Seven years on and they were living in a two bedroom apartment on the second floor of a luxury block in Ocean Village, Southampton and life could not have been better. Erin had passed her Detective exams eighteen months ago and Sarah had successfully completed a training course on teaching children with learning difficulties, which would widen her scope for one day progressing to the Headteacher role she coveted. Sarah's father had still not accepted that his daughter was a lesbian, but then that was a different story altogether. Erin's parents had passed away in a plane crash when she had been eighteen. But none of that mattered, because, when they were together, they didn't need anybody else.

Sarah was planning to cook a garlic ciabatta as a starter that evening, followed by a rich spinach and ricotta cannelloni main meal and zabaglione for dessert; she already had a chilled bottle of Pinot Grigio in the fridge. Erin was due home at seven, and Sarah planned to have the food on the table for when she arrived. She had also been to a lingerie shop to buy a seductive one-piece that she planned to put on for the evening. She tingled, thinking of what was to come.

Sarah was still smiling to herself, when she spotted Erin approaching the classroom, through the same door from which the children had exited moments earlier. She didn't look happy; in fact the expression on her face was grim. There were two other people walking with her, the first being Mrs McGregor, the school's Headteacher and a balding man whom Sarah knew only as Vin-sent.

'Erin? Is everything okay?' Sarah blurted out, instinctively.

'Sarah,' said Mrs McGregor, in her warm, soothing, Scottish brogue, 'the police need to talk to you.'

'What about, what's going on?' she replied, her mind racing with thoughts about what might be so wrong.

'It's about Natalie Barrett,' offered Vincent. 'She is

missing and we believe she may have been abducted.'

'Oh dear God,' whispered Sarah, as the realisation dawned on her that one of her children had been taken. It was like a cold, sharp knife piercing through her heart.

4

'She's been abducted?' gasped Sarah, trying to come to terms with what Vincent had told her.

'We don't know what has happened yet,' countered Erin, frustrated with how Vincent had broken the news to her girlfriend, 'but, it is possible that somebody has taken her, yes.'

'I can't believe it. She's such a nice girl,' stated Sarah, putting a hand out to steady herself.

'I know this must have come as a big shock to you but we need to ask you some questions about Friday,' continued Erin.

'Of course, of course,' replied Sarah, suddenly realising how her behaviour must have appeared.

'Mrs McGregor, would you be able to fetch a cup of hot, sweet tea for Sarah? It's good for shock,' Erin suggested.

'Yes, of course,' cooed Mrs McGregor before shuffling off out of the door, in search of a kettle.

'Do you want to sit down?' asked Erin, waving her arm in the direction of Sarah's teacher's chair at the far side of the classroom.

'Thanks,' she mumbled and the three moved towards the desk. Noticing that there was only one adult-sized chair, Vincent and Erin lifted down a couple of the children's chairs from a nearby desk and sat uncomfortably on them. Vincent looked like a large owl perched perilously on a small twig, about to crack. If the circumstances had not been so serious,

Sarah probably would have laughed.

'What can you tell us about Friday?' Vincent asked Sarah, keen to get straight to questioning.

'Where do you want me to begin?'

'Tell us how Natalie seemed. Was her behaviour different in any way?'

Sarah thought for a moment. Had Natalie's behaviour been any different?

'I don't remember anything strange,' said Sarah thinking through the events of the day.

'There didn't appear to be anything troubling her? She wasn't withdrawn from the other children?' continued Vincent.

'No, quite the opposite, to be honest. Natalie was, is, a very popular girl. She gets on really well with all her classmates and has a very pleasant way about her that rubs off on others.'

'So she didn't seem scared or nervous about going home?' asked Vincent as he adjusted his uncomfortable sitting position.

'No. As I said, she seemed her usual, bubbly self.'

'Can you talk us through everything that happened on Friday, starting when she arrived in the morning?' asked Erin calmly, keen to progress the interview but in a softly-softly approach.

Sarah glanced at her girlfriend and smiled to acknowledge that she knew she was there for support.

'Well, the children all arrived, as usual at nine a.m. and went straight in for an assembly. Every Friday morning, Mrs McGregor leads an assembly, where she talks through some of the children's achievements of the week. You know the kind of thing, where a pupil has drawn a great picture or has gone out of their way to do something kind for another pupil? Mrs

McGregor calls the pupil's name out and explains what they have done and then everybody claps, to congratulate them. The assembly lasted about fifteen minutes and then we all came into the classroom and I took the register.'

'Was everybody in?' interjected Vincent.

'Yes, we had a full class on Friday; no absentees.'

'What happened next?' asked Erin, soothingly.

'The whole day was themed around the Olympics and the children had been encouraged to wear their own clothes, instead of their uniforms, so they were all a bit hyper.'

'Hyper?' quizzed Vincent.

'The children get used to wearing their uniform every day and it becomes something of a ritual,' explained Sarah. 'Every now and again, they are given the chance to wear their own, non-uniform, clothes to school and they find it quite thrilling, so they appear more excitable than usual.'

'Continue,' beckoned Erin.

'Anyway, there was lots of talking and giddiness, particularly from the boys, who seemed keen to show off their new trainers and the like. They had been told to wear something sports-related, so most were sat in football shirts and tracksuit bottoms.'

'What was Sarah wearing?' asked Vincent, interrupting again, causing Erin to shoot him a look of disdain.

'I think she had an England football shirt on and some stripy leggings.'

'Did she have a coat when she left?' asked Vincent.

'I assume so,' said Sarah trying to recall. 'It was a wet day from what I remember so she probably had her red coat with her. It's the same coat she wears every day to school.'

'What happened next?' asked Erin.

'Well, as I said, the day was Olympics-themed so there was a change to the usual teaching programme. Mrs McGregor had arranged for a local celebrity to visit the school, to help launch our Olympics project, and he came and met all of the children over the course of the day.'

'Local celebrity?' asked Vincent, his intrigue spiked.

'Johan Boller, from Southampton Football Club.'

Vincent looked quizzically at Erin, to verify that this man was indeed a celebrity. Vincent didn't really follow football. Erin nodded quickly to confirm.

'Mrs McGregor wants us to base our classes and assemblies on the Olympics in the run up to summer,' continued Sarah. 'To launch it properly, we decided that Friday would be a fun-filled day, allowing the children to get an understanding of what the Olympics means to them and to encourage further sports-participation. I think Mrs McGregor's husband has some contacts at the football club. The children were so excited and I think that's probably why we had a hundred percent attendance on the day.'

Mrs McGregor returned to the classroom and placed a mug of steaming tea in front of Sarah.

'Oh,' said Mrs McGregor when she realised what she had done. 'I didn't think to ask if either of you wanted a cup of tea.'

'We're both fine,' answered Erin before Vincent started pestering her for drinks.

'I was just telling the detectives about the footballer who visited us on Friday,' Sarah said to Mrs McGregor.

'A lovely boy,' replied Mrs McGregor, 'quite

handsome too. It was great to see the children so excited. It seems like a lifetime ago, given what we have learned today.'

'How long was he here for?' asked Erin to nobody in particular.

'He was with my class between one and two, I think,' recalled Sarah. 'I'm not sure where he went after that.'

'I think he may have gone to see the Year-5s after but I can't really remember,' stated Mrs McGregor, picking up where Sarah had left off. 'You don't think he had something to do with this?'

'No, no,' answered Erin quickly. 'But if he was still around after three, it's possible he might have seen something or someone hanging around.'

'Well, Mr Stanley is the head of Year-5 so I can go and ask him now if he remembers what time Mr Boller left the school,' said Mrs McGregor eagerly.

'I'll come with you,' said Vincent, before standing and following Mrs McGregor out of the classroom.

'Are you okay?' asked Erin when the other two were gone. She placed a reassuring hand on Sarah's knee and caressed it tenderly.

'It's just such a shock. I mean, you see things like this on the news every year, but it's always some other place in the country, so it doesn't seem real.'

'I know what you mean. There are hundreds of missing children cases across the UK every year, but we only really hear about them when they make the news. Most of the cases that don't reach the media end with the child returning, having just run away for attention.'

'Do you think Natalie has just run away from home?' asked Sarah hopefully.

'It's possible,' said Erin reluctantly, 'but unlikely. Most of those cases, where the child returns home, are resolved within forty-eight hours. Natalie has been missing for seventy-two hours already, which might suggest there is something more sinister going on here.'

The two ladies sat in silence, considering Erin's last statement.

'I suppose my only other question to you would be, did you see anyone suspicious lurking around outside of the school?' asked Erin eventually.

'Not that I remember,' answered Sarah honestly. 'I left here just before four on Friday. The street was pretty empty, from what I remember, but then it's only ever busy when the children arrive and leave. It's not a well-travelled thoroughfare, at other times of the day.'

'Okay, then,' said Erin standing, 'let me know if you do remember anything else about the day. I better go track down Vincent and head back to the station.'

'Okay,' said Sarah, forcing a smile. 'What time will you be home tonight?'

'Not sure yet. By seven, hopefully.'

'Okay. I love you,' said Sarah as Erin moved towards the exit door of the classroom.

'I love you, too,' replied Erin before disappearing around the corner.

5

Neil and Melanie Barrett's home looked like any normal, council-owned, house in Southampton: three bedrooms, a garden at the front, concrete yard space out the back and a satellite dish clinging to the now redundant chimney pot. As a suburb of Southampton, Sholing had become something of a melting pot for residents, who couldn't afford the affluent housing on the west-side of the city. Largely detached from Southampton, and only joined by the famous Itchen toll-bridge, Sholing wasn't much to write home about. Had Betjeman visited the area before he had seen Slough, maybe he would have invited the friendly bombs to fall here instead. Whilst some people in the area were prepared to stand on their own two feet, and privately acquire a property in one of the more pleasant, quieter closes, the majority of the housing available in Sholing, was still council-owned or worse, formerly-council-owned.

As Erin pulled up the squad car on the grass verge outside of the Barrett's semi-detached-hub, it amazed Vincent how many nearly-new cars were parked in driveways and along the street. If the people living here couldn't afford to pay monthly mortgage arrangements, how the hell could they afford such expensive cars?

'How do you want to play this then, Guv?' asked Erin as she removed the keys from the ignition.

Vincent remained staring out of the window, but

said, 'you do the softly-softly and I'll interject with some observations.'

Vincent really didn't want to be here right now, but he knew that it wouldn't have been fair to send Cookie by herself, particularly considering how emotional the Barretts were likely to be. Something didn't sit right with Vincent, and it was a feeling he was finding hard to shake.

The two officers walked up the short driveway to the shiny, maroon-coloured front door and pressed the doorbell. It didn't make a sound. Erin pushed the button a second time, but still no sound was emitted. She was about to try for a final time when Vincent pounded his fist on the door.

Melanie was the one to open the door, her face resembling that of a panda, clear that she had been crying not long ago.

'Mrs Barrett,' began Erin. 'We spoke yesterday? I am D.C. Erin Cooke and this is my colleague, Detective Inspector Jack Vin-sent.'

Vincent waved his warrant card photo I.D. in front of her.

'Yes?' came the response, clouded in confusion. 'Have you found her?'

'No, not yet,' Mrs Barrett,' replied Erin. 'Would you mind if we came in? It's just to confirm some further details about Friday afternoon.'

Without a word, Melanie Barrett opened the door wider and beckoned for them to follow her. The doorway led into a short, narrow hallway with a small kitchen, off to the left, a staircase to the right, a dining room, at the end to the left and a living room, at the end to the right. Melanie Barrett walked zombie-like into the living room and took a seat on the long, dark brown leather settee. Neil Barrett was sat on a second leather sofa, idly watching whatever happened to be on the television.

'Good afternoon, Mr Barrett,' offered Erin, making eye contact with him. He nodded acknowledgement, but didn't speak.

'How are you both?' Erin asked, naively, and immediately regretted it. Neither Barrett responded, but they both glared up at her, silently cursing her presence there.

'Sorry,' Erin muttered, 'Stupid question.'

Vincent moved slowly into the room, across the floor and to the back wall, where he stared out into the stark yard space. There was a small pink tricycle tipped on its side, a barbeque going rusty from under-use and wet weather, and a small, blue, child's trampoline that looked like it too had seen better days.

'D.I. Vincent and I wanted to ask you both some further questions about Friday afternoon, if that's okay?' asked Erin, taking a seat on the sofa next to Melanie. 'How did Natalie seem on Friday morning when you dropped her at school?'

'She was fine,' said Melanie, resolutely. 'She was excited about being dressed in her own clothes for the Olympics day-thing that the school were doing.'

'She didn't appear nervous, or worried about anything?' Erin persevered.

'No, not that I noticed. Neil, did you notice anything?' Melanie asked, glancing at her husband for support.

'No,' he said quietly, refusing to move his eyes from the screen.

'Have either of you noticed anyone strange hanging around? Have there been any unusual phone calls? Anything like that?' asked Natalie.

'I told you yesterday, we haven't noticed anything out of the ordinary,' replied Melanie, her voice starting to crack under the strain. 'What does this have to do with Natalie? Do you know who has taken her?'

'We have yet to establish if anyone has taken her, Mrs Barrett,' said Vincent, matter-of-factly, but without turning around. His tone caught them all off-guard.

'Where the hell is she then?' demanded Neil Barrett, suddenly deciding to enter the conversation.

'That's a very good question, Mr Barrett,' replied Vincent, slowly turning around to face the seated group. 'You claim that your daughter wouldn't be silly enough to climb into a stranger's car, yet she is missing. You claim she was happy and playful, and not the kind of girl who would run away from home, yet where is she?'

Neil Barrett was about to stand up and leap across the room at Vincent when he spoke again, 'What was the argument about on Valentine's Day of this year?'

'Valentine's Day? What?' asked Melanie, confused by the change in the line of questioning.

'Two uniformed officers were called to this property at ten past nine on Valentine's evening as a neighbour had reported the sound of violent banging and shouting. Can you explain what it was about?'

Melanie glanced at her husband, who was quietly seething in the corner.

'We had an argument, so what?' replied Neil, eager not to say anything incriminating.

'What was the argument about, Mr Barrett?' asked Vincent, calmly, yet directly.

'What does it matter what the argument was about? It has nothing to do with Natalie,' he shouted in response.

'Temper, temper,' Vincent said, as condescendingly as he could. 'I think we'll be the judge of whether it has something to do with your daughter's disappearance. Okay, if you don't want to tell me about that one, how about the night of March first? Uniformed officers were called out again because of a neighbour reporting a disturbance. What was that about?'

'It's that bloody bitch at number fourteen,' stated Melanie, between gritted teeth. 'That cow is always sticking her nose in where it doesn't belong!'

'Number fourteen?' Erin gently pushed.

'Yeah,' replied Melanie, practically spitting the words out. 'Her, with her two BMWs and son at medical school. She is so up her own arse, it's untrue.'

'Do you not see eye to eye?' asked Erin, acting the innocent.

'We never have,' replied Melanie, sensing an ally in Erin. 'Ever since we moved to the street, she's had it in for us: moaning that Natalie was pulling flowers out of her garden, or that Neil was washing the car without a top on. Any reason she can find and she is round here, putting us and the world to rights. She should mind her own bloody business!'

'Number fourteen is across the street, isn't it?' enquired Vincent, knowing full well it was.

'And?' retorted Melanie.

'I'm just thinking,' mused Vincent, looking around the room, before making direct eye contact with the blonde, sat on the couch. 'It must have been a bloody loud argument for the woman across the street to have heard it!' Vincent caught himself, as he sensed his voice had risen.

'She's got a dog,' chipped in Neil. 'She walks her dog around the street every night and pauses outside people's houses while it pees or shits, just so she can listen to what is going on, or to peer through open curtains. I've even caught her in the act before, though of course she denied it.'

'Shall I make us a cup of tea?' suggested Erin, sending a signal to Vincent with her eyes. 'Melanie, would you be able to show me where I would find cups and tea bags?'

Vincent forced himself not to smile. He really was pleased with the progress Cookie was making as an officer. He knew her tea-suggestion was a ploy to get Melanie away from Neil, for a quiet, informal chat about what had been going on. Oblivious to the ploy, Melanie stood up and led Erin to the kitchen.

Vincent looked down at Neil Barrett, who was still seated on the sofa, looking uncomfortable. It was as if he knew that Erin had planned a 'divide and conquer' strategy that had worked perfectly; Neil was uncomfortable, as he had been left in the room with the 'bad cop' in the partnership.

'Can you tell me where you were on Friday afternoon, Mr Barrett,' Vincent began.

'I told the other woman, I was on a call out.'

'And where was this 'call out'?' Vincent continued.

'Near junction-1 of the M27 near Cadnam.'

'Near Cadnam? That's a bit out of the way of Sholing, isn't it? Do you do many call outs that far away?'

'Not really, no. Not always. It depends. If someone calls us from a distance, and we're not too busy, then we might take the call.'

'So was it quiet on Friday afternoon?' Vincent asked, trying to sound innocent.

'I guess it must have been,' replied Neil.

'What was the name of the person on this 'call out'?'

'I don't remember.'

'You don't remember? Okay, how about this one: was it a man or a woman?' Vincent asked.

'A man.'

'And what car did he drive?' asked Vincent, eager to fire the questions quickly at Neil Barrett, in an effort to catch him in a lie.

'A BMW. A black one.'

'A black BMW? What series?' Vincent fired.

'What series?'

'Yes. What series? A three series? A five? A seven?'

'A five, I think,' said Neil, blinking rapidly, trying to process the rapid questions.

'You think? Well don't you know? You were there, weren't you? You must remember what type of car was in need of repair? How about this one: What was wrong with the car?' Vincent was almost shouting now.

'It wouldn't start.'

'Why not? How did you fix it?'

'The wire between the ignition switch and the battery was damaged. I made a temporary repair with some insulating tape and told him to take it to a garage for a proper repair,' replied Neil Barrett, squirming in the chair. He did not like the way Vincent was speaking to him.

'And how long did all this take?'

'About an hour, I think.'

'An hour?' Vincent asked. 'What time did the call come in?'

'I don't know. About two thirty maybe. A lot has happened since Friday, I can't recall everything. Check the log at the office. That will confirm all the details.'

'I already have, Mr Barrett,' Vincent replied, smiling. 'I just want to check the accuracy of the record, by testing your recollection of events.'

'Why are you interrogating me?' shouted Neil, standing up and going nose-to-nose with Vincent. 'I had nothing to do with my daughter's disappearance. You should be out there trying to find the son of a bitch who has taken her, not in here pestering us.'

At that moment, Erin and Melanie Barrett re-entered the room, Erin carrying a tray with two mugs on top of it.

'Neil!' admonished Melanie. 'What are you doing? Sit down!'

Neil looked over at his wife, and sensing that she was right, returned to his seat like an injured dog licking his wounds.

'Sir, I just had a call. We are needed back at the station. Pronto,' said Erin, nudging her head, to indicate they should leave.

Vincent looked confused at first, as he hadn't finished questioning Neil Barrett, but when Erin cocked her head again, he understood that it was time to leave.

'Thank you for your time, Mr Barrett,' Vincent said, as he strode across the room. 'We'll be in touch.'

Erin led the way back to the car, and once they were seated inside, she said, 'Melanie told me what the arguments have been about. To cut a long story short, they've been arguing about Neil's brother, Jimmy.'

'What about Jimmy?'

'Melanie says he always comes home drunk, shouts things in his sleep, and is generally making their life quite difficult. She told me she argues with Neil about when Jimmy is going to move out, so they can get on with their own lives. Apparently, they had been talking about having another baby, before Jimmy rocked up on the scene, but that's gone out the window now. The argument on Valentine's Day was because Jimmy had originally agreed to babysit Natalie, so Neil and Melanie could go out for dinner, but then Jimmy arrived home late and drunk as a skunk, so they had to cancel their plans. Melanie said she instigated the argument as she felt it was the last straw. The loud banging that the nosy neighbour heard, was Melanie throwing several plates at the wall, out of frustration.'

'Do you believe her?' Vincent asked, calmly.

'I do, Guv, yes,' replied Erin. 'I don't think the Barretts had anything to do with Natalie's disappearance, Melanie certainly not. She opened up to me in the kitchen, and she was far too upset to have done anything to her daughter.'

'Okay,' replied Vincent, 'but I still don't trust Neil Barrett. There is something he's not telling us; I can sense it. We need to find out what the brother was up to at the time as well.'

'What do you want to do next then?'

'We'll ease up the pressure on the Barretts for now, but I'll assign someone to do some further digging into Neil Barrett, quietly. If he is hiding something, I want to know what it is. Same goes for Jimmy.'

'Okay.'

'I also want someone to talk to the nosy neighbour. What number did they say she lived at, fourteen? We'll get someone to question her, and check up on the other side of the story,' Vincent replied.

'I'll do it, if you want, Guv?' offered Erin.

'Okay, Erin. That's not a bad idea. What was the call from the station, you received?'

'Oh, yeah,' said Erin, remembering why they had left. 'Apparently, the D.C.I. has arranged an urgent press conference with local media agencies. He wants the Barretts to make a heart-felt appeal for information. Oh, and he wants you to chair the conference.'

'Bloody brilliant!' muttered Vincent, under his breath.

6

'Are you ready to go?'

It was a strange question to be asked at this point in proceedings. Vincent stared down at the white cards he had scribbled his notes on, checking that the numbers scrawled in the top corners were in sequential order.

'Ready as I'll ever be,' he replied, glancing up to the composed eyes of D.C. Erin Cooke, who had posed the question.

Both were stood outside the communications suite at the Police Central Headquarters in Southampton. Despite the obvious chill from the draft of the corridor in which they were stood, Vincent felt overly warm. He ran the tips of his fingers in the small space between his shirt collar and his neck, desperately trying to widen the gap. Why did it feel so tight? He decided to undo the top button of his shirt and readjusted his tie, with note cards still between his fingers. He could feel a small wall of sweat forming at the edge of his hair line and opted to use his handkerchief to wipe it away.

'Are you sure you're okay, Sir?' asked Erin, aware that her boss was not a big fan of public speaking, especially in front of the country's media.

'How many times, Cookie, I'm fine. It's just another press conference.'

'Cookie' was the nickname that Erin had acquired during her eighteen month spell in D.I. Vincent's team. She knew that most of the men in the team fancied her, but she had been quick to point out that her interest clearly lay elsewhere. At first there had been some awkward moments, with the team getting to grips with having a lesbian within the ranks. It wasn't homophobia, they didn't have an issue with the fact that Erin liked other women: their issue was knowing what to say, so as not to offend her. The modern day police force had been so bombarded with political-correctness that most officers didn't dare breathe in the wrong direction, for fear of offending some minority group: blacks, gays, single parents, religious types. The modern day police force truly was a diverse population of individuals.

Those first few weeks had been wrought with tension, as even Vincent had been careful with his words and the requests he had made of Erin. It didn't seem to matter how many times she had said it, they just seemed unable to relate to her as a fellow officer. About six weeks into her new role she had been called in, on her day off, to take part in an armed raid of a house in nearby Chilworth. Chilworth was an affluent part of Southampton, where your annual income needed to be above six figures just to view a property in the area. The raid had been intended to locate and arrest a Southampton-based man, accused of laundering money at the bank where he worked and who had allegedly murdered the owners of the property being raided. The team had successfully caught the assailant in bed, and he had been tried and convicted within four months of his arrest. Erin had made sure she was one of the first officers through the door and had held the suspect down while cuffs had been fastened around his wrists.

The team had headed out into Southampton city centre that evening and had hit several bars and clubs, celebrating the success of the operation. Erin had tagged along, and had more than held her own when it came to drinking games, and once everyone's inhibitions had been lowered, she had happily shared some insights from her life. By the end of the evening, she was no longer a woman whom the team needed to be careful around: she was 'Cookie', one of the guys who didn't mind when her colleagues fawned over passing women. Over the last year she had proved herself to be more than adept at detective work and had earned her colleagues' respect.

Vincent looked back at Cookie and smiled. He really was proud of the officer she was becoming. She was bright, sharp and very articulate. He had big plans for her and had already spoken to his D.C.I. about her applying to sit the Sergeants' exam in the coming months. He did envy her a little, though: at least she didn't have to go out and talk in front of the gathered masses of journalists currently setting up cameras and recording equipment, just the other side of the door he was stood next to. Vincent pulled his jacket sleeve up and looked at his wrist watch. It was nearly six.

'Is it time to go in?' asked Erin, noticing him looking at his watch.

'Yes it is,' croaked Vincent, before clearing his throat and repeating the line.

Erin twisted the door handle and pulled the door open, allowing Vincent to enter first. There was a loud hum in the room as journalists continued to talk to each other in loud whispers. Erin couldn't distinguish what was being said only that everyone seemed to be talking at the same time. Cameras began to flash, as some of the group noticed Vincent approaching the long table at the front of the room, behind which were four chairs and a large plasma monitor attached to the wall. Vincent ran his right hand over his dark moustache, checking to ensure that he had cleared the sweat, and then he pulled out the chair closest to him and sat down. The remaining three chairs to his right-hand side would be filled when the Barretts were escorted through.

A silence befell the room as each of the conversations ended simultaneously and the journalists prepared to ask the hundred and one questions they already had, without hearing what Vincent was about to say. They already knew what this press conference was about, although Vincent had no idea how they could have found out, as there had been no contact between the police and the media prior to this point, but then they always seemed to know. Vincent wished some of his team had the contacts on the street that some of the local press did; they were always one step ahead.

The Communications Suite was a long room, able to comfortably seat about thirty journalists with room for video-cameras and camera stands. It had been built for this very purpose: a press conference where the police would be able to appeal to the public for help with a specific case. Vincent had chaired several such meetings in the past, but even he had never seen this many journalists crammed in, there was at least twice the usual number. He didn't like speaking in front of a dozen strangers, let alone the thirty or so that had turned up today. It seemed the D.C.I. had called in some favours, as there were representatives from SKY, the BBC, Meridian and Channel 5, as well as representatives from local radio stations, the Daily Echo and other London-based newspaper agencies.

Vincent rechecked the sequence of his note cards again and cleared his throat, ready to speak.

'Ladies and gentlemen of the gathered press, my name is Detective Inspector Jack Vin-sent. Thank you for attending this evening's press conference.'

Vincent paused, as he took a sip of water from the glass on the table in front of him. Thankfully, there was also a jug full of additional water on the table, which he had a feeling he was going to need: his throat felt so dry.

'Every year in the U.K. approximately one hundred and fifty thousand children go missing from their homes. That is one child every three and a half minutes on average. The reason I am sat before you here this evening, is that a child from Southampton has gone missing and we believe she may have been abducted.'

Vincent paused for effect, to allow the masses to take in the news. He half-expected extreme in-takes of breath or gasps but instead all he heard was the snapping and popping of camera lenses and flashes. He sighed; what had the world come to that the news of an abducted child could be met with silence and a total lack of surprise? Vincent nodded his head, the signal that the image of Natalie Barrett's face should now be beamed to the large monitor above his head, on the wall behind his chair.

'Natalie Barrett was last seen walking from St. Monica's Primary School in the district of Sholing, between three p.m. and half past on Friday. She is seven years-old, has bright blonde, shoulder-length hair and was wearing a bright red coat. It is likely that the hood of the coat was pulled up over her head as it was raining on Friday afternoon. We have begun door to door enquiries of all the houses between the school and Natalie's house, which is a mile from where she was last seen.'

Vincent paused for a further sip of water before continuing, 'Natalie was a very bright and popular child and had no history of running away from home, which is why we are treating this case as abduction and not as any other missing child case. We will be sharing images of Natalie with you and my officers will shortly pass you a wallet of information and contact points that we would like you to use, in helping us uncover additional information to aid this case.'

'D.I. Vincent, Marshall Lancaster from the BBC,' said a ginger-haired man in the front row. 'Are you presuming the child has been taken by a stranger?'

'We are making no presumptions at this time, Mr Lancaster. We want to gather as many leads as possible and will consider each and every piece of evidence, as it surfaces.'

'D.I. Vincent, D.I. Vincent,' chorused several other journalists.

'Please, ladies and gentlemen,' said Vincent raising a hand to restore calm, 'there will be time for questions at the end. Now, Natalie's family are here and wish to read a statement.'

Vincent turned and looked over his left shoulder to where Erin was stood. He nodded at her, to indicate she could now bring the family through. Erin disappeared out through the door they had both entered minutes before, and returned through an alternate door to Vincent's right, with Neil and

Melanie Barrett and Neil's brother, Jimmy. Erin ushered for them to sit in the three chairs next to Vincent, and this was greeted with a further flurry of popping camera flashes, as the hungry journalists got their first look at the parents.

Melanie, a bleached-blonde woman in her late thirties was the picture of despair, her eyes full of tears, ready to drop at the merest nudge. She was wearing a long, black woollen dress with short sleeves, giving the impression she was on her way to a funeral, rather than a press conference. Neil, also in his late thirties was wearing dark blue jeans and a blue and cream lumberjack shirt. His curly hair had been brushed but maintained the unkempt look it always did. Melanie was sat in the chair closest to Vincent with Neil next to her and making up the threesome was Natalie's Uncle Jimmy.

'Begin when you're ready,' whispered Vincent to Melanie, with a hint of empathy.

Melanie didn't respond, but did move her hands to the table so that she could pick up the piece of white A4 paper, which had been left on the table prior to the arrival of the press. The paper was a prepared, typed statement that had been hastily put together by Vincent's team, with the help of an on-call duty solicitor.

'This is a plea to the person or persons, who have taken our daughter,' Melanie began. 'Please return our daughter, unharmed. Natalie is a beautiful, funny and friendly little girl. She deserves to be at home with her family...' She was unable to finish the sentence before the flood-gates opened and the tears flowed down her cheeks. She pushed the sheet of paper to her husband and leaned into his arm for support. Neil Barrett wiped a tear from his own eye and put a loving arm around his wife's shoulders and picked up the piece of paper with his free hand.

'The police believe that Natalie was taken on Friday, between the school finishing and three thirty. We are also appealing to anybody who may have seen our little girl in her red coat, walking or being approached by anyone. Even if you only saw her, at least that might help the police better pin-point the moment she was taken.'

Neil leant over and kissed the head of his wife, who was still sobbing uncontrollably.

'Unless you have sat where we are now,' he continued, 'you cannot begin to imagine the anguish we are currently going through, not knowing what has happened to our little angel. We are begging people to look closely at the image of our daughter, and to try and remember if you saw her on Friday afternoon. If you do remember anything, no matter how small, please contact the police immediately and pass on the information.'

Neil placed the piece of white paper back on the table in front of them and placed his second arm around his wife so that he was now fully embracing her. Vincent took a sip of water from his glass, before topping it up from the jug. He then signalled to Erin again, this time it was the nod that she could begin distributing the prepared packs to the journalists in the room.

'My colleague will now provide you with the images and contact points and again we would ask that you include the *CrimeStoppers* telephone number in any articles or reports that you run over the next few days.'

Vincent turned to the Barretts and whispered that it would probably be best if they now left the Communications Suite so that he could receive questions from the press. Jimmy was the first up and out of the door, glad to be out of the glare of the lights and was quickly followed by Neil and Melanie.

'Okay, now you can ask questions,' said Vincent addressing the crowd, ready to be inundated.

'D.I. Vincent, D.I. Vincent,' shouted almost every reporter.

7

Sarah's mobile phone vibrated on the kitchen table, behind her. She didn't hear it at first, as she was singing along to the radio at the top of her voice. It wasn't often she dared stretch her vocal chords, such was the feedback she had received in the past about her unique range. However, when she was alone, in the kitchen and cooking, it was as if she was auditioning for a talent contest. It was just her way of making cooking-time pass more swiftly. Sarah had returned home an hour earlier. And after a quick shower she had thrown on a pair of jogging bottoms and an old t-shirt, out of fear that the tomato sauce she was preparing would splash up and ruin what she had planned to wear at the meal. Sarah was no *Masterchef* and had gone to great lengths to find as easy a recipe as possible for the spinach and ricotta cannelloni she had decided to cook. Erin would appreciate her efforts, she knew.

The mobile phone vibrated a second time, a reminder to the recipient that she had an un-viewed message. This time, Sarah did hear it, as the song on the radio was coming to its end. Sarah turned the knob on the stove to reduce the gas flame, so that the tomato sauce would continue to simmer. She then turned and moved to the small, wooden kitchen table that she had yet to set with cutlery. She unlocked the phone's screen and saw that the message had come from Erin. She smiled as she opened it. The message read: 'N.B. Press Conference on SKY news at 6:30. Can you record for me? Will be home ASAP. Luv U x'

Sarah hadn't realised that Natalie Barrett's disappearance would warrant a press conference, and checked the time on the clock over her shoulder. It was nearly six thirty already, so Sarah quickly moved from the kitchen to the living room, grabbed the television remote and flicked through until she found the news channel. A scrolling, red banner, at the bottom of the screen, indicated that the press conference would be the next story on the screen. Sarah pressed the record button on the remote and was about to turn the television off, when she saw Erin's face appear on the screen walking behind that other detective she had met earlier. Erin's note hadn't said she would be on the screen as well. Sarah gushed; she was dating a television star now! Well, not quite, but it was a nice thought and she would probably tease Erin about it later.

The detective with the dark, bushy moustache sat down at the table in the room where the broadcast had come from and took a sip of water. Erin was no longer in shot and Sarah secretly hoped that she would feature again later. The detective introduced himself to the screen, and explained that he was there to appeal to the public for information about a missing school girl, Natalie Barrett. Sarah felt the cold knife pierce her heart once again, as the reality that Natalie may indeed have been abducted, hit home. She took two steps back and sat down on the sofa behind her, carefully dropping her mobile phone on the seat next to her.

Images of a smiling, innocent Natalie flashed up

on the screen while Vincent's voice continued to speak in the background, but Sarah wasn't really listening to him, she was too caught up in the images. What kind of sick bastard would snatch such a sweet child?

The image of Natalie disappeared and was replaced by Erin once again, this time leading Natalie's parents, Neil and Melanie, into the room. The picture then cut to show four people sat at the table: Vincent at the far right of the screen, with Melanie, then Neil and then the man Sarah recognised as Uncle Jimmy. Melanie began to read from a piece of paper, in front of her but stopped after less than a minute and passed the paper to her husband, who continued to read from it. Melanie looked inconsolable and Sarah felt her heart lurch and had to quickly wipe a tear from her own eye.

The cameraman continued to focus on the four people at the table, but Sarah could not take her eyes from Uncle Jimmy. He looked at least ten years older than Neil and had long scraggly, ginger hair that hung below his shoulders. He was wearing a creased grey suit jacket, which was covering an equally creased, white shirt. Even from where Sarah was sat, she could make out distinct stains on the shirt, which suggested it either hadn't been washed prior to today's appearance, or was just so old that those stains had become a permanent fixture. Never had Sarah seen a man looking so uncomfortable. He had a weird squint and his mouth hung down at the left-side of his face. It reminded Sarah of when she had been a child and seen her grandfather after his stroke. There was just something not quite right about Jimmy Barrett.

Sarah continued to focus on him, until the image

on the screen flashed back to the reporters in the studio who advised that they would be looking at the day's sports stories after a commercial break. Sarah decided to watch the press conference over again and pressed the rewind button on her remote control and watched once more as Erin led the three Barretts into the room. As Jimmy took his seat, Sarah saw that his hair was thinner than she had first realised and that he was, in fact, partly bald on top. The bright lights behind the cameras also seemed to reflect off his forehead, suggesting that he was sweating, during the proceedings. She watched the whole press conference through to the end again and then switched off the screen. As she stood to return to the kitchen, she felt a shudder shoot through her shoulders and down to her feet. Jimmy Barrett looked like the sort of person Sarah would not want to meet on a dark night; he really gave her the creeps.

Sarah suddenly became distracted by a smell of burning and remembered her tomato sauce was still on the stove. She rushed over to it and gripped the wooden spoon, which was sat in the pan, in her hand. A searing pain shot through her hand, and she realised that she probably should have removed the spoon when she had originally left the kitchen. She quickly grabbed at a single oven glove, which she slipped over her right hand and stirred the sauce. Pieces of chopped onion were stuck to the bottom of the stainless steel pan and it was this that was giving off the burnt odour.

Sarah cursed under her breath: she had messed up yet another meal. Oh well, she thought, she'd use the sauce anyway and just leave the pan to soak; hopefully the burnt taste would be covered up by the garlic and cheese-infused béchamel sauce. Sarah placed each of the cannelloni tubes, which she had already stuffed with the spinach and ricotta mixture, in an oven-proof dish and poured the tomato and then the béchamel sauce over. She then grated more parmesan on the top and placed it in the oven, ready to be cooked when she knew Erin was on the way home.

Sarah walked over to her tall fridge and opened the door. She removed an open bottle of white wine from the door and poured herself a large glass. It had turned out to be a stressful day, finding out about Natalie's disappearance and then seeing the monstrous-looking Jimmy Barrett at the press conference. A thought struck Sarah like a lightning bolt, nearly causing her to drop her glass of wine. It was the memory of Natalie's picture that was hanging in the classroom. The picture of the princess, trapped in the castle, waiting for the knight to save her. The image of the dragon in Natalie's picture, now reminded her of Jimmy Barrett. Was Natalie's innocent-enough painting, in fact, a cry for help on that rainy Friday afternoon? Was she scared of her Uncle Jimmy? Was it in fact her Uncle Jimmy who stopped her returning home? Sarah drained the entire contents of her glass and vowed to discuss it with Erin in the morning.

TUESDAY

8

Sarah heard the bedroom door open and the shuffling of a pair of feet in slippers. She was aware that somebody was bustling about the room, but her eyes were glued shut, by a mixture of sleep and dried make-up. She tried to assess why she still felt so tired and why one of her arms appeared to be jutting out to her left, while the other was contorted and jutting out to the right. There was something soft, beneath her cheek, but, as she began to adjust her head's position, her cheek came into contact with a damp patch and her lips pulled themselves into an involuntary grimace: drool. She pulled her right hand up to her face and wiped the corner of her mouth.

Something heavy plonked down on the bed next to her, so that it was touching her bottom through the duvet. The action made Sarah roll over, to see what the intrusion was and as her eyelids cracked apart, she could make out the figure of Erin, sat in a navy blue trouser suit, staring adoringly back at her. Sarah tried to smile, but her facial expression looked more one of pain than pleasure, so much so that Erin asked, 'Are you okay?'

Sarah attempted to say, 'Yes,' but it came out as more of a grunt.

'I made you some tea,' said Erin, rubbing Sarah's leg through the duvet. 'I also brought you up a glass of water, as I thought you might need it.'

Sarah rolled over from her front to her back, and

then into a sitting position, so that her back was resting against the soft headboard. She was about to speak when a stabbing pain tore through her head, as if somebody had just stabbed her with a meat skewer. She instinctively moved her hand to her forehead, to protect herself.

'Head hurting?' enquired Erin.

'Yeah,' Sarah replied through the pain.

'I thought it might, judging by the empty bottle of wine I found in the kitchen. I'll fetch you some painkillers.'

With that, Erin padded out of the room, still in her slippers, returning moments later with a plastic bottle of pills in her hand. She removed the child-safety cap and tipped a couple of white pills into Sarah's grateful, extended hand. Sarah threw the pills into the back of her throat and washed them down with a large gulp of water from the glass that Erin had brought up and put on the bedside table.

Erin sat and waited for Sarah to regain some of her focus before saying, 'I'm sorry about last night.'

Sarah left the statement hanging while she tried to remember what had happened the previous evening that was making Erin apologise. Then it hit her, causing further stabbing pains as her memory cells started firing. Sarah had watched the press conference and had been eagerly waiting for Erin to arrive home but, when she still had not returned by eight p.m., Sarah had decided to put the prepared cannelloni in the fridge, ready to cook on Tuesday instead. It wasn't the first time that Erin had not been home in time for dinner and it was the one thing that Sarah detested about her partner's chosen profession: the unsocial hours. Sarah had continued to drink the wine, and given that she hadn't eaten since lunchtime, she was soon quite drunk. In all honesty, Sarah was usually pretty tipsy after one glass of wine, so she was in no fit state to do anything by the end of her third glass. With no word from Erin, Sarah had headed for bed and a paralytic night of sleep. Well, at least that explained the headache and nausea.

'After the press conference,' continued Erin, when Sarah didn't say anything, 'we started getting all sorts of calls from people claiming to have seen a little girl in a red coat, waiting outside the school and walking past shops, around the corner from the school. Vincent asked me to accompany him to interview one supposed witness, who claimed to have seen her getting into a blue van. We got to her house, just after eight, and she gave us a description of the car and driver, and we were about to radio it in when the woman's son arrived and explained that his mum suffered with dementia, and couldn't possibly have seen the little girl, as she had in fact been out to dinner with him at the time. Vincent nearly went ballistic, and was ready to charge her with wasting police time, but I managed to get him out of there before he said something he might regret.'

Erin paused to check that Sarah was still listening before continuing, 'We got back to the station just after nine and heard from the rest of the team that they had also experienced prank callers and had no new, tangible leads to work with. It was just a waste of time. By the time I got home, you were already in bed and from the way you were snoring, I knew you must have had a drink, so I slept in the spare room. I'm really sorry I didn't phone to let you know what was going on, but Vincent gets a bit funny about us making personal calls when on duty. I'll make it up to you tonight, I promise.'

'It's fine,' said Sarah, unable to hide the disappointment in her voice. 'It was for your birthday, so you don't need to make anything up to me.'

'But I know you went to a lot of trouble to cook for us and I feel bad that I wasn't here to enjoy it.'

'What time is it?'

Erin looked down at the small watch on her wrist. 'It's just coming up to seven. I thought you might want to jump in the shower before school starts.'

'Oh shit. School,' said Sarah, wondering how she was going to make it through a day of energetic children, with a hangover. 'Do you want some breakfast?'

'I've already eaten, I'm afraid,' replied Erin. 'Vincent wants us in by eight so I'll have to go in a bit. I can fix you some toast if you'd like?'

'That would be great,' said Sarah smiling, grateful for the offer and starting to feel less upset about the previous evening's spoiled date.

'Okay,' said Erin, standing and patting Sarah on the leg, once more. 'Jump in the shower and I'll have the toast ready for when you get out.'

Erin disappeared out of the room again and Sarah pushed the duvet back and headed for the shower. Ten minutes later, feeling cleaner and more awake, Sarah threw on a dressing gown, wrapped a towel around her hair and charged towards the kitchen, eager to catch Erin before she left the house. Sarah had recalled the press conference and the connection she had made to Natalie's painting.

'Oh thank God you're still here,' said Sarah, when she saw Erin stood at the counter top, buttering toast.

'What's wrong?' asked Erin, noticing the concerned look on her girlfriend's face.

'There's something I need to tell you,' answered Sarah, calming her breathing. 'While watching the press conference last night, I remembered something Natalie did on Friday.'

'What is it?' asked Erin as she looked for a piece of paper to jot some notes on.

'On Friday afternoon, I asked the children to write a story and paint a picture, depicting a scene from the story. Natalie wrote about a beautiful princess who was trapped in a castle that was being guarded by a fire-breathing dragon. In the story, a brave knight slays the dragon and rescues the princess.'

'And?'

'What do you mean, 'and'? Don't you get it? It was a cry for help!' replied Sarah, confused at how Erin couldn't see what she was saying.

'A cry for help? The story sounds like every child's story I've ever read. What makes you think that it has anything to do with her disappearance?'

'I was watching the press conference and saw Natalie's Uncle Jimmy there. I think he is the dragon from Natalie's story.'

'That's a bit of a stretch, don't you think?' asked Erin.

'No. Think about it. What do you know about Jimmy Barrett?'

'I can't really discuss this with you, Sarah. It's an active investigation.'

'Come on, Erin, humour me.'

'No, Sarah, I can't do that.'

'Fine,' said Sarah realising that Erin wasn't going

to budge. 'I know Jimmy has returned from active duty in Afghanistan in the last year. He is currently living with Natalie's parents. They live in a three bedroom terraced house; it can't be easy. Natalie is not the sort of girl who would get into a car with a stranger. What if Jimmy had come to pick her up? She'd have got in a car with him, wouldn't she? He's family, after all.'

'Maybe, but how does the fire-breathing dragon fit into it?'

'In child psychology, they say that a fire-breathing dragon depicts a monster, right?' said Sarah. 'What if Jimmy was hurting Sarah or threatening her, wouldn't a child deem that person a monster?'

'It's still a bit of a stretch, Sarah.'

'Is it, Erin? Is it? What about that family up North a few years back who claimed their daughter had been abducted and then she turned up at some uncle's or neighbour's house? Do you really think it isn't possible that he might know more than he is letting on? Did you see how nervous he looked during the press conference? He seemed guilty about something, if you ask me.'

'I can't go to Vincent and say we should issue a warrant for Jimmy Barrett's arrest because of a child's painting. He'd probably kick me off the team,' said Erin, honestly.

'I'm not saying you should present it to him straight away. Just do some digging into Jimmy Barrett's background, will you? Find out where he was or what he was doing on Friday afternoon. Do it for me, Erin. Please?'

Erin looked at her girlfriend and could see the sincerity dripping from her eyes.

'Okay, Sarah. I'll do some digging. But I'm not going to Vincent yet; not till I have found something.'

Sarah smiled at Erin and said, 'Thank you.'

9

Sarah paced from the kitchen to her bedroom, and back. She had an important phone call to make, but, like with most important phone calls, her stomach was tense, with a mixture of nerves and excitement. She had been meaning to make this call for several weeks now, and had persistently put it off, feeling that the time just wasn't quite right, but she couldn't put it off forever.

Sarah had hardly spoken to her father since her mother had passed away, three years earlier. To say their relationship was strained, would be an understatement. They sent each other the obligatory Christmas and birthday card, but neither bothered to phone the other to say thanks for the gesture.

Alan Jenson lived in the town of Fortuneswell, on the island of Portland, which is on the edge of Weymouth, along the Southern coast of England. This was where Sarah had grown up and had been keen to leave, as soon as she turned eighteen. It was a nice enough town; with a long pebbled beach that stretched for miles. It was a pleasant bus ride into Weymouth itself; when the desire to shop struck, but that was as much as Fortuneswell had to offer. Sarah understood why her father liked the peaceful way of life there, but to an eighteen year old girl, discovering her sexuality, it was like a pit of quick sand that needed to be escaped from.

Her father had been a prison guard at HMP

Verne, which sat on top of a large hill, over-looking the town like a medieval King; surveying his people. The prison was actually buried within the hill top, providing even greater security to local residents. It was opened in 1949, on the site of a military barracks, and only one known escapee had been recorded in historical documents, but that inmate was subsequently recaptured two days later. The prison housed Category-C inmates, who were deemed a danger to the public, but unlikely to attempt to escape from their incarceration. Alan Jenson had always had a sense of pride in working at the prison, and Sarah had often overheard him telling her mother that most of the inmates preferred being locked away, so that they could not bestow any harm on the public. Sarah couldn't imagine what it would be like to be locked away and governed under strict rules for a substantial period of time. It was probably his experiences with inmates that had led her father to be so strict with her upbringing. She could still remember the look of disapproval her father had given her on her seventeenth birthday, when the local Police Constable had escorted her home from a nearby park where she had been caught drinking alcohol underage. The Police Constable had given her an informal slap on the wrist, but her father had refused to speak to her for more than a week, such was his shame at having his daughter caught breaking the law.

She had always got on better with her mother, even though her mother was a vicar's daughter. But her mother had always been there for her, ready to lend a shoulder to cry on when things had seemed difficult at school, or a welcome ear, when all Sarah needed was to be listened to. The cancer had been diagnosed too late for surgery and had aggressively attacked her mother's body, until it actually seemed the kindest thing when she passed away: at least the pain was gone. Her father had taken a leave of absence from work, in the two weeks before the passing, in order to make her as comfortable as possible, but there had been very little he had been able to do for her. Sarah managed to secure a week's compassionate leave to return home for the funeral, to cook and clean for him and he had seemed grateful.

Sarah had been nervous about telling her mother she was gay, but actually the conversation had ultimately been very easy, with her mother giving that understanding smile that she always seemed to be able to produce, when it was most needed. Telling her father had been something she had avoided, until the day of her mother's funeral, when she had just decided to bite the bullet and explain that the friend she had brought along for support was, in fact, her girlfriend. Erin had warned her that it was probably not the greatest time that she could tell him, but Sarah had been adamant that she was no longer going to keep it a secret. In hindsight, telling her father that she was gay, on the day he buried the woman he had loved for more than thirty years, was probably not a great move.

She had waited until the service and wake had ended, and the three of them were back in the old family home, before sharing her news. He had looked shocked but had remained silent. She hated his inability to display his emotions, and how he maintained his stern expression, regardless of the situation. He had eventually commented that it was her life and she was big enough to make her own decisions. It was such an impassive response that she had been angered with him. She had not expected him to jump for joy, but at least if he had shouted at her or thrown her out of the house, she would have known how he felt and would have been able to move on with her life. But the lack of facial expression or words gave her no indication of his opinion, and to this day it drove her mad.

Sarah had been an only child, and on some days, she did feel guilty that she did not stay in better contact with him. In truth, she had no idea what he currently did with his life, who he saw or what health he was in. She was aware that he had retired the year before, but only because a friend from the old neighbourhood had mentioned it to her in passing. He, too, had been an only child so there was no family around to check on him. She often wondered whether she would just receive a phone call one day saying he had been found dead in his home, and that the body had not been discovered for several days.

Still, she had to make the phone call to him and let him know what was going on in her life; it was the least he deserved, for bringing her into the world. She fished her mobile out of her handbag and scrolled through her contacts till she found his number, and hit the call button. It rang several times before a gruff, male voice said, 'Yes.'

'Dad, it's Sarah,' she began, hoping he might have changed and might have sounded pleased to hear from her.

'What can I do for you?' was his response, as if he were talking to a cold-caller.

'I thought I'd phone and see how you are,' Sarah

continued. She had already determined that she would try and sound as upbeat as possible, so he would know that she was in a happy place in her life and might care to share in her pleasure.

'I'm fine,' he replied, leaving an awkward silence hanging in the air.

'Good,' she said when no further statement was forthcoming. 'Have you been up to much?'

'This and that.'

Sarah wanted to shout at him down the phone, to tell him to take a fucking interest in her life and ask how she was, but she knew there was no point.

'Okay,' she said, deciding to surrender her chirpy attitude, 'well I thought I would just let you know that I might be getting married in the next year.'

'Oh right,' he responded, followed by a dour, 'Congratulations.'

'Thanks,' she said, sarcastically, before adding, 'I am planning to propose to Erin tonight.'

'Okay,' he replied with no emotion. No questions about how she planned to pop the question, what type of venue they would be looking at, or even when they were planning the ceremony; none of the normal questions a father might ask his daughter on receiving such news.

'Right,' said Sarah dismissively, 'well, I just thought I would let you know.'

'Thank you.'

Sarah couldn't be bothered to try anymore and disconnected the call. His stubbornness riled her. Her original plan had been to ask him to attend the ceremony and do the honourable thing and give her away, but his cold reaction to the news had changed her mind. He had been little more than a bit-part in her life story since the funeral, and, as far as she was concerned, he didn't need to be any more than that in her future. So long as Erin was there on the day, nothing else mattered. She was the one she wanted to settle down with. If her father wasn't prepared to accept the olive branch she was offering, then he didn't deserve a part in her future.

Sarah had originally planned to propose the night before, after dinner, and had planned to hide the engagement ring in the zabaglione. She wanted the mood to be just right. She had set up a playlist of Erin's favourite songs that she would play in the background and would then get down on one knee and ask her the question. Butterflies danced in her stomach as she thought about the moment when Erin would say yes, and they would disappear off to the bedroom to consummate their love. This feeling totally banished the negative thoughts she had been experiencing about her father and caused her to smile as she left the house and began her journey to work.

10

Ten minutes later, in the Police Headquarters building, Detective Inspector Jack Vincent was pacing at the front of the Major Incident room. He had pulled the whole team in for this morning's briefing, to establish what progress had been made in the investigation into the disappearance of Natalie Barrett. As usual, his sleeves were rolled up, revealing his dark, hairy arms. His tie was pulled down an inch, allowing him to unfasten the top button on his shirt. Vincent was the sort of man who found pacing a great thought-provoker.

'What have we got, people?' he began, talking to nobody in particular.

His question was met with silence. The group knew that nobody had yet discovered the vital clue that might lead to the recovery of the missing girl, but they also knew that Vincent would not be happy with this news. Senior members of the team glanced at each other nervously, hoping that someone would take the lead and feel the full force of Vincent's anger.

'Come on, people,' Vincent repeated. 'Somebody give me something; anything. Marsden, what happened with that witness who lives near the school?'

Marsden's face dropped, as he realised he was in the firing line, and had nothing to defend himself with. He removed a small notebook from his trouser pocket and flipped through the pages. He wasn't looking for anything in particular; it was just a delaying tactic while he tried to work out how to phrase his response in the most positive light.

'You mean, Mrs Jones, Guv?' Marsden replied.

'Does she live near the school?' Vincent questioned. In truth, he had no idea what the witness' name was, as it was irrelevant.

'She lives across the road from the school, Guv.'

'And what did she see?' Vincent demanded, frustrated that he was being forced to manually extract the information from the tubby Marsden.

'She claimed to see a red car outside the school around half past three, but could only confirm the colour. Her eyesight is pretty poor and given her age, she was unable to provide make, model or description of the vehicle. All she said was that it was *different*.'

'How old is she?'

'In her early eighties, Guv,' Marsden replied, pleased that Vincent had yet to shout.

'Did you speak to her neighbours, to see if any of them recall seeing a red car parked outside the school?'

'Not yet,' said Marsden, gulping.

'What? Why not?' shouted Vincent.

Marsden dropped his eyes as he tried to justify this latest oversight in what had been a far-from-distinguished career to date.

'Well, the Jones woman wasn't even able to confirm if the girl got in the car. All she witnessed was a red car parked outside the school. It could have been anyone and may not be related to the case.'

The rest of the group seemed to take a collective step backwards, as they waited for Vincent to explode.

'It may not be related to the case?' Vincent

bellowed. 'A witness saw a red car parked outside the school, at the time the girl was abducted and you think it *may* not be relevant? Are you fucking stupid? The first thing you should have done was to try and verify the account with the other residents in the street.' Vincent stopped pacing and turned so that he was able to address the whole room. 'Come on people. You are the best Hampshire has to offer; surely you don't need me to do your jobs for you? We need to think smarter: faster.'

Vincent began pacing again, taking deep breaths to calm himself down. He knew he shouldn't have sworn at Marsden, but the pressure of the case was starting to get to him. No, it was the lack of progress that was getting to him.

'What else have we got?'

'I spoke with that footballer,' offered a quiet voice, from near the back of the room. It caused Vincent to stop pacing again so that he could try and pick out who had spoken. The voice belonged to a young lad, who was being borrowed from uniform to support the investigation.

'Davies isn't it?' Vincent asked to check he was speaking to the right person.

'Davies, sir, yes. John.'

'What did the footballer have to say?' Vincent asked.

'Mr Boller says he left the school a little after three. He said he vaguely remembers seeing a girl in a red coat, stood by the school gates alone. He said he was surprised that she was stood outside of the school, as he would have expected her to be waiting for her parents inside the school gates.'

'Can he be any more specific about the time he

left?' asked Vincent.

'He said he finished talking to Mr Stanley, the head of Year-5 as the school bell rang. Then he took a phone call from his agent, which lasted about ten or so minutes, after that he started the engine and drove home,' replied Davies eagerly.

'So that means she was still stood at the gates at about quarter past three?'

'Yes, Guv.'

'Good,' mused Vincent. 'That narrows our window a bit more. Marsden, did Mrs Jones recall seeing the little girl stood near the school after the red car had moved?'

Marsden was still licking his wounds following the last attack, and was surprised to hear his name mentioned so soon after. He didn't quite hear Vincent's question and had to replay it in his head, before he eventually spoke up.

'No, Guv. She was adamant that there was nobody stood by the gates once the car had moved.'

'How can she be so certain of the time?' asked Erin, suddenly intrigued by the red car angle of the investigation.

'She was watching Countdown on the telly and whenever it went to an ad break, she glanced out of her window to see what was going on,' replied Marsden. 'She said the car was there at the second break but gone by the third.'

Vincent's eyes narrowed as he did the maths in his head. He then turned to face the three dry-wipe boards behind him, where the team had been updating facts of the case. Vincent grabbed at a marker pen and wrote '3:15 to 3:45'. Satisfied with his work, he turned back to the group. 'Here it is, people.

This is our window. Natalie Barrett was abducted between three fifteen and three forty-five. I want you to go out and re-canvas the area. I want you to knock on every door, talk to every shopkeeper. You are to ask them to recall that timeframe. Any sightings of the little girl or the red car.'

Vincent looked pleased with himself. 'What else have we got?' he asked. 'Have we established the whereabouts of all the perverts on our patch yet?'

A few snickers echoed around the quiet office.

'There's one person of interest, Guv,' said Davies, when the rest of the team had confirmed alibis for those they had spoken with.

'Go on,' Vincent urged.

'Miles Heath, Guv,' offered Davies. 'No answer at his house on the three occasions I drove by yesterday. I spoke to his neighbour and she said she hasn't seen him since Friday morning.'

'Tell me there's more than that?'

'Yes, Guv. He was seen loading a suitcase and some boxes of food into a camper van, before heading off. The thing is Guv, he hasn't checked in with his handler to say he is going on holiday. He lives in Thornhill, less than a mile from the school.'

'Any idea of his whereabouts at the moment or when he is due back?'

'The neighbour said she wasn't sure, but it didn't look like he'd packed much stuff, so she assumed he would be back in about a week. I spoke to the dairy company that delivers his milk, and he's cancelled it until Thursday, so he should be back on Friday, I guess.'

'Good work again, Davies. I want you to do some digging about. Find out the registration of the camper van, see if you can track it through the city's cameras and find out where he was heading. On Friday, I want you at his place early, so you can bring him in as soon as he surfaces.'

'Yes, Guv,' replied Davies, nodding his agreement.

'What about the parents, Guv?' shouted another voice from the group. 'Are we certain it's not them?'

'Who said that?' asked Vincent glancing around the group.

'Capshaw, sir,' replied the voice.

Oliver Capshaw was another officer on loan from uniform and was stood next to Davies. Having seen Davies receive praise for his efforts, Capshaw wanted in on the action.

'Melanie Barrett's alibi has been verified by her client,' replied Vincent. 'We have checked local traffic cameras and the route described by Melanie Barrett was chocker-block on Friday afternoon so we're satisfied she's telling the truth.'

'And what about Neil Barrett? Have we checked the garage's records yet?' asked Capshaw again.

'Yes,' answered Erin, speaking up. 'D.I. Vincent and I located the client who confirmed Neil Barrett arrived at his car at half past three and was with him until after five, when he received a call from Melanie, explaining that Natalie was missing. We're pretty sure it's not the parents.'

'Oh,' was all Capshaw could reply, disappointed that he hadn't progressed the investigation any further. Unlike Davies, Capshaw had a strong desire to leave uniform and work for Vincent on a more permanent basis. He had taken the National Investigator's exam four times already without success and was secretly hoping that Vincent would take him under his wing and act as mentor.

'Any other ideas?' Vincent asked his team of fifteen officers, with varying degrees of experience. The question was again met with silence. The truth was, none of them had any real idea who had taken Natalie Barrett. Vincent attempted to make eye contact with each of them, desperate for someone to shout out the solution to the problem but nobody was forthcoming. Vincent was about to wrap up the meeting and send them out to continue their enquiries when Erin stepped forward.

'Yes, Cookie?' Vincent asked, causing fourteen pairs of eyes to turn and stare at her.

'What about Jimmy Barrett?' she asked.

'What about Jimmy Barrett?' replied Vincent, surprised by the question.

'Have we got an alibi for him yet?'

'What are you thinking?' asked Vincent, intrigued.

Erin had been reluctant to step forward with Sarah's theory, particularly as it was her girlfriend's theory and if she admitted as much she would be laughed out of the office.

'Well,' she began, 'we've been advised that Natalie wasn't the sort of girl who would get into a car with a stranger, right? Well, what if the driver of the red car wasn't a stranger?'

'I understand what you're saying, Cookie, but what makes you think Jimmy Barrett is the driver?' asked Vincent.

'Natalie's teacher told me that Natalie wrote a story and drew a picture of a monster on Friday and she believes it might have been a cry for help from Natalie.'

The response was met with sniggers from her colleagues, particularly those that had figured out Erin was referring to her girlfriend, without directly naming her. Vincent didn't look happy.

'Look, I know it's a stretch,' continued Erin, eager to defend her theory. 'We know that Neil and Melanie have been arguing recently from the reports filed by uniform, following neighbour complaints. The arguments only started up a few months ago, around the same time that Jimmy Barrett returned from active duty and moved in with the family. It's a small house; it can't be easy having three adults and a child under the same roof.'

Vincent's expression still hadn't softened, so Erin continued, 'What if Jimmy Barrett is suffering from some kind of post-traumatic stress? He thinks he is doing his brother a favour by collecting Natalie from school. Maybe she has a go at him because he is causing her parents to argue. He shouts at her, maybe strikes her, goes too far and dumps the body. I know it's thin, but we should at least check out what he was doing at the time.'

'Jimmy Barrett didn't do this,' answered Marsden, laughing. 'I can vouch for him. I regularly see him down *The Swan*. He hasn't got PTSD.'

'Why? Just because he can throw beer down his throat? Show some objectivity, Marsden,' replied Erin defensively. She wouldn't have minded if the challenge had come from any of her other colleagues, but she despised Marsden, whom she considered a dinosaur from a bygone era; more interested in working nine to five than doing real investigative police work. In fairness, he wasn't her number one fan either.

'I need to be objective? What about you, taking advice from your girlfriend on how to solve this case?' he replied.

'Sarah is the best witness we have to Natalie's state of mind on the day of her disappearance, and has studied child behavioural psychology, so she's certainly more qualified than you to comment on this case,' replied Erin angrily.

'That's enough!' shouted Vincent, interrupting the argument before it spiralled out of control.

Marsden looked hurt and angry but knew not to go against Vincent's wishes. He would get his revenge on her in the future, he vowed.

'Okay,' continued Vincent when silence had returned to the room. 'Cookie, go and interview that nosy neighbour. Find out why she really called uniform in. Then go and speak with Jimmy Barrett. Find out what he was up to on Friday afternoon and do some digging into why he left the army when he did. The rest of you go start asking some questions. We meet back here at five tonight, and I want some progress!'

Vincent then turned his back on the group to study the dry wipe boards once more. The group knew this was the indication that the briefing was over and that they had been dismissed.

11

Erin knocked on the door of number fourteen. She had been anxious not to let on to the Barretts that she was following up on the previous day's interview, so she had parked her unmarked squad car, around the corner. There was no obvious doorbell to press, but there was a gold-coloured door knocker, so Erin used that instead. She didn't even know the name of the nosy neighbour, as the Barretts had not offered it, and it would have given the game away to have phoned and asked. She had checked if the patrol officers had a name for the person who made the complaints that they had been called out on, but they had told her the calls had been anonymously made.

After a sixty second delay, the door to number fourteen was opened and a very average-looking, grey-haired woman appeared in the door frame.

'Yes?' enquired a voice, oozing snootiness.

'Hello, are you the owner of this property?' asked Erin, not quite sure how to fish out the woman's name.

'I don't buy things at the door, dear. Thank you anyway,' replied the woman, starting to close the door.

'Oh no,' said Erin pushing the door to prevent it closing. 'I'm not selling anything. I'm a police officer.'

Erin produced her warrant card from her pocket and held it up for the woman to see.

'Wait a second,' said the woman, who then

shuffled off back into the house. Erin was unsure whether she should follow or stay where she was. She was about to ask, when the woman returned clutching a pair of reading glasses. She slipped them onto her nose and grabbed at the warrant card, snatching it from Erin's grasp.

'Can't see a thing without my glasses,' she said, scanning the card, looking for signs of authenticity. Erin's I.D. couldn't have been more than three inches from the end of the woman's nose, and she was tempted to suggest that the woman should increase the prescription of her glasses, when the warrant card was thrust back towards her.

'Right, Detective Cooke,' said the woman, matter-of-factly. 'What can I do for you?'

'Would it be okay if I came in, please?' asked Erin, keen to avoid the chance the Barretts might spot her.

'Whatever for?' asked the woman.

'It's about your neighbours, the Barretts? I'm investigating the disappearance of their daughter, Natalie. Do you know her?'

'Horrible little brat,' the woman said, looking down her nose at Erin. 'I suppose you better come in,' she added, pulling the door open for Erin to enter.

Erin walked along the narrow corridor, to the room at the end, which she quickly identified as the living room. The layout was very similar to the Barretts' house, although the kitchen and staircase were on opposite sides. Erin sat down on the edge of a sofa and, once the woman was sat down as well, said, 'Can I take a note of your name, please?'

'Mrs Norris. N, O, double R, I, S.'

'Thank you, Mrs Norris,' replied Erin. It was standard practice to take a first name as well, but Erin was pretty confident Mrs Norris wouldn't be so willing to part with it. 'Can you tell me what the Barretts are like?'

'They're not really my sort of people,' replied Mrs Norris. 'I can't say we see eye-to-eye on most matters. To be perfectly honest, I try to avoid any contact with them if possible.'

'I see,' said Erin, pretending to write something in the notepad, she had just pulled from her pocket. 'Were you aware that the police were called to their property a couple of times in the last few months?'

'Yes, I saw them there.'

'You wouldn't happen to know who phoned the police on those occasions would you?' Erin asked, drawing a small doodle of a flower on the notepad.

'Well, yes,' replied Mrs Norris. 'Since you ask, it was I whom called the police.'

'Can you tell me what led to you phoning them?'

'I told the officer on the telephone why. Don't you people keep records of your calls anymore?' Mrs Norris replied.

'Of course, we do, Mrs Norris, but the report is limited to only a brief description of the purpose of the call. You know, like, 'domestic disturbance', that kind of thing. I was hoping you could confirm what you saw or heard, in your own words.'

Mrs Norris paused for a moment, clearly trying to decide how much to share. Eventually, she said, 'They argue, a lot. There are always loud voices and loud, crashing noises, when I am out walking little Petra.'

'Petra?' asked Erin, already aware of the answer.

'Petra. My chihuahua. They really do make the most horrendous sounds when they are fighting. Anyway, I was concerned that the arguments were becoming more heated and more frequent, so I called you people, to report it. It was only the right thing to do, in my opinion. For the good of the street.'

Erin jotted down 'snooty cow' but quickly scribbled over the top of it, in case Vincent asked to see her notes at any point. Mrs Norris reminded Erin of Patricia Routledge's character, from *Keeping Up Appearances*.

'Was there anything specific that happened that caused you concern, Mrs Norris?'

'Such as what?'

'You mentioned at the door, that you knew of young Natalie. Was there anything about the Barretts that made you worry about her safety?' asked Erin.

'Oh, I see,' said Mrs Norris with a knowing look in her eyes. 'You're here to talk about that brother of his.'

'That's right,' said Erin, playing along, not quite sure where Mrs Norris was now leading the conversation.

'Grubby lay-about, that one,' said Mrs Norris. 'They never should have taken him back in. Just looking at him, you can tell he's trouble.'

'Can you tell me what happened?' asked Erin.

'This should all have been in the report, as well,' replied Mrs Norris, sighing.

'In your own words, remember, Mrs Norris,' coaxed Erin.

'Well, it must have been about six weeks ago, I suppose,' said Mrs Norris, raising her eyes, as she tried to recall the memory. 'I was out the front, tending to the garden. I looked up and saw the brother stood on the driveway, drinking from a can of something or other; beer, lager, cider, who knows?

Anyway, he seemed to be draining the can so he could dispose of it in the brown recycle bin. I mean, this was at ten o'clock in the morning. What kind of man is drinking alcohol that early? Disgraceful!'

Mrs Norris waited for Erin to nod agreement at the statement before proceeding, 'The little girl came out of the house and walked over to him to say something I couldn't hear, and he bent over, grabbed her wrist and started shouting something at her.'

'What was he shouting?' asked Erin, now eagerly writing down notes, pertaining to Jimmy Barrett.

'I couldn't really make it out, but the girl's reaction said it all: she ran from him into the house in tears. When he stood back up, he saw that I was observing what had happened and he shouted a rude obscenity in my direction, before marching off down the road, probably in search of the nearest pub or off licence.'

'What did he shout at you, Mrs Norris?'

'I would prefer not to repeat it, if it's all the same to you. It was very rude!'

'So you don't know what his rant at Natalie was about?' Erin persisted.

'No. As I said, I couldn't really hear the words, just the intonation of what was said. He was definitely shouting, and he definitely grabbed her wrist.'

'And did you report that incident to the police as well?'

'I tried, but this time the young man on the line told me I would have to give my name if I suspected any kind of child abuse, but I did not wish to, so I disconnected the call.'

'Right,' said Erin, standing suddenly, eager to share this new item with Vincent. 'Thank you for your time, Mrs Norris. I'll leave you a card with my telephone number on. If you remember anything else, please give me a call?'

Erin fished her business card out of her purse and handed it over. Mrs Norris took the card and placed it on a coffee table to her left.

'I'll show myself out, Mrs Norris,' said Erin, turning on her heel. 'Thanks again, for your help.'

12

Sarah waited until the last of her class had disappeared out of the door, before she sat down and let out a satisfied sigh. She had made it through the morning intact and the lingering headache that had been with her since she had woken up, hung-over that morning was finally dissipating. She reached out and picked up the plastic bottle of water that she had been taking regular sips from all morning, flipped the lid and poured the remaining contents into her mouth. She knew that the pain killers she had taken were controlling the ache in her head, but she was also convinced that her attempts to rehydrate were probably playing their part too. She made a mental note to ensure she topped up the bottle before the children returned from their lunch break.

In preparation for the evening's planned big meal, Sarah had brought a small cheese sandwich with her, as a snack for the lunch period, and was just about to pull it out of her bag and head to the staff room when she heard a familiar voice at the door.

'I hope I'm not disturbing you?'

Sarah was startled by the sudden noise and looked up to see the smiling face of Johan Boller standing in her doorway.

'That's fine, Johan, come in,' she beckoned, smiling back. 'What can I do for you?'

The handsome, Swiss footballer walked into the room and perched himself on the edge of a table, opposite Sarah. He must have been in his mid-twenties, by Sarah's estimation.

'I came in to speak with Mrs McGregor about a further appearance she wants me to make, before the school breaks up for the summer,' he explained. 'She's asked me to hand out medals at the school sports day, which I think you are having, at the end of the Olympics initiative?'

'That's right,' she affirmed. 'The last day of term is scheduled to be an all-day sports event for the children, competing in a range of Olympic-type events. She mentioned to me that she was hoping you might come back to close the project as you opened it.'

'Yeah,' he said. 'I told her it should be okay but it depends whether I get called up to play in the European championships, if I do I won't be able to be here.'

'Sorry, I don't really follow football, is that likely?'

'I hope so,' he replied honestly, 'but it would also be great to see the children again. I enjoyed myself last Friday.'

'Good,' said Sarah. 'The children loved having you here. They talked about nothing else yesterday.'

'That's nice,' he said smiling again. Sarah had to admit, he did look cute, even if he wasn't her usual type. 'I thought I should come and see how you are.'

'How I am?' she asked, surprised.

'Yes. The police told me that one of the children went missing on Friday afternoon?'

Sarah couldn't believe she had allowed Natalie's disappearance to slip from her mind.

'That's right. She is such a sweet girl. God knows what kind of sick bastard is capable of that kind of thing.'

Johan didn't reply and Sarah suddenly became conscious that her language may have offended the footballer.

'Sorry,' she said. 'It just gets to me.'

'That's okay. I can understand how you feel. The police told me that I may have been the last person to see her, before it happened.'

'Really?'

'Yes,' he continued. 'I saw her stood by the gates as I left at about three fifteen.'

'Did you see anyone else around?' asked Sarah, keen to know as much as she could about who might have abducted her little star.

'As I told the police, I wasn't really concentrating as I left. I remember seeing a girl in a red coat but that is all. I was setting up my navigation system, as I still don't know the roads around Southampton. I was more concerned with not getting lost, than I was on who might be around.' He hung his head in shame, 'I know how bad that sounds.'

'It's not your fault, Johan,' she said, keen to make him feel better. 'You weren't to know that she was in any danger.'

'That's kind of you to say,' he responded, 'but if I had been more alert, I might have noticed something.'

An awkward silence followed, before Johan spoke again, 'How are the other children? Do they know what has happened?'

'They seem okay. After last night's press conference, we had to make an announcement this morning. Those that didn't see it on the news would have eventually heard about it through playground gossip. We tried to keep the level of detail as vague as possible, so as not to scare them anymore than they already are.'

'I suppose they should be warned, in case the person strikes again.'

'That's true,' Sarah agreed, 'but I don't believe it will happen again.'

'You don't? Why not? Do you know who took her?'

Sarah looked around to check that nobody had popped into the room to overhear them. When she was satisfied that nobody was listening, she said, 'I have my suspicions about who has her and have told the police. I reckon he'll be caught soon enough and hopefully she'll be returned.'

'Oh, so you think she is still alive?' Johan asked.

'Yes, maybe, I don't know. Do you not?' replied Sarah, thrown by the question.

'I don't know,' said Johan throwing his hands up in mock defence. 'These things don't always end well, do they?'

'I hope this one does,' Sarah said.

'So do I,' he echoed, hoping that he had not inadvertently upset her.

She looked up at him and he smiled weakly to test the waters and was relieved when she smiled back.

'I should go,' he offered, standing up.

'Thanks, yeah. I need to prepare everything for this afternoon.'

'Are you busy later?' he asked.

'What? Sorry?' said Sarah, again surprised by the directness of the question.

'Are you busy later?' Johan repeated. 'I thought maybe we could go for a drink?'

'Go for a drink?'

'Yes. A drink, in a bar, talking? It's what people do?' he replied sarcastically.

'You want to go for a drink? With me?'

'Yes I do,' he said, smiling again. 'I like you, Sarah. I'd like to get to know you better. Do you not want to?'

Sarah was flattered by the request but uncertain how to respond. She knew she had to let him down, but wanted to do it as gently as possible.

'It's a very kind offer, Johan, but I already have a partner.'

'Oh, I see,' he responded cautiously. 'There is no ring; I thought you might be single.'

Sarah glanced at her left hand and acknowledged that indeed there wasn't a ring on her finger, but couldn't help but giggle at thinking there very well could be a ring there tonight.

'Is it serious between the two of you?' he asked, knowing that he had managed to convince other women to drop their boyfriends for him in the past.

'Pretty serious, yes.'

'And you won't change your mind?' he asked, smiling as broadly as he could.

'I am flattered, Johan, really, I am, but there is no way you can convince me to change my mind. Even if I wasn't in a relationship, I'm not sure we would have much of a future.'

Mistakenly, sensing that she was softening, he asked, 'And why not?'

Sarah noticed that he didn't seem to be getting the hint so blurted out, 'I'm gay, Johan. I am in love with another woman, so your smile, as cute as it is, just isn't going to work.'

Relieved that it wasn't that she found him

unattractive, Johan held his hands up in mock surrender again and said, 'Okay. I understand. You can't blame me for trying, can you?'

'Not at all. As I said, I'm flattered that you would ask.'

'Well, I should go,' he said, as he started to walk towards the door, before turning back and saying, 'you are not offended?'

'No,' she said, smiling.

'Good,' he replied and disappeared out of the door.

Sarah smiled to herself at the thought she had just been asked out on a date by a famous celebrity. She imagined herself as a footballer's WAG and shuddered at the thought. It would make a great story to tell Erin later. Sarah reached down and picked up her handbag. She really didn't fancy eating the cheese sandwich, but knew it was a good idea to eat something, even if it was just to soak up the remaining alcohol in her system. She stood and left the classroom, heading for the staff room.

13

Erin pulled her car into a marked bay in the car park, beneath the Central Police Headquarters building. It had been a long day and, in fact, it felt like it had been a long week, even though it was only Tuesday. She knew Vincent would sort it, so that she got credit for the additional hours worked over the two days, but she was upset that she had missed out on the birthday meal Sarah had been attempting to cook for her, the previous evening. Even though she had promised to be home by seven tonight, she knew there was a danger she wouldn't be able to keep that promise.

Erin glanced up at her reflection in the rear-view mirror. She didn't look as tired as she felt, and she thanked the miracle-workers, in factories across the globe, that churned out the various moisturising creams she applied daily, to keep her skin taut and fresh. She felt the vibration of her mobile phone in her pocket and pulled it out to see that she had received a text message from Sarah. Erin laughed as she read it; apparently Johan Boller had visited the school and made a pass at Sarah, but she had let him down gently. Erin knew how lucky she was to have found Sarah, and really appreciated their relationship: It didn't matter how bad things got at work, Sarah was always there to comfort her. She had considered proposing to Sarah, to cement their love, but after the death of Sarah's mother three years ago, she had wondered whether Sarah would ever wish to get married. It didn't bother Erin if they didn't marry, as she was certain of Sarah's feelings for her, but, like most women, she had dreamed of her big wedding day since she was a child.

The digits on the dashboard clock showed that it was just coming up to six p.m. Erin was back at the station to file a report of what she had learned that afternoon. She had managed to eventually track Jimmy Barrett down and in hindsight she probably should have checked that location first: *The Swan* pub, where Marsden had mentioned seeing him. Naively, Erin had spent an hour trying to get hold of Neil and Melanie Barrett to see if they knew his whereabouts, but both had been rather dismissive in their responses, Melanie more so than Neil, indicating that perhaps there was something more to Sarah's theory. Clearly, Melanie was not her brother-in-law's biggest fan.

Neil Barrett had named a handful of local pubs that his brother was likely to frequent, assuming he wasn't at the bookies. Neil didn't paint a particularly pleasant picture of his brother and yet he had not seemed to be doing it out of malice; if anything, it was pity.

Erin had found the pub in question and sure enough, as she had entered, she saw Jimmy Barrett sat on a stool at the bar, nursing what looked like a pint of lager. Erin had walked straight up to him and offered to buy him a drink. She had decided that her approach should appear friendly, and she told him that she just needed to check a few background details of his whereabouts on Friday afternoon. When he looked up at her with an expression of anger, she quickly re-assured him that it was just a formality, and that she knew he had nothing to do with Natalie's disappearance. Even though she was in a public place and was the figure of authority in the exchange, he was a bulky man and if he were suffering some kind of post-traumatic stress, she didn't want to be on the receiving end when he lashed out. Given what Mrs Norris had told her earlier that afternoon, she knew he was capable of violence.

He accepted the drink and told her that he had been at a bookies in nearby Woolston, until four thirty on Friday, and had then come down to *The Swan* to spend his winnings. Erin estimated it was probably a fifteen minute walk from Woolston to *The Swan*, and that the bookies would have witnesses capable of validating or contesting Jimmy's alibi.

Vincent had told her to look into the background of Jimmy Barrett, as well, to identify if he could indeed be the monster from Natalie's picture, but neither Neil nor Melanie Barrett had been particularly forthcoming with the reasons that Jimmy had left the armed forces so suddenly. This meant Erin would have to ask him outright, but without appearing threatening. She ordered herself a soft drink and pulled up a stool to sit on, next to Jimmy. His defensive body language showed that this was going to be a cagey conversation. Erin lied that her father had served in the Falklands, but had left the service when she was born, as he was too worried about missing her growing up. Erin's father had in fact worked for a bank, but she saw the untruth as the best way to open Jimmy up. It worked.

Jimmy asked about what unit her father had served in and she made out that she wasn't certain, as he had rarely discussed his years in uniform with her, before his early death. She sounded just vague enough to pass as believable. She asked tentative questions, such as what had made Jimmy join the army to begin with and how much of a culture shock he had found it. He explained that he had signed up with a couple of friends, as he had not done very well at school, and the army didn't seem to care about his past. He actually smiled at times and Erin continued to buy him drinks to keep his lips moving. The more he drank, the more he opened up. The smell of his alcohol-stained tongue made Erin want to retch, but she smiled through the pain, pretending she couldn't smell it. It was a smell she knew all too well, as a recovering alcoholic herself.

After the fifth pint she had bought him and his umpteenth cigarette break, he confided that he had been asked to leave the army after an incident with his superior officer. A court martial hearing had been convened after he punched the officer during an argument at the barracks bar. A psychiatrist at the hearing ruled that Jimmy was indeed suffering from PTSD, following his stint in Afghanistan, and the decision was made not to dishonourably discharge him. However, it was decided that Jimmy would be unable to continue serving with his present condition. Having spent the last fifteen years serving, leaving the army and returning to a 'normal' way of life had actually been a greater culture shock than when he had first signed up.

Before she left the pub, Erin had had a private word with the man behind the bar, to see if he could remember what time Jimmy had come in on Friday afternoon, but he had explained that it had been his day off but could confirm that Jimmy was a regular. Erin left her telephone number and asked him to arrange for someone to call her and confirm what time Jimmy arrived on Friday afternoon. The bartender indicated he would see what he could do.

Erin left the pub with lingering doubts in her mind about Jimmy Barrett. In one way she pitied him for his fish-out-of-water status, but at the same time he had admitted to having a violent streak, and she could easily imagine that he was indeed the dragon in Natalie's painting. But did that mean he was capable of taking her? Mrs Norris would probably think so, but she wasn't so sure. She had left *The Swan* at the wrong time really, as she had hit rush-hour traffic over the Itchen toll bridge and had literally crawled back to the station. She determined that she would file her report with Vincent, as quickly as she could, and get herself home. If she worked it right, there was still a chance she could make it home by seven.

Erin found Vincent in his office, pouring over witness statements that had been produced by the team over the course of the day. Erin's face at the door was a welcome relief and, as she entered, he offered her a drink of the scotch that he kept hidden in the bottom drawer of his desk, for those occasions when he deemed it necessary. Erin declined, but told him she wouldn't be offended if he wanted one. Vincent poured himself two-fingers' worth of liquor into a glass tumbler and savoured the taste as it washed down his throat.

Erin proceeded to tell Vincent everything that she had learned from Mrs Norris, the Barretts and then Jimmy. When she had finished Vincent asked, 'What does your gut say?'

Erin had known he would probably ask this question and that whatever response she offered, would be taken, as salient as fact, so it was important that she felt comfortable with her conclusion.

'I have to be honest, Guv,' she began. 'I think Jimmy Barrett warrants further investigation. Do I think he abducted Natalie? No. Do I think it's possible that he collected her from school as a kind gesture for Neil and Melanie and that something could have gone wrong and he stashed the body? Maybe. I definitely think there are question marks over his mental state.'

Vincent seemed to ponder her response for a moment and Erin took advantage of the silence to plough on, 'How did this afternoon's interviewing of potential witnesses go? Any leads?'

The question worked and threw Vincent's attention back to the reams of paperwork in front of him.'

'Not yet,' he responded, picking up various bits of paper in his hands to show how much he had already reviewed. 'Nobody else has mentioned a red car, or seeing Natalie walking, so it's a bit of a dead end. Seems everyone was too busy, watching that footballer, to notice a little girl walking alone.'

'What about the crossing guard?'

'Didn't notice a thing, she told me,' he replied, sighing.

'Maybe we just need to take a break from it all; look at it with fresh eyes in the morning,' suggested Erin, conscious that she had been sat with Vincent for half an hour already and was keen to get home.

'Maybe you're right, Cookie,' he said, accepting defeat. 'Have you got plans for this evening?'

'Sarah's cooking me a birthday meal,' she replied, smiling.

'It's your birthday? I can't believe I forgot,' Vincent replied, feeling incredibly guilty.

'That's okay, Guv. You've had a lot on with the case and all.' She didn't have the heart to tell him it had actually been her birthday the day before, and that he had caused her to miss the celebration.

'Well, I'm sorry, anyway,' said Vincent, offering an apologetic smile. 'You better get yourself off home.'

As he said it, a thought struck Erin. It was so ridiculous that she almost laughed out loud, but then, the more she thought about it, the more the thought grew.

'Something funny?' Vincent asked, when he saw her smiling to herself, lost in her own little world.

'No, Guv,' she said, quickly realising where she was. 'Just a theory.'

'A theory? About the case?'

'Mmm,' she replied as she continued to work through the angles.

'Care to share it?' Vincent asked, ever hopeful for a breakthrough.

'It's probably stupid,' she answered, not wishing to get herself booted off the team. 'Let me check something out on the way home and if I think it has legs, we can chat about it in the morning. It's just a feeling at the moment, too circumstantial.'

'Okay,' said Vincent, not wishing to prohibit his young star's creativity. 'Don't spend too long on it; I don't want you to miss your birthday dinner.'

'Don't worry, Guv,' Erin said standing and heading towards the door. 'There's no danger of that.'

Vincent smiled and then added, 'By the way,

Cookie, you might want to take a shower. You smell like a brewery.'

'Thanks, Guv,' she replied. 'That's Jimmy Barrett for you. Good night.'

With that she disappeared through the door, closing it behind her. Vincent took a sip from his tumbler and allowed his eyes to re-focus on the paperwork in front of him.

14

Sarah sat bolt upright as she heard the distinct sound of a car pulling up outside. It took her a moment to get her bearings. The room was dark and the limited light emanating from the translucent curtains only revealed dark shadows instead of objects. She certainly wasn't on her bed, which ruled out her being in the bedroom. She blinked several times as she tried to encourage her eyes to adjust to the darkness. She felt exhausted and assumed she must have been in quite a deep sleep when the sound of the car had disturbed her. It was very dark, which would suggest it was quite late, so why was she not in bed?

As her eyes adjusted to the darkness, she recognised her television, coffee tables, lamps and the sofa she was stretched out on: She had been asleep in the living room. She swung her legs from the sofa, so that she was in a sitting position, and then leant forward so that she could run her hands over the carpet in an effort to locate her mobile phone. Despite her efforts, her fingers merely brushed the fibres and found nothing. She decided to put the light on and reached over to the coffee table, beside the sofa, pressed the switch on the light cord and the room illuminated. She quickly spotted the mobile phone on the coffee table, and pressed a button to display the time. It was nearly midnight, which explained why it was so dark outside.

Where was Erin? The plan had been for Erin to be home at seven. But Sarah had not been surprised to receive a brief text message explaining that she was running late again. She had been disappointed, as usual, but Erin's message had indicated that she would be home by eight at the latest, so Sarah had poured a glass of wine and put the television on. Clearly she must have dozed off. Sarah noticed the empty wine glass on the table, along with a packet of painkillers and a new memory popped into her mind. She had taken a couple of pills to help clear that lurking headache, which had returned once school had finished. It must have been a mixture of those and the wine that had knocked her out.

It still didn't explain where Erin was and why she had not returned home at eight, as indicated. Sarah flicked through her mobile phone until she located Erin's mobile number and she pressed the screen to call the number. It went straight through to voicemail, which suggested Erin's phone was turned off. Sarah screwed up her face; this was very odd, as Erin never turned her phone off, even at night. It was possible that the battery had gone dead, if she had been using the phone all day, but if it had, it would have been the first time. Besides, Erin had a charger for the phone in her car and surely would have plugged it in, if the battery were nearly dead.

Sarah checked through her text messages and emails, and the only thing she had received from Erin was the text message saying she would be home by eight. Sarah started to worry. It wasn't out of character for Erin to be late home, and to not tell Sarah in advance, but even Erin was usually home by this time. Sarah thought about calling Erin's desk phone but the last thing she wanted to do was phone up and embarrass Erin at work. Sarah knew Erin had worked hard to win over her colleagues and a panicked call from 'the little lady at home' would probably lead to ridicule.

Sarah went to the kitchen and filled her empty wine glass with cold water from the tap and took a big gulp. At least the headache had passed. She moved back to the living room and retook her seat on the sofa, willing her phone to ring. She heard car doors open and slam shut outside and assumed they belonged to the same car that had pulled up earlier. She moved to the window to see if she could identify who might be moving about outside at this late hour, but she couldn't really see from the angle her apartment window faced.

Sarah jumped and nearly dropped her glass when she heard the door buzzer go. She was filled with relief: Erin must have left her keys at home but at least she was here. Sarah moved across to the door and opened it.

'What have you done with your key, you silly… ?' Sarah said as she swung the door open, but she was unable to finish the sentence, as it wasn't Erin stood in the doorway. Instead, there were two men in dark uniforms with bright yellow, high-visibility coats on. Both men were wearing flat caps, and Sarah's heart skipped a beat as she realised they were police officers.

'Miss Jenson?' said one of the officers.

'Yes?'

'Miss Sarah Jenson?' said the officer again.

'Yes,' Sarah replied as her mind raced with a thousand terrible thoughts about why the police were stood at her doorstep so late at night.

'May we come in, please?'

'What's this about?' challenged Sarah. If only Erin was here, she thought; it was Erin who was best at handling these types of situations.

'It would be best if we could come in, please, Miss Jenson.'

Sarah decided not to argue, as she pulled the door open wider, and allowed the two men to enter. They seemed to find the living room instinctively and sat down on the sofa opposite where Sarah had been perched, moments earlier. The officer, who had been doing the talking, removed his hat and indicated for his colleague to follow suit.

'What's this all about?' asked Sarah, failing to hide the obvious fear in her voice.

'Take a seat, please, Miss Jenson,' the officer instructed, and Sarah dropped down to the sofa, without question. 'There is no easy way to say this, Miss Jenson, so I will just tell it how it is. Erin Cooke has been involved in a car accident.'

'Oh, God, no,' Sarah gasped. 'Is she okay?'

The officer took a deep breath and then said, 'It was quite a serious accident. Miss Cooke's car was found in a ditch near Dibden. It appears that the car left the road at some speed and rolled several times. Miss Cooke was extracted from the car and has been taken to the General Hospital. She is in a critical condition.'

'Oh, God, no!' screamed Sarah throwing her hands up to her face as tears formed deep pools in her eyes and began to trickle down her cheeks.

'Miss Jenson?' asked the officer as Sarah began to sob uncontrollably. 'Miss Jenson, please? I know this has come as a shock but it is vital that we get you to the hospital. Immediately.'

Sarah didn't hear him as she rocked backwards and forwards on the sofa. This couldn't be real, could it? Was this just Erin's way of playing a horrible practical joke? Sarah wished that Erin would jump out from wherever she was hiding and shout, 'Fooled you!' But she didn't. Sarah continued to rock on the sofa until one of the police officers stood up and moved across to her and put his large arms around her. She didn't even know his name but right now she welcomed the embrace. The officer tried to soothe her with gentle words and gradually the rocking stopped.

'Listen to me, Miss Jenson,' the officer said, ensuring he had made eye contact and had her full attention. 'I want you to pack any items you need, change of clothes, that kind of thing. Go now and pack a bag. When you're ready, we'll drive you straight to the hospital.'

Sarah nodded her understanding and ran to the bedroom, where she grabbed a t-shirt, pants, socks and trainers. She was still wearing the dress she had put on for the evening meal and as she pulled it over her head, sequins flew all over the carpet. She didn't care; she just wanted to get to the hospital, to check on Erin's condition. She threw on a pair of jeggings, the t-shirt, socks and trainers and rushed back to the living room.

'All ready?' asked the officer gently.

'Yes,' she replied and the three headed for the door.

The officer who had done all the talking, whose name was Caldicott, put the car's flashing lights and siren on and drove through every red light. D.I. Jack Vincent had given him specific instructions to get Sarah Jenson to the hospital as quickly as possible to say her goodbyes to the one she loved.

WEDNESDAY

15

Sarah sat on a plastic chair, in a corner of the room, in utter silence. To anyone watching, she looked like she was asleep with her eyes open. Her body was sat bolt upright and was unmoving; it was as if she was playing musical statues and nobody had told her that the game was over and that she could now move again. Sarah had been sat in this pose for more than two hours now, staring at the body stretched out on the hospital bed before her.

The surgeon, a stern-looking woman who went by the name Dr Habib, had advised Sarah that Erin had sustained serious head trauma during the accident and this had caused intra-cranial haemorrhaging and was the likely cause of the coma. Apparently, a '999' call had been placed anonymously shortly before nine p.m., advising that a car had been spotted careering off a road, near Dibden, just outside of Southampton. By the time Paramedics had arrived on the scene, there was no sign of who might have placed the call, or even what might have caused the accident. From what she had overheard Vincent and Caldicott discussing, there had been no skid marks on either side of the road, which suggested that another vehicle had not been involved, leaving one conclusion: Erin had simply lost control of the car. But that was so unlike Erin; she was a very safe driver.

So many questions were racing through Sarah's head that she was struggling to keep up with her own thought processes, hence why her body was as still as stone. What was Erin doing near Dibden? Why had she lost control of the car? Who had placed the '999' call and then scarpered? If the car had careered off the road, why were there no skid marks? Had she simply not braked? But the biggest question that kept bursting through all the others was: *why*? Why Erin? Why now?

It was so unfair. Sarah was finally at a point in her life when she felt genuinely happy. She was madly in love with Erin, even ready to propose to her, to make that promise to spend the rest of her life with her. Work was going well for both of them and although they didn't own their apartment, they were making enough money to live quite comfortably in a rented property in a nice area of Southampton. Only hours earlier, she had been planning how she would propose to Erin and now her whole world had been turned upside down. Still the question persevered: *why*?

Erin had been placed in an individual room, away from other patients, to ensure she received the right level of care. Vincent would never tell Sarah, but he had pulled a few strings to get the room for Erin. Erin's body had not moved since she had been wheeled back in, following an M.R.I. scan, just before midnight. It was difficult to make out who was buried beneath the wires, tubes and other various apparatus attached to the lifeless body. In fact, Sarah would have questioned if it was even Erin, had she not been told by Vincent. Amongst Erin's injuries, she had dislocated her right shoulder, fractured her pelvis and broken her ankle. Were these injuries even consistent with a car accident? Sarah didn't know but it was another question rattling around her head. So many questions, it was difficult to keep track of them.

Dr Habib had said the results of the M.R.I. would be ready by about four a.m. That deadline had passed over an hour ago, and yet Sarah was still none the wiser about the condition of her soul-mate. There was a steady bleeping noise and then the intermittence of what sounded like a small vacuum cleaner. Sarah had no idea what all the medical apparatus was, or what it was doing, but so long as it was keeping Erin alive, she didn't care.

A knock at the room's only door disturbed Sarah's questions. In walked Dr Habib in bright blue scrubs, a blue surgical cap and a white, cotton mask over her mouth and nose. She removed the mask as she approached Sarah's seat. Dr Habib found a vacant chair nearby and scraped it across the floor until it was positioned in front of Sarah and then the surgeon sat down. She took Sarah's hands in her own and forced Sarah to make eye contact. Dr Habib needed Sarah's full attention for what she was about to say, and could not afford for the young lady not to be listening.

'Miss Jenson?' the surgeon began. 'Miss Jenson? I need you to listen to me as I have an update for you and some questions. Is that okay?'

Sarah nodded, petrified about what might follow. She had a hundred and one questions to ask the doctor but knew that her chance would come, eventually.

'Right,' said Dr Habib, taking a deep breath before she continued. 'Erin has undergone an M.R.I scan, which allows us to take a picture of what is going on inside her head. Erin sustained several blows to the head, most likely the result of bashing the frame of the car, as it rolled. These blows have caused bleeding inside her head that we have been trying to stem with drugs as a limiting measure. So severe were the blows that Erin's brain has swelled in size, making it impossible for us to safely operate and have a proper look at what has happened. We had been hoping that the swelling would decrease with the drugs, but the M.R.I. suggests they are not working.'

Sarah tried to process everything Dr Habib was telling her, but she was struggling. So far all she had picked up on was that Erin was in a pretty serious condition.

'Miss Jenson?' said Dr Habib to ensure she still had Sarah's attention. 'Erin is not currently breathing by herself. That machine that looks like an accordion in a fish bowl is breathing for Erin. I have consulted with my colleagues and we do not believe that Erin's body is capable of breathing of its own volition. Do you understand what I am saying?'

Sarah continued to stare blankly back at Dr Habib, not quite realising that she was being asked a question.

'What? Sorry?' Sarah said when she noticed that the doctor was waiting for a response.

'What I said was that Erin is not currently able to breathe without the aid of that machine. The damage to her brain is so substantial that she may never regain consciousness. Do you understand what I am telling you?'

Sarah remained staring blankly, sub-consciously she knew exactly what the doctor was telling her, but the barrier her own consciousness had created was blocking the thought from getting through.

'You're saying she is going to need a lot of care?'

'Miss Jenson, I need you to understand this and I don't wish to sound blunt but the truth is: Erin is unlikely to ever wake up and recover from this accident. I am telling you that we could leave her on the ventilator for the next decade and she probably would not wake up.'

The conscious barrier collapsed and Sarah burst into tears.

'I'm so sorry, Miss Jenson but we believe the kindest thing to do would be to turn the ventilator off.'

'What?' screamed Sarah through her sobs. 'No! No way!'

Sarah pulled her hands away from Dr Habib, stood and moved to look out of the small window next to where she had been sitting. She moved her hands up to her face to prevent the world from seeing the waterfall of tears flowing down her cheeks.

Dr Habib watched Sarah for a moment to sense if she was likely to regain her composure, but after a minute decided it would be best to return later. The doctor stood and walked back towards the door. She found the suited police officer who had been sat outside the room the whole time and provided him with an update of the situation. He looked distraught with what she told him, but confirmed that he would go and talk to Sarah to try and make her understand.

Sarah turned, as she heard Jack Vincent open the door and cough to get her attention. He didn't know what to say. Seeing the total devastation in Sarah's eyes in stark contrast to the vulnerability of Cookie, unconscious in the bed; it was all he could do to stop himself from crying as well. He had to remain strong, his grieving could follow later.

'Miss Jenson,' he began, trying to stop his voice from showing emotion. 'I am so sorry...' but before he could finish what he had been rehearsing to say, Sarah moved straight across the room and wrapped her arms around his broad shoulders, put her cheek onto his shoulder and wept. It was the most human contact he had experienced in quite a while, and he felt uncomfortable as he put his arms around her and held her still. They remained, locked in this embrace until Sarah's crying subsided and she pulled away from Vincent, embarrassed that she had allowed herself to breakdown in front of a virtual stranger.

'Take a seat,' Vincent suggested and Sarah sat back on the chair in the corner of the room. Vincent then sat in the chair that had earlier been occupied by Dr Habib. Vincent was about to start talking when Sarah said, 'What happened?'

Vincent thought about how best to answer the question and then chose to be as honest as he could, 'The details are still sketchy at the moment. We know the car left the road near Dibden at some considerable speed. It rolled several times as it fell into a ditch by the side of the road. Cookie was brought in by paramedics and once her warrant card had been located, I was called in.'

'I don't understand what she was doing in Dibden,' Sarah countered. 'She was supposed to be home for dinner at seven. Why did you send her there?'

The tone in Sarah's voice was accusatory and immediately put Vincent on the defensive.

'I told her to go home and see you,' he began. 'She said she had something she wished to check out, but that she would then be heading home. I've no idea what she was doing anywhere near there!'

'She was a safe driver. I don't see why she would have lost control of the car,' challenged Sarah, raising her voice.

'I may have an answer for that,' Vincent reluctantly replied.

'Well?'

'It is standard practice for doctors to take blood samples from victims of car accidents that are brought in, in an unconscious state. Dr Habib has just provided me the results of the toxicology report have been released.'

'What are you going on about?' asked Sarah not realising what Vincent was building up to.

'Cookie, sorry, Erin, was twice above the acceptable blood-alcohol level when she was brought in. She was drunk,' he said, shuddering, disappointed to be saying the words.

'Don't be ridiculous. She is a recovering alcoholic! She hasn't touched a drink in nearly two years! There is no way she was drunk!' Sarah was shouting now, unable to believe that this man was claiming Erin had crashed because she was drunk.

'I didn't want to believe it at first either,' he countered, 'but, when I last spoke to her, her clothes did reek of booze and cigarettes. She had spent the afternoon in a pub, interviewing a suspect. As you said, she is a recovering alcoholic; can you really be sure she would have avoided temptation?'

'I know, Erin,' Sarah shot back. 'Her alcoholism stemmed from a troubled childhood. She is in a happy place in her life so I know she would not have slipped back into old ways. I know it!'

'I can show you the results of the blood test,'

Vincent argued. 'Believe me, she is one of my best officers, I don't want her name unfairly slurred, but the facts are the facts. She was drunk!'

Vincent suddenly became aware of how loud he was speaking and tried to switch to a calmer tone.

'Listen,' he said, 'I won't allow this to affect her memorial. I will make sure the toxicology does not appear in the write up. We will simply say that she lost control and that will be the end of it.' He smiled as warmly and as empathetically as he could but Sarah didn't buy it.

'What do you mean by 'her memorial'? She is still alive for God's sake!'

'I thought Dr Habib had spoken to you,' said Vincent glancing towards the door, outside of which the surgeon had earlier told him that she had filled Sarah in on the seriousness of Erin's condition.

'She suggested turning off the ventilator but I told her I didn't want to,' shouted Sarah, unable to control the anger building in the pit of her stomach: Not only was the woman she loved in a coma, but now they were claiming it was because she was drunk and that she should be allowed to die. It was like a nightmare.

'The decision is not yours to take, Miss Jenson,' replied Vincent pointedly. 'The surgeon was not asking for your permission to turn the life-support off, she was giving you the courtesy of choosing the time of when it will be switched off. I thought you understood this?'

Sarah's heart broke as she turned to stare at the lifeless body of Erin again. Even though she had heard what the doctor had said, she believed it was merely an over-reaction. Only now, did Sarah realise that she would never get to hear Erin's voice again, would never get to hold her again, that they would never grow old together. Sarah dropped to her knees and wept again.

*

At ten thirty, Dr Habib returned to the room where Sarah continued to watch Erin, praying that she would wake up and make everything better, in that way she just had about her. But despite the prayers, she continued to lay still, her chest rising and deflating as the ventilator beeped next to her.

Sarah had an impossible decision to make. In spite of what Vincent had told her, it wasn't actually within Dr Habib's power to switch the ventilation machine off, not without next of kin consent, or a court order. The doctor had already made it abundantly clear an hour ago that she would pursue such an order if Sarah did not make the decision first.

Sarah had requested a second opinion and this had led to her meeting Dr Habib's senior registrar, a short, uptight man by the name of Mr Ramsay. He had seemed almost angry that his presence had been demanded for such an insignificant meeting, insignificant to him probably, because it had cut his game of golf short. Sarah had thought he was a clear example of someone suffering with small-man syndrome, using his power to make up for his lack of presence. He had told Sarah, in no uncertain terms, that all the tests indicated very minimal brain activity and, whilst they could not predict the future, he could say the prognosis of survival and recovery were very slim.

Dr Habib and Mr Ramsay had left her an hour

ago, saying they would give her time to reach a decision but it looked like that time had now run out.

'Miss Jenson?' Dr Habib asked carefully, unsure about how Sarah might react to her presence. 'I need to know if you've reached a decision.'

Sarah looked up from the chair she was sitting in, which was still in the corner of the room where it had been earlier. Sarah had done a lot of thinking, in the last hour, along with a lot of crying, and now felt physically exhausted. The truth was, she was still in shock that Erin was in this condition. Twenty-four hours earlier they had been laughing and smiling in their kitchen, and now she was being asked for consent to turn off Erin's life support machine. It still felt like a bad dream, one Sarah wished she could wake from soon, as she was past the point where she could cry anymore.

'Miss Jenson?' asked Dr Habib again, when no response was forthcoming.

'Okay,' said Sarah with a sharp intake of breath.

'Okay?' asked Dr Habib, not quite understanding whether this was consent or just acknowledgement of her question.

'Okay,' Sarah repeated, and felt a shiver shoot through her body. 'I will give my consent.'

There was a calmness about Sarah's tone that revealed an inner strength she didn't know she was capable of.

'Is there anyone you wish to call?'

Sarah thought about the question. Erin's parents were both deceased and she had been an only child. Sarah thought about phoning her own father, but after the coldness of his reaction to her engagement announcement, she didn't see the point. Sarah had been an only child as well so there really was nobody that she needed to call.

'I don't think so,' replied Sarah.

'Okay,' Dr Habib said empathetically. 'There is some paperwork that you will need to complete, but I will get that prepared for you now.'

Dr Habib turned to leave the room.

'How will you do it?' Sarah asked.

Dr Habib stopped short of the door before turning back to answer her. Sarah's eyes looked heavy, dark rings had formed around them but there was a determination that surprised the doctor.

'We will make Erin as comfortable as possible with some morphine, before we remove the tube from her oesophagus and then we will wait and let nature take its course.'

'Will she feel it?' asked Sarah.

'No,' replied Dr Habib emphatically. 'She won't feel a thing, she will just drift away.'

'Can I be here when it happens?'

'It can be a very distressing thing for family members to watch,' said Dr Habib, frowning. 'Most people prefer to say their goodbyes and then leave the room while we remove the equipment. If you really want to be here, however, then it can be arranged.'

'Yes,' replied Sarah. 'I want to be here.'

'Okay,' said Dr Habib, nodding. 'I will make arrangements. Erin's boss is still sat outside the room. Would you like me to send him in?'

'Yes,' said Sarah, glad that there was someone else in the world who seemed concerned by Erin's demise.

16

Vincent looked at the clock on the wall behind the head of Mrs McGregor. It was just after midday and he had been sat here with her talking non-stop, for the last ten minutes but he hadn't really been listening. Instead, he had been reliving the moment when he had watched D.C. Erin Cooke slip away, after her life support machine had been switched off. It was a moment, he was sure, would stay with him for the rest of his life.

Unfortunately, the modern police force didn't have time to grieve, not when there was still the case of a missing child to be solved, and so Jack Vincent was about to watch a live re-enactment of the last sighting of Natalie Barrett, as it was filmed.

'And so, you see, Detective Inspector,' said Mrs McGregor, recapturing his attention with her warm, Scottish brogue, 'I am not sure that using Natalie's classmates as part of the reconstruction is very sensible.'

'Well I appreciate what you are saying, Mrs McGregor,' lied Vincent, 'but we want to make the reconstruction as real as possible, and seeing the actual children leaving the school might help trigger somebody's memory. I believe it will be best to use her actual classmates, so we will.'

Vincent was in no mood to pander to the whimsical wishes of this wet woman and he was determined that he would get his own way, especially today.

'And you also think that using Sarah Jenson is wise, considering what she's been through?' persevered Mrs McGregor, showing genuine concern for one of her members of staff.

'I spoke with her earlier and suggested we use an actor in her role,' he fired back, 'but she was adamant that she wanted to help find out what had happened to Natalie, and would play herself. To be honest, this is a common trait in grieving people; they find it easier to bury themselves in work, to avoid dealing with the emotions of what they are going through.'

Mrs McGregor didn't really look satisfied with either response, but guessed she was on a hiding to nothing if she continued to argue, so she waved him away dismissively. Vincent was happy to leave the room and to get the filming underway. He left Mrs McGregor's office, heading towards Sarah Jenson's classroom. One of his team had been briefing the children in what they were expected to do, since Vincent had arrived at the school. They had been briefed to pretend that it was in fact the end of the day, and not lunchtime, so that when the school bell sounded, they would pack up and head for the school's exit, instead of for the playground. The children were acting like excited beavers, with all the camera crew stood around hanging cables, setting up microphone recording equipment and testing the lighting. In truth, the only person not excited by the presence of a film crew was Vincent himself. For him, it was a means to an end.

'Are you okay?' he asked, approaching Sarah.

She pulled her lips tight, in an effort to force a smile, but it was clear she was still in shock with the morning's events.

'I'll be fine,' she responded.

'Good,' said Vincent, eager to press on. 'We want you to carry on like you did on Friday. It is important that you speak, not that your voice will necessarily be used for anything more than background noise in the final cut, but it needs to look real.'

'I understand,' she said, nodding. 'Where is the girl who will be playing Natalie?'

'She is receiving final instructions from the director and will be here in a minute,' he replied.

'Where did you find her?'

'The film crew provided her,' he replied. 'I guess she is a young actress. Not really sure, to be honest. We gave them a picture of Natalie, along with estimated sizes and then they produced the little girl.'

'She looks quite like her,' said Sarah as a little blonde haired girl entered the classroom with a man in a scruffy t-shirt and jeans, whom Sarah knew was the director. The little girl sat down in Natalie's chair, and said hello to the other children sat around her.

'Are we ready to go?' asked the director, approaching Sarah and Vincent.

'I believe so,' replied Vincent and allowed the director to steer him towards a space at the back of the room where he could observe the scene.

The decision to film a reconstruction had been the brainchild of D.C.I. Young, Vincent's overbearing boss. He detested working for a woman, especially one who had spent more of her career in a classroom than out on the streets fighting actual crime. She was one of a wave of new senior officers who had entered the force via graduate schemes. She had put a call in to an acquaintance at the BBC and they had agreed to send a film crew down and film the scene, which would be broadcast in the next edition of *Crimewatch* in a week's time. An interview with Vincent was required as part of the filming, which he was dreading, but knew that, as lead officer, was essential. That would come once the reconstruction had been filmed. A second unit was already set up outside the school gates to capture the children as they streamed out of the school. Parents had been contacted and asked if they could spare the time to collect their children for the purposes of filming. Vincent had been surprised by the positive response received: it seemed that there was no end to the lengths people would stoop to in order to get their face on the television.

'Action,' shouted the director and Sarah began to speak to the children about the story she had just read, not that she had actually read a story, but the children had been briefed to play along. Two minutes later the school bell sounded and the children packed their things up, grabbed their bags and headed for the cloakroom, before proceeding to the exit. The director had decided to film the sequence in a continuous take and had a monitor with him in the classroom, which gave a live feed of what was being filmed outside.

The little girl playing Natalie, whose real name was Emily, had been told to leave the school slowly, and to take up a standing position next to the school gates. The plan was to film the scenes of Natalie walking from the school, once the director was satisfied with the group shots. That way, all the children would be back inside, out of shot, which is how it would have been on Friday afternoon.

'Cut,' shouted the director, and then spoke into a

walkie-talkie that linked him with the second unit director, outside, 'Let's go again. This time I want you to zoom in on the face of Emily as she exits the school.'

A crackling from the radio evidenced acknowledgement, and the school children slowly began to return to the classroom to re-film the shot.

The director was finally satisfied with the fifth take and advised the children that they could now commence their lunch-break. With nothing better to do, and in the interests of not being left alone to consider the implications of this morning, Sarah moved outside with the film crew to watch the filming of the Emily-only scenes.

'Hello, stranger,' said a familiar voice behind her.

Sarah turned to see the smiling face of Johan Boller.

'Johan, what are you doing here?' Sarah asked, with a confused look on her face.

'The police asked me to come down and watch, to see if I could remember anything else'

'Oh I see,' said Sarah. 'That makes sense, I guess. Did you remember anything else??'

'No, I did not.'

'Oh,' said Sarah, 'at least you tried. Maybe you'll remember something later. You know, like when you stop thinking about something, and suddenly the answer jumps out at you?'

'Like déjà vu,' he said nodding.

'Not exactly,' replied Sarah but decided not to try and explain what she meant.

A young looking man in a baseball cap ran over to where they were stood.

'Mr Boller,' said the young man, 'the detective

wants to know what you thought.'

'I better go,' Johan said to Sarah. 'It was good to see you again.'

'You too,' said Sarah, instinctively and then he was gone. She checked her watch. It was nearly one o'clock but she still didn't feel very hungry. She was about to walk back into the school, in the direction of the staff room when a thought struck her. It was a memory that she had long since buried in her subconscious, but which had suddenly decided to reappear.

Sarah didn't give it a second thought as she opened up into a sprint and ran towards the school. The memory was a moment of total clarity and she knew it was time to go home: not the home she had shared with Erin in Southampton, but the home she had been raised in back in Fortuneswell on the island of Portland. If she was quick enough she could be on a train heading for Weymouth inside an hour. She would phone Peggy McGregor once she had her ticket.

17

Sarah managed to catch the Weymouth-bound 14:25 train service from Southampton, and with a small gym bag filled with enough clothes to last until the weekend, she was on her way. The journey was likely to take about ninety minutes so Sarah had bought a magazine and chocolate bar to try and help pass the time. The magazine wasn't her usual choice, filled with photos of celebrities in the latest fashion trends, but it had been on special offer and she had decided she wasn't in the mood for reading, so looking at the photos would have to do. But despite her efforts to concentrate on the glossy images, her mind kept returning to the memory that had entered her mind back at the school. No matter how hard she tried, she could not shake the name Ryan Moss.

Sarah had known Ryan since she was eleven, having attended the same secondary school as him. He had been a popular lad, competing in the school's football and cricket teams and being brighter than the average sports jock that attended the school. He was six-foot tall with broad, powerful shoulders, a slightly crooked nose, the result of a sports injury, and with a wave of wispy, brown hair atop his head. He had not been the best-looking lad at the school, but he did have his fair share of admirers, including Sarah for a brief time. They had dated during sixth form, a time when Sarah was still trying to convince herself that her attraction to other girls was just a phase. As an awkward teen, she had thrown herself at several boys to try and prove to herself that she was 'normal' but by the time she had left sixth form, she had found the courage to accept who she was. Looking back on it now, she couldn't help but laugh at how silly her behaviour had been.

An annual prom was held every year at the school for students in their final year. Students in the first year of sixth form were allowed to attend, but only if they were there as a date to one of the final year students. Ryan had asked Sarah if she would go with him. He was in the year above and as they had been on several dates and were nearing the point of becoming an item, she had agreed, nearly to her detriment. She was excited at being one of the few girls in her year to be attending the event, and her mother had happily bought her a pretty blue dress for the occasion.

Two weeks before the big night, Ryan started acting very strangely. He missed a couple of days' school without explanation and had been spotted, unwashed, down at the park, drinking cheap cider. He was back at school by Thursday but seemed detached and not willing to really talk to his friends. He avoided Sarah, making excuses to be somewhere else whenever she tried to instigate conversation with him. He was referred to the school's psychologist, and she made recommendations that he see somebody who could devote more time to seeing him.

On the night of the prom, Sarah didn't know whether Ryan was still taking her or not as she had been unable to get a response from him. Her mother had suggested she get ready, just in case Ryan showed up. So, Sarah put on the blue dress and allowed her mother to curl her hair and apply a limited amount of make-up and then she sat and waited. Sarah was in tears by nine o'clock when Ryan had still not shown up or phoned to say what was going on. Sarah's father had been working a night shift so Sarah's mum had cracked open a bottle of wine and a box of chocolates and had set Sarah straight on a few things about how boys behaved and how even as men, they could still be utter bastards. It had made Sarah laugh seeing her mother so relaxed and liberal in her use of expletives. In fact, that was probably Sarah's fondest memory of her late mother.

A little after ten, Sarah's dad had rung home in a panicked state, eager to know where Sarah was. Her mother had explained that she was at home as Ryan hadn't showed up to collect her. Her father had been a relieved man, and had then advised her mother that Ryan had been arrested for attempted murder.

The story was all over the local newspapers for weeks. Apparently, Ryan's mental state had been far worse than the school psychologist had estimated. A physician later recorded that, in the two weeks prior to the attempted murder, something had snapped in Ryan's head and he had entered a particularly dark place in his mind. He had turned to drink to deal with what he was going through, which in turn had led to the truancy and shunning of friends. On the day of the prom he had been seen leaving his home at the crack of dawn, and had not been spotted again until just after six p.m. the same day. He was down at the park again but this time he was not alone.

Chloe Greene was something of a celebrity in Portland, having been crowned 'Young Miss Portland' in a local beauty pageant. She was only ten years old and, even to this day, Sarah had no idea how the pageant hadn't been banned for the exploitation of youngsters. But it was an old-fashioned competition, set in an old-fashioned town. The winner of the pageant was responsible for making a series of public appearances, over the course of the year, including opening church fêtes, attending charity days and of course handing over the winner's crown at the following year's pageant.

Chloe had been out playing with classmates, when the time arrived for them all to return home. She too lived in Fortuneswell and had begun the slow journey home, up the steep hill. Her friends lived in the opposite direction and bid her farewell, confident that she would arrive home safely as she had done dozens of times before. Unfortunately, Chloe ran into an unhinged Ryan Moss, who had been knocking back cheap whiskey for most of the afternoon. Exactly what happened, between Chloe waving goodbye to her friends and later being found with Moss, may never be known. Ryan was undergoing a full psychotic breakdown and was unable to tell police later what had happened. Chloe was so traumatised by the events that she could not give an accurate account of how, or why, she had agreed to go to the park with Ryan Moss.

When Moss had been found at the park just after six, his t-shirt had been covered in blood and he had been knelt down beside Chloe's body. Bruising around her throat showed that somebody had attempted to strangle her having already raped her, causing a massive haemorrhage. Initially, witnesses thought that Moss had actually killed Chloe, and it was only when paramedics arrived on scene that it was discovered she was still breathing. She was rushed to hospital and doctors were able to stem the bleeding and save Chloe's life. Unfortunately, such inoperable damage had been done to Chloe's sexual organs that it was predicted she would probably never be capable of conceiving a child later in life.

Moss was immediately taken into custody and evaluated by a team of psychiatrists from London, to determine whether he was capable of appearing in court. Despite question marks remaining over his mental state he was deemed fit to stand trial and was sentenced to twenty years behind bars. As Moss had turned eighteen during his trial, his sentence was to serve time in adult prison and this had led to his residence in HMP Verne ever since. Chloe didn't attend the following year's 'Miss Young Portland' pageant to hand over her crown as she was undergoing rehabilitation at a specialist hospital, somewhere up North, where her parents had relocated to. Sarah had no idea what had become of her, but deep down hoped that she would one day find peace.

As for Sarah, herself, she was quizzed by the police to see if she knew what Ryan was capable of and, was questioned even more extensively by her friends at school when she returned. The overall consensus was that she had been very lucky to have avoided the clutches of 'The Psycho' as he had become known. Sarah had done her best to put the whole incident behind her and had vowed to live her life to the full, which had probably helped influence her decision to leave home, to attend university. She had been keen to reinvent herself, in more ways than one, and so the memory of Ryan Moss had been buried deep in her subconscious for many years. That is, of course, until she had seen the actress playing Natalie walking down the road from the school. It had reminded her of a picture she had seen in a newspaper all those years ago of a smiling Chloe Greene, totally unaware of what fate had in store for her.

18

Sarah's train arrived at its final destination, Weymouth, just before four p.m. The train station sat on the edge of the strip of shops that makes up Weymouth's main high street and about a five minute walk from the beach. The island of Portland, which was linked to Weymouth by a long road, was the other side of the town, past the main multi-storey car park. Fortuneswell, on the island of Portland was a good twenty minute drive from the train station in Weymouth so Sarah decided to use a taxi to make the journey up there.

Sarah hadn't been back this way since her mother's funeral, three years before, and was amazed at how much development had gone on in Weymouth in that time It now looked like a proper British seaside resort, with plenty for all the family to do, if they came to visit for a weekend. Fortuneswell, by contrast, had hardly changed since Sarah had left over a decade ago. The main road was less than half a mile long and had more vacant properties than it had shops. It made Sarah feel sad for the residents of the town, and she pitied anyone who didn't have a car to take them to the mainland. There were a couple of takeaway restaurants, a newsagent, a small convenience store and a hair-salon. There were still one or two pubs and a local working man's club, but these all looked quite run down, and in dire need of a good lick of paint to brighten them up.

Sarah asked the taxi driver to drop her by the working man's club, which had been the venue for her mother's wake. It had also been the hang-out for her father for as many years as Sarah could remember. It still looked the same as it had done three years ago, the windows lined with yellow from where people had previously been allowed to smoke inside. As she opened the door, she was once again greeted by the stale, musty smell, a combination of male sweat, damp corners and beer. The building was split into two parts. As she walked through the door, she turned to the left towards where she knew the bar was. To the right was a door into a large back room, which had, in the past, been used to host quiz nights and private parties, including her mother's wake. Sarah had no guarantees that he would be in there, but wasn't surprised when she spotted the familiar face of him talking to someone behind the bar. The pint glass in his hand was nearly empty so, as she walked up behind him, she said, 'Can I buy you another?'

At first he didn't seem to recognise her and was about to tell her it was a members-only club, when he realised who she was.

'What are you doing here?' he asked, with little excitement in his voice.

'Let me buy you another drink and I'll tell you,' she said, determined not to allow her disappointment, at his lack of emotion, show.

Her father turned back to the man behind the bar he had been talking to and said, 'I'll have another bitter, please Les, and she'll have a cola.'

'I'll bring them over,' said Les, smiling towards Sarah, realising she must be his daughter.

Alan Jenson turned back to his daughter and put

his arm out, indicating an empty table they could go and sit. Once they had taken their seats and their drinks had arrived, Sarah said, 'How are you?'

'As well as I was yesterday when I spoke to you on the phone. Did I give you cause for alarm?'

'Alarm? No, what makes you say that?'

'Well, you phone me out of the blue one day, and come and see me the next. It just seems a little odd, that's all. What do you need, money?'

Sarah could feel herself already growing frustrated with her father and challenged, 'What makes you think I need anything?'

Her father took a sip from his drink while he considered his daughter. 'Call it intuition,' he said.

'Are you still in touch with any of your former colleagues up at the Verne?' Sarah eventually asked when she could think of no other small talk.

'Sure,' he replied. 'I see Pat and James every Thursday night at darts.'

Sarah could still remember Pat O'Connell and James Dale who had been her father's best friends for several years. They had also acted as pall bearers at her mother's funeral.

'Really?' Sarah replied. 'Have they not retired yet?'

'You forget that they were both a couple of years younger than me. Pat is due to pack it in next summer, but James is planning to work on a couple of extra years on a part-time basis to support his pension. Why do you ask anyway? What's your interest in the Verne?'

Her Majesty's Prison Verne was locally referred to as 'the Verne', owing to its domineering presence on the island's landscape.

Sarah wasn't sure how much to tell him, partly for

how crazy she might sound, but partly as she wasn't sure he would be interested. She decided to tell him everything, as she really wasn't sure how to provide an abridged version of the week's events.

'Do you remember Ryan Moss?' she asked.

Alan Jenson slowly lowered the pint glass from his lips and observed his daughter and asked, 'Why the interest in him?'

'Do you remember him?' she repeated.

'Of course I do. He was on my wing. You're not planning a reunion with him are you?'

Sarah chose to ignore the facetious comment. Alan Jenson had never liked Ryan Moss, had never trusted him and he had not approved when Sarah had begun dating him. His judgement had been truly vindicated by what had happened to Chloe Greene, but, in his defence, he had never gloated over his foresight.

'Something happened at my school on Friday night,' Sarah continued. 'A little girl from my class was abducted while walking home from the school and she hasn't been seen since. It reminded me of what Ryan did to that little girl here.'

Her father nodded slowly, remembering the scandal and how it had affected the neighbourhood, 'A truly despicable crime,' he surmised.

'The police are canvassing Southampton, looking for clues and witnesses, or anybody who can throw any light on who might have taken her or what might have become of her.'

'And you think it's Moss who is responsible?' her father asked taking another sip from his drink.

'No,' Sarah answered affirmatively. 'I thought that if I could speak to him, to find out what he had been thinking when he abducted Chloe, I might be able to get an idea of how the person's mind works, and figure out what might have happened to Natalie.'

'Natalie?' her father asked. 'Is that the girl's name?'

'It is,' Sarah nodded. 'She is such a bright child.'

'Why don't you just leave it to the police to do their job? I'm sure they are more likely to figure this out than you.'

Her father raised his glass towards Les behind the bar to indicate he was ready for another drink.

'Nobody knows Natalie as well as I do,' Sarah protested.

'What about your little friend? Can't she look into it for you?'

Her father was clearly referring to Erin; he was old school and wouldn't bring himself to acknowledge that Erin was Sarah's life partner.

'Erin's dead,' Sarah said bluntly.

'What?' asked her father, his face a contorted portrait of angst. 'When?'

Sarah could feel the tears welling up in her eyes. It was the first time she had said the words: to admit that Erin was gone and would never be returning. She wanted to speak; to tell him that Erin had died this morning, but, even as she tried to open her mouth, the words would not appear. Sarah felt the emotion get the better of her and she began to sob. She so desperately wanted him to scoop her up in his arms and tell her that it would all be okay but she knew he wouldn't. As if her prayer had been answered, Alan Jenson stood, moved around the table, wrapped his large arms around his daughter's shoulders and held her there. It made the emotion of the moment even stronger and as surprised as she was, Sarah embraced the connection and pulled his arms in closer to her.

'I'm so sorry, Sarah,' she heard him say and knew he, too, was crying, from the crack in his voice.

19

Jack Vincent poked his head out of the door of his cramped office and, on seeing that the outer office was empty, he re-closed the door and headed back to his desk. It was just after six p.m. and he felt shattered. He had only managed a couple of hours sleep in the last thirty six, and all he wanted to do was close his eyes and shut out the rest of the world. The team had put in an incredible effort, so far this week, to try and find a break in the Natalie Barrett case, but they still had nothing concrete to go on. Vincent had decided to send the whole team home for a good night's rest with an impassioned plea that they return first thing in the morning and review all the facts of the case again, looking for possible suspects and motives. He should have taken his own advice really and headed home too, but 'home' was not really somewhere he wanted to be.

Vincent lived in a one bedroom studio flat in the Shirley area of Southampton, but the flat was bare of any homely touches. It had a bed, a tiny kitchen and a shower cubicle that only seemed to pump out hot water between five and six a.m. It lacked a woman's touch but then, in truth, so did Vincent. He was forty-three years old, with an ever-increasing patch of baldness spreading across the top of his head. He did his best to brush the few dark, stray hairs that remained, back across the baldness but it was there for all to see. He knew his chances of meeting someone to share his life with were getting slimmer by the day, but, like most of the people he had joined the force with, he was married to his job.

A couple of years ago, he had still been kidding himself that he was capable of going out of an evening and meeting young, attractive women, but things had changed in the last couple of months. No, correction, he had changed in the last couple of months. He no longer felt satisfied meeting women in bars. Those women, who would offer him more than a second glance, were getting older and more-desperate and it just wasn't the same.

When he had been a younger officer, he had used his uniform to get his way with younger women and had been guilty of letting charges slip to achieve what he wanted. As promotions had come and he had started to rise within the ranks he had understood that he could no longer be seen to dabble in such circles, but he had actually found that his position within the force had been something of an aphrodisiac for women of a certain age. Not anymore.

In late December, a mere five months ago, he had lost one of his officers in a botched undercover operation. D.C. Alison Jacobs, 'Ali' to her friends, had been one of the brightest officers Vincent had come across during his time in the force. He had disliked her when they had first met, as she had been young, overly-ambitious and incredibly hot-headed. She had seemed so keen to get out of Hampshire and make a name for herself in London and he had resented this streak in her. She had managed to wangle herself a small secondment to a special arm of the Serious Organised Crime Unit, and had been placed undercover, as a prostitute, in a Russian mafia family.

The role had taken her to London and then seen her return to Southampton shortly after Christmas. Vincent was not aware of all the details of the case as things had quickly been brushed up and the case file sealed by the security services. What Vincent did know is that Ali had been arrested, on suspicion of killing the lead officer of the unit she was working for, and Vincent had been asked to take her back to Southampton, in his custody. He had planned to offer Ali a post in his new team of detectives when she had slipped his custody, and had ended up being caught in the cross fire between Russian and Irish gangsters in a hotel. She had died in his arms, with him helpless to do anything about it.

Losing Ali had affected Vincent more than he had ever realised it would. He had seen a spark in her that he admired but was too late to tell her of his respect. He had seen a similar spark in Cookie and now she too was gone. Vincent had read a tribute at Ali's funeral at the request of the D.C.I. and, having spoken to friends and family of the fallen officer, it soon became clear how little he had known about her life. It had spurred him on to take a greater interest in his team's personal lives, within reason, of course.

D.C. Erin Cooke was a lot different from D.C. Ali Jacobs. Cookie was ambitious, but didn't have a desperation to make a name for herself. Instead, she was keener on achieving the respect of her colleagues. Vincent had had high hopes for Cookie. He was sure she would pass the forthcoming Sergeant's exam and he had already put in a good word for her with the D.C.I. There was rumoured to be an acting-Sergeant's role coming up, and Vincent had recommended Cookie as a potential candidate.

Vincent removed the nearly empty bottle of brown scotch whiskey from his bottom drawer and unscrewed the cap. He usually only saved the bottle for special occasions, but today he just wanted to forget: to forget the two officers that he had failed to protect. Vincent put the bottle between his lips and took a large swig as he felt tears start to roll down his cheeks. He felt ashamed that he was sat in his office, crying, but he couldn't stop himself. He felt like a failure. He was unmarried and child-less, which he was sure disappointed his ageing mother who had always longed for grandchildren. He had allowed Ali to get killed while on the job, and now he had allowed Cookie to die. It was all his fault, he determined. It was his decision to send Cookie off to meet Jimmy Barrett in a pub. How could he have been so careless, sending a recovering alcoholic to a pub to interview a suspect? Of course she would be tempted. What made it worse was that he was still no closer to solving the disappearance of little Natalie.

Cookie's lover, Sarah Jenson, claimed that something untoward had happened to her, that she wouldn't have given in to temptation but the theory was absurd. Wasn't it? Vincent began to wonder exactly what Cookie had been doing in Dibden. He had assumed she was checking on something that Jimmy Barrett might have said, but why would she have ended up out that way? It wasn't a long drive from Southampton, but it was by no means the kind of place you visited on your way home, not if you lived and worked in Southampton as Cookie did. It made no sense, but Sarah had been adamant that Cookie would not have yielded in her rehabilitation.

Vincent took another slug from the bottle and

wiped his running nose with the back of his hand. How had he messed his life up so much? He decided to take another drink from the bottle, but it was empty. Would nothing go right with his life, he thought? Now he couldn't even have a fucking drink! Vincent smacked the bottle down on the desktop and was pleased when he heard it smash into several pieces. Light from the overhead halogen bulbs reflected off the large shards of glass on the desk before him, making them almost sparkle in his teary eyes.

A dark thought swept through Jack Vincent's mind and he took a deep breath in through his nose to stifle another sob. Maybe there was an end to this misery he thought as he picked up the nearest shard of glass and examined its rough edge with his thumb.

Vincent had been present during several investigations into suicides and he was wise enough to know that to successfully attempt the act, it was important to move a sharp instrument up, along the arm, rather than across the wrists. Having spoken to several survivors, he also knew that the pain didn't last very long as the sudden loss of blood tended to numb the mind.

Vincent continued to survey the edge of the glass shard, considering his options. It would be so easy. A quick swipe here, another swipe there and the journey would start. Nobody would be due back in until seven, at the earliest, and by that time it would be too late. There would probably be a big mess, but that would be out of his control.

Vincent was still considering the ease of what he was contemplating when the telephone on the edge of his desk started to ring. It startled him and he dropped the shard of glass, quickly trying to compose himself, wiping the tears from his eyes and clearing his throat.

'Vincent,' he shouted into the receiver as he put the handset to his ear.

'Oh, Sir,' came the reply from a nervous sounding uniform in the radio room, 'I'm glad someone is up there.'

'What is it Constable McIntyre?' Vincent asked, sounding his usual gruff self, annoyed by the interruption. He would recognise the Australian twang of D.C. Phil McIntyre anywhere.

'We've just had a call from a member of the public. She's found a coat, half buried in some woods near Dibden golf course,' replied the Aussie.

'And?' asked Vincent, not making the connection.

'It's a child's coat, Sir, a red coat.'

20

Sarah watched as her father spoke with Les, behind the bar. They seemed to be laughing or joking about something that she couldn't quite hear, but at this moment she didn't care. She had learned more about her father in the last hour than she had in the previous thirty years of her life.

She had been really moved by his embrace when she tried to explain what had happened to Erin. He had hugged her tightly and she had felt so safe with him there. It had been as if the warmth of his body was acting as a force field against all the evils of the world. He had cried too, which had come as a massive shock. She couldn't tell what had brought on his tears, as he had never shown any real consideration for Erin, so she could only assume it was his seeing her so upset that had caused it. None of that mattered now, anyway.

He had pulled a chair up close to her, so that he could still hug her from a seated position and then he had started asking her questions about what had happened to Erin, along with several other questions about her life: had she been happy, did she enjoy being a teacher, was she good at her job, that kind of thing. It was the most interest he had shown in her life and, whilst it frustrated her that he hadn't shown more willing in the past, it delighted her that he was opening up and making an effort at last.

She had explained how she had met Erin; how it

had been an affirmation of the confused feelings she had felt as a youngster but been too scared to admit. She had explained how Erin's fine cookery skills were starting to rub off on Sarah too, and she was starting to experiment more in the kitchen. She told him where they lived and described the lay-out of their small but adequate. It had been strange, once she had started talking and telling him about her life, she couldn't stop. He had ordered them both a couple of whiskies, 'for the shock,' he had explained but knew that was for her benefit only. She had sipped hers and enjoyed the feeling as the smooth liquid scorched her throat on the way down. She had cried so much in the last twenty four hours that she felt all cried out and it allowed her to talk quite openly about Erin, without breaking down in tears as she had done earlier.

He had asked her how Erin had died and she had been strong enough to tell him what D.I. Vincent had explained to her, but she had told her father that she definitely didn't believe what the police were saying. Her father had asked what Sarah thought had really happened and she had to admit she had no idea. She told him that there was no rhyme or reason for Erin to have been driving near Dibden, when she knew Sarah was cooking a special meal and it was the lack of reason that Sarah was finding so difficult to accept. Her father had asked whether it was possible that Erin had found a clue and was going to look for the missing girl. Sarah hadn't really considered the question before, but like a bolt of lightning, the question made everything seem clearer.

Vincent had told Sarah that Erin had planned to check on something before returning home and that she had been questioning that creepy Jimmy Barrett in the afternoon. Sarah joined the dots in her head and wondered whether Erin had found something out about Jimmy and had gone to question him again and it had cost her, her life. It was a stretch, and didn't explain where the car was found, given that Jimmy lived in Sholing with Natalie's parents, but it made more sense than Vincent's claim that she was drunk behind the wheel. At the very least, it gave Sarah some further questions to ask Vincent when she returned to Southampton at the end of the week.

Peggy McGregor had been really understanding when Sarah had phoned her from the train. She had told Sarah to take as long as she needed. Sarah had booked a return train for Friday lunchtime, intending to try and visit some old school friends in Weymouth before returning to organise Erin's funeral, a task she was dreading. Alan Jenson had told his daughter that she was welcome to stay at the house, for as long as she needed, though he did admit that he would need to whip the Hoover around first.

Sarah decided she would take the opportunity to ask her father some questions next. It had always annoyed her how cold he was towards her, and she decided that now was the best time to confront him. Alan Jenson returned to the table with another two tumblers of whiskey.

'I haven't finished the last one yet,' she protested as he placed one of the glasses in front of her.

'Best you get a move on, then,' he said, smiling.

'Dad,' she began, 'can I ask you some questions now?'

'Of course you can, love,' he said taking a sip from his glass.

'And will you answer honestly?' she asked,

nervous about what she was going to ask, but determined to continue.

He eyed her cautiously, curious about where this might be going before saying, 'Sure.'

Sarah had about one finger's worth of scotch still in her first glass and decided to knock it back quickly, grimacing as she did. She justified it as Dutch courage.

'Do I embarrass you?' she asked.

The directness of the question caught him off guard, but he resolved to be as honest as she had demanded, 'For heaven's sake, what makes you say that?'

'At mum's funeral, when I told you about Erin, you seemed so disinterested, and you've hardly said two words to me in the three years since. I wondered whether you were ashamed to have a lesbian for a daughter.'

Alan Jenson looked her up and down, and put his glass down before reaching out and taking both her hands in his. He said, 'I have never been more proud of you than I feel right now. I am ashamed at myself if my behaviour has made you think that I could ever be embarrassed about you.'

It wasn't the response that Sarah had expected, though it was what she had hoped he might say.

'So why were you so dismissive when I told you about her?' Sarah persisted.

He thought for a moment, keen to get the words straight in his mind before responding. 'You've always been a very independent young lady, Sarah. Even when you were a teenager, you always knew what you wanted to do and achieve from life. When you were born, I promised your mother that I would protect you until the day I died. But, as you grew up, you seemed to need me less and less, and you would always go and speak to your mother if something was bothering you; it felt like there was no place in your life for a dotty, old codger like me. When you told me that you had fallen in love with another woman, at your mother's funeral of all places, I knew that you were really telling me that you no longer needed me in your life; that you had moved on. I accepted your decision and have tried to stay out of the way, so as not to be a burden.'

Sarah stared at him, speechless, moved by his admission. 'Is that what you really thought?' she eventually asked.

'You don't realise how strong you are, I think,' he replied, smiling warmly. 'I knew there was nothing I could offer you that Erin couldn't, and that you no longer needed me.'

'You don't know how wrong you are,' said Sarah as she felt tears starting to build up in her eyes. She fought them back down, determined not to break again so quickly. 'I needed you more than ever, after mum passed away and you just weren't there.'

'Oh God, Sarah,' he said, sighing. 'If you had asked for my help, I would have gladly come running for you.'

'I shouldn't have needed to ask for your help!' she practically shouted back. 'You are my father; you should have been there for me, without me having to ask for your help.'

'You're right,' he said, keen to diffuse the situation. 'I am here for you now, Sarah. I know it's probably too late but I need you to know it. I love you and I want you to understand that.'

Sarah remained angry and relieved in equal

measure, but decided that another argument would not solve matters. They both sat in silence for the next five minutes, taking occasional sips from their drinks. An old-looking, box, television sat on top of the bar, caught Alan's attention.

'That's nothing to do with you, is it?' he asked waving a finger towards the television set so Sarah could see what he was referring to.

She turned to see where he was pointing. On the small screen she could just about make out the face of a reporter stood in front of blue and white police cordon tape. A banner running along the bottom of the screen read, 'Body Discovered in New Forest.'

Sarah put her glass down and ran over to the television screen. She searched desperately for a volume button, and, not finding one, she looked up towards Les for help.

'Do you have a remote?' she asked urgently.

Les felt down behind the bar and produced a remote control that he passed to her. Alan Jenson had since moved across to where his daughter was stood, shaking. She was turning the volume up on the story as it flashed back to the face of a fierce-looking woman sat behind a news-desk.

'And so, Marshall,' said the news-presenter, 'Have the police been able to identify the body yet'

The image on the screen returned to a man in his early fifties, with a mop of ginger-coloured hair. Another banner appeared, identifying him as Marshall Lancaster. 'The body is still in situ at the moment but should be removed from the crime scene shortly. I managed to speak to Detective Inspector Jack Vincent, who is leading the investigation into the disappearance of missing local school girl, Natalie

151

Barrett. He told me that they cannot confirm or deny if it is Natalie's body until tests have been carried out. He was able to say that the body did match the description of the missing school girl.'

'No!' screamed Sarah as she dropped to her knees and began wailing. Her father tried to lift her up, surprised by the sudden collapse of his daughter, but he wasn't strong enough. Instead, he got down on his knees and held her tight.

'What is the matter, child?' he asked. 'What's wrong?'

'No,' sobbed Sarah. 'Not Natalie, as well. Not Natalie!'

'Is everything okay, Alan?' asked Les, peering over the top of the bar at the strange woman crying beneath the television and his friend, who seemed to be cradling her. Alan looked around the room and could see that everyone was staring at them.

'It's okay,' he offered the staring eyes. 'She's just had some bad news.'

Alan then looked back down at Sarah and added, 'Come on, love. Let's get you home. We can watch the television from there.'

Sarah didn't want to move anywhere but knew her father was right so she allowed him to manoeuvre her up and then they headed out of the bar, and into the cool, evening air.

THURSDAY

21

Sarah awoke with a start and it took her a moment to remember where she was: in the bedroom she had grown up in. The room had hardly changed and still had a Peter Andre poster hanging inside the wardrobe from when she had been twelve; she had never had the courage to hang a poster of a woman in the months before she had packed up and moved to university. The room was at the top of the house, on what could be considered the second floor of the rickety old house. Technically it was more like the loft space than a second floor as it was a single room at the end of a steep, winding staircase that led up from the first floor.

The house was typical of those in Fortuneswell: very narrow at street level but extending back a decent way for adequate living space. The smaller bedroom on the first floor was barely big enough for a double bed and Sarah had actively encouraged her parents to convert it into a spare bathroom, but her dad had said something about the floor not being strong enough to support an additional water tank; so the room had remained a guest room, although Sarah wasn't sure if a guest had ever stayed in it, with the exception of Erin when they had returned for Sarah's mother's funeral.

Sarah's room was large enough, but had very creaky wooden floorboards, meaning any chances for naughty goings-on, when she had been a teenager, had been out of the question. Sarah suspected that this was the reason her father had refused to get the floorboards changed.

Sarah rubbed her eyes. Her head felt woozy and she swayed a bit as she tried to stand. She had only had a couple of shots of whiskey the night before, but had no recollection of going to bed or why she felt so odd. She decided to walk down the two flights of stairs to the kitchen on the ground floor, to fix some breakfast. The stairs creaked as much as the other floorboards in the house, so she wasn't surprised to hear her father shout out, 'Morning, love,' as she approached. Alan Jenson was sat on a small, two-seater sofa in the lounge, which was the first room she reached from the foot of the stairs. He was wearing his reading glasses and had a newspaper open on his lap. He smiled as she entered the room.

'How are you feeling, love?' he asked.

'Fine, I think,' she said, rubbing her forehead with the back of her hand.

'Can I get you a cup of tea?' he asked, folding the newspaper in half and placing it on the seat next to him, ready to stand and go to the kitchen.

'Can I have a coffee?' she asked, stifling a yawn.

'Certainly,' he replied. 'I might join you actually. Did you sleep okay?'

'Fine, I think,' she repeated, following him from the lounge, through the small dining room and out into the kitchen at the back of the house. Like the house, itself, the kitchen was narrow but long.

'Well, you've been out for a good ten hours by my calculations,' he said, as he turned the kettle on and found a couple of mugs in a cupboard above where the kettle stood.

'That whiskey must have been strong,' Sarah replied, unable to stop the yawn this time. 'I usually only sleep for about six hours.'

'Oh,' said her father, looking sheepish, 'I may have been the reason for the extra sleep.'

'What do you mean?' she asked, frowning.

'Well,' he began. 'When we got back from the bar last night, you were pretty inconsolable. We watched the news, but you wouldn't stop crying. I suppose it's only natural, given the ordeal you've been through. Anyway, I slipped something into your tea to help you sleep.'

'You drugged me?' she asked, incredulous that her father would do such a thing, and concerned about where he might have got his hands on illicit substances.

'Don't overreact,' he replied defensively. 'It was something your mother used to take when she had one of her migraines. It used to help her sleep, so I knew it was harmless.'

Alan Jenson offered his daughter a reassuring smile, 'It worked didn't it?'

The old man had a point and Sarah found it hard to disagree with him, especially when he was showing so much concern for her.

'I suppose you're right,' she said, before adding, 'I don't suppose there is any toast going, is there?'

'Is wholemeal, okay?'

'Wait a second,' she said in mock judgement. 'You've got wholemeal bread? Mum tried for years to get you to switch from white bread, and you always refused. What changed?'

Her father's eyes darted around as if he was checking that nobody was in ear-shot. 'Doctor's orders,' he eventually whispered, placing two slices of bread in the toaster to his side. 'Says it will keep my bowel movements regular.'

'Too much information, dad,' she said. It was incredible how much he had changed overnight. From someone who had barely said two words to her in the last three years, to a man quite happy to share the inner workings of his digestive system.

'You're keeping healthy then?' she asked.

'Oh yes,' he replied. 'See the old doctor once every three months for a check-up. He says I am in pretty good condition for my age.'

He seemed quite proud of himself at this statement.

'And your drinking? What does he say about that?' she asked, the disapproving school teacher in her coming to the fore.

'All is fine in moderation,' he replied, winking.

'And how many times do you go up to the club in a week?'

'Only when there's nowt I want to watch on the telly,' he said. 'Relax,' he added seeing the concern in her eyes, 'Dr Willoughby gives me a blood check on liver function whenever I see him, and it all looks good. Don't worry. I'm as fit as a fiddle!'

The toast popped up from the toaster and he placed the two slices on a plate for her and told her that he had left a pot of butter on the table. He apologised for not having any jam, but did offer a jar of honey, which she gratefully accepted. He sat with her at the small, wooden dining table, sipping his coffee until she had finished the toast and her head began to clear.

'I was thinking of going up to the Verne this

morning, to see if I could get a visiting order to see Ryan Moss. I thought he might be able to give me some insight into the sort of person capable of abducting a young girl.'

'Good luck with that,' her father laughed.

'What do you mean? I know I haven't seen him in a while but I reckon he'd agree to see me.'

'That's not what I meant, Sarah,' he replied. 'Moss isn't at the Verne anymore. He was released two months ago, for good behaviour.'

'What do you mean he was released? He was supposed to be inside for twenty years!'

'That's how these things work, Sarah,' her father said. 'He may have been sentenced to twenty years, but it is rare that an inmate ever serves his full sentence, unless of course they misbehave inside, or attempt to escape.' He paused, while she digested what he was saying, 'Moss was a model prisoner, never in trouble, avoided the bad apples, and attended worship every Sunday. He accepted what he had done was wrong and had turned over a new leaf. He is a free man now.'

Alan Jenson eyed his daughter nervously. 'What's troubling you, Sarah?' he asked. 'You look worried.'

'Why didn't you tell me this last night?' she asked, standing and heading towards the lounge.

'I don't know,' he replied, standing and following her out of the room, 'I thought I had. Sarah, stop a second,' he pleaded, trying to catch up with her. 'What's wrong?'

She paused as she reached the foot of the stairs, ready to ascend, 'Don't you see, dad? Don't you get it?'

'See what?' he replied. 'Get what?'

'It's him,' she said, frustrated at having to spell out what seemed abundantly obvious. 'It's Moss. He's the one who abducted Natalie.'

Her father laughed out loud and only stopped when he saw Sarah glaring at him.

'You're being silly, Sarah,' he said in a condescending tone. 'What makes you think it's Moss?'

'Fourteen years ago, Ryan Moss abducted and tried to kill little Chloe Greene. This man was released into the general public two months ago. On Friday, a pretty, young child was abducted on her way home from my school and may have been murdered. Don't you see the connection?'

'No, I'm afraid I don't,' he replied. 'There must be hundreds of abductions every year across the U.K. What makes you think these two are linked?'

Sarah turned and ran up the stairs, shouting back over her shoulder, 'I'm the link, dad. Moss was dating *me*, when he abducted Chloe and now Natalie has been taken from *my* class.'

'That's just a coincidence, Sarah,' he shouted after her, but it was too late. She had already made it to the second flight of stairs and was bounding up them; her intention to pack as quickly as she could. She returned ten minutes later, bag in hand, now sporting a pair of faded, blue jeans, a grey t-shirt and a thin faux-leather, black jacket.

'Where are you going?' her father asked, from where he had re-taken his seat on the sofa, with his newspaper.

'I'm heading back to Southampton. I need to stop him,' she replied, a determination in her voice that reminded Alan of a younger version of himself. He knew that trying to convince her of the error of her ways was pointless.

'Okay,' he said, looking her straight in the eye. 'Let's just say, you're right and he has been harbouring some deep resentment against you for all these years. And let's just say he was the man who abducted that little girl from your school on Friday night. What do you think is going to happen next?'

'I don't know. I know it sounds crazy, dad, but I just have a feeling in my stomach that I know who took her. If he did take her, then I think he will strike again. I have to stop him.'

'What makes you think you can stop him? Or even find him? You've not spoken with him in over a decade,' he protested.

'I know what he looks like, dad,' she replied. 'I can tell the police who they are looking for and widen the net for him. I have to try.'

'Okay, Sarah, okay,' he said admitting defeat. 'I'll ask Pat and James what they remember about him, when I see them tonight. Maybe they can shed some light on where he was planning to move to, once he was released. I'll let you know what I find out, if anything.'

She smiled a reassuring smile in his direction. 'Thanks, dad. I appreciate your help.'

'Look after yourself, Sarah,' he called after her as she opened the front door and headed out into the street. 'I want to see you again, and soon. Be careful!'

The door closed and she was gone.

*

Sarah had phoned a local taxi firm while she had

been getting dressed and packed and the taxi she had booked was waiting for her when she stepped out of her father's house, into the cobbled, and incredibly narrow, steep road that the house was located on. She clambered into the taxi and told the driver that he was to head for Weymouth train station. They reached their destination twenty minutes later and Sarah was just in time to buy a single ticket to Southampton and board the 10:20 train. It wasn't a struggle to find a seat and once she was settled, Sarah pulled the Smart phone from her pocket and started to search for articles about Ryan Moss. She wanted to review all stories relating to the abduction of Chloe Greene, to satisfy herself that she wasn't jumping to conclusions, and to try and find some tangible evidence linking Moss to Natalie Barrett.

Sarah found various articles covering the abduction and read each one so that she had every angle covered, in her own mind at least. He also appeared in a feature story that Sarah had had no clue about. It appeared that Ryan Moss had featured in a *Panorama* programme on the BBC about prison inmates who were benefiting from the rehabilitation of incarceration. The programme had been aired nearly four years ago and, as it wasn't the sort of programme that Sarah would watch, it was hardly surprising that she had missed it. She had a vague memory that Erin had mentioned such a programme, but then not knowing who Moss was, there was no reason that Erin would have made a connection to Sarah.

Sarah found several images of Moss as well in a search engine. Some of the photos were shots taken while they had both been at school, but there weren't many recent photos, with the exception of images used within the *Panorama* programme. Moss hadn't aged well. The one-time good-looking teenager that Sarah had once dated was now rather bloated with a round face; gone were the well-defined arms and chest, replaced by a portly belly of a man that looked ten years older than he really was. There was a look in his eyes that gave Sarah the creeps; a dead look.

The train journey flew by, as she continued scouring for as much information as she could find and she was surprised when the guard announced through the speaker system that the next stop was Southampton Central. Sarah put her phone in her pocket, grabbed her bag and headed for the nearest exit. Her plan was to return home, have a shower, and then write down everything she had learned about Chloe Greene's abduction and how it linked in with Natalie Barrett's disappearance. Her thinking was that it was better to approach Jack Vincent with a tangible story than the wittering of a grieving school teacher.

Rain was starting to fall gently as Sarah emerged from the train station. Thankfully there were several taxis at the taxi rank outside the station, so she jumped into the first one and told the driver her address. The driver sped away and for the first time in three days, Sarah felt like she was finally making progress.

<u>22</u>

Jack Vincent didn't like hospitals. The aroma of disinfectant, tinged with stewed vegetables, made his stomach turn. The odour was even worse down in the morgue where the added influence of death was enough to make any sane person ill. It amazed him that people actually worked down here. Vincent wasn't a squeamish man, but even he had to admit to getting the creeps when he was stood near dead bodies. In his eyes, there was something quite unnatural about seeing the dead. It was the part of his job that he loathed the most, but being a man of principle, he endeavoured not to show it.

Dr Neil Spinks had worked in the morgue of Southampton General Hospital for the past five years. A fifty-year-old man, he didn't allow himself to get haunted by the lives of the victims that he tended to. Back in school, he had always had a fascination with the way things worked. From an early age, he had spent countless hours with his grandfather, a clock-maker, in his workshop observing how the old man's gentle hands could place various cogs and thin strips of metal together, to create something magical. The young Neil Spinks had hoped to take over his grandfather's business one day, but after the old man had passed away, Neil's father had sold the business and that dream had vanished. The fascination with the make-up of machines developed through puberty as an adolescent Neil was given his first taste of biology.

He was a natural when it came to dissecting frogs and earned himself a strong grade for Science and in turn set himself along the road to medical school.

Dr Spinks had spent several years in various areas of medicine, general, psychiatry and surgery before he had finally decided to specialise in forensic pathology. He had since written several papers of note on the art of identifying cause of death. One such paper, *Knowing your Victim* is still used as a teaching paper in universities today. He had settled on the outskirts of Southampton, as he liked the idea of living near a big city but having the coast on his doorstep too.

What helped Dr Spinks to work in an area where he was surrounded by death was his propensity to talk to the bodies that came his way, like they were living patients. It was quite eerie and had led to some complaints against him from other medical professionals, as well as police officers. However, despite their objections, he really wasn't doing anything wrong. He argued that it helped him formulate a better idea of his patient and that led to achieving quicker results, about what may have caused their untimely demise. Vincent found the practice a bit disturbing as well, but Dr Spinks did deliver results much faster than his colleagues and had helped Vincent crack many a case thanks to his speed.

'Good morning, Detective Inspector,' Spinks hummed cheerily as Vincent walked through the door to the laboratory.

Vincent struggled to understand how the pathologist stayed so relaxed. 'Good morning, doctor,' he replied gruffly.

Vincent hadn't slept since the call had come in the previous evening, confirming that a body had been discovered in the woods. After he had received the phone call in his office, stating that a red coat had been found, he had dispatched two patrol cars to the area to preserve what evidence there might be and had also put a call into the local Scene of Crime specialists. At that point no body had been discovered but in his gut, he knew one would be. Sure enough, within ten minutes of the patrol cars arriving, he received a call on his mobile to confirm that the body of a young girl had been located. He had already been in the car on his way to the site.

The Scene of Crime Officers cordoned off the area and began to take samples of footprints and fibres in and around the body but, as the light started to dim, emergency lighting was produced from strong, halogen bulbs that the SOCOs always carried for late night discoveries. They had worked into the night, and Vincent had stayed to observe and to see if any new evidence had been uncovered that could help what had now gone from an abduction case to a murder investigation.

He was still awaiting an official time of death from Dr Spinks so that he could arrange for a canvas of new witnesses who may have seen the killer dumping the body. That was why he had come down now, hopeful that the good doctor had prioritised the case as Vincent had requested over the phone in the early hours of the morning. Spinks was the on-call specialist, and had been more than happy to come into the laboratory early to start work. He had been here since a little after three.

Vincent had learned very little from the SOCOs. From all accounts, the body had been quite stiff when it had been discovered, which suggested it was days, rather than hours since she had been killed. In a way, he was relieved. It seemed likely that the child had been killed over the weekend; he wouldn't be held accountable if Natalie, if indeed it was Natalie, had been killed before he had even taken over the case. This was scant consolation, however.

'Have you managed to look at the little girl yet?' asked Vincent, eager to move along the discussion and get back out to the crisp, odourless air of the outside world.

'I have begun a primary examination of Betsy, yes,' replied Spinks grinning. He had a tall, thin frame with white, not grey, hair. He was well over six feet tall, with wide shoulders, but there was barely a morsel of fat on his body. As Vincent observed him, smiling as he wheeled a trolley over towards Vincent, he reminded the detective of Lurch from *The Adams Family*.

'Betsy?' Vincent questioned.

'Yes,' replied Spinks, with an even broader grin. 'Whenever I get a young patient without a name, I call her Betsy if it's a girl and Bobby if it's a boy. It just helps, you know?'

Vincent nodded his acknowledgement, even though he disagreed with the logic.

'And what have you learned about...' Vincent began, unable to refer to the girl as Betsy.

'Betsy?' Spinks completed for him.

'Yes.'

'Betsy is between the ages of six and seven, judging by the length of her limbs and under-developed breasts,' Spinks began, raising the glasses, which had been hanging around his neck, to the end of his nose. 'Rigor mortis is evident, which would suggest she has been dead for some time.'

'Can you be any more specific?' Vincent interrupted.

'Patience, Detective Inspector,' Spinks countered. 'Anyone would think you didn't want to be down here,' Spinks chortled to himself. 'My initial estimate for time of death would be Saturday or Sunday, just passed, forgive the pun.' He laughed to himself again.

'And cause of death?' Vincent persisted.

'In due course, Detective Inspector,' Spinks hummed.

Vincent shrugged his shoulders to express that the doctor should continue.

'Remember, this is just my preliminary examination. The results of the toxicology reports will take a couple of days to produce.'

'Toxicology?' Vincent asked. 'Do you believe she may have been drugged?'

'It's too early to say,' Spinks replied, 'but I have reason to believe that something foreign may have been administered.'

'What makes you say that?' Vincent asked, intrigued.

'Betsy has been sexually assaulted,' Spinks replied matter-of-factly.

'You're certain?' Vincent asked.

'I'm afraid so,' said Spinks. 'There is bruising and dried blood around the vagina and Betsy's mouth. The contusions are classic signs of assault and from the looks of the damage sustained, it would seem the assault lasted several hours.'

Vincent felt sick. What kind of bastard could rape a little girl, let alone for several hours?

'Betsy appears to have lost a fair amount of blood,

but I'm not sure the SOCOs will find much blood at the site,' Spinks continued.

'How come?'

'Betsy's body was moved, post mortem,' Spinks replied. 'There are markings on the back that have been caused after death that would suggest the body was thrown from a height to the location of discovery.'

'Are there any clues as to where the assault may have happened?' Vincent asked.

'Not yet, I'm afraid,' Spinks replied, frowning. 'When I have completed the full examination, I may have more information, if I can find any fibres secreted on the body, but I wouldn't hold your breath.'

'Are there any traces of... ?' Vincent was struggling to get the words out. 'Are there any traces of…semen…on the victim?'

'Not that I have found at the moment,' Spinks replied. 'There are traces of lubricant, which would suggest a condom or two were used during the attack. The assault on the vagina is quite severe and the victim would have been in significant discomfort, which is what leads me to think a sedative of some kind may have been used. The toxicology report should be able to confirm that information.'

Vincent could feel himself welling up. He had never felt so emotional about a case. It made him even more determined to catch the killer of this little girl.

'There is also significant bruising on the face, the nose appears to be broken and there are scratch marks on Betsy's upper thighs,' Spinks continued. 'It may be wise not to show the victim's parents her face.

She appears to have a birthmark of sorts on the back of her left leg so probably worth seeing if they can identify her with that,' Spinks suggested.

'Okay,' Vincent agreed. 'So, was cause of death the loss of blood?'

'No,' Spinks replied abruptly. 'She was strangled. The bruising around the neck suggests the strangulation was inflicted by a large pair of hands, suggestive of a male perpetrator.'

'Is there anything else?' Vincent asked, hopeful the answer would be 'no'.

'I think that's all for now, Detective Inspector,' Spinks replied, satisfied with what he had discovered in such a short time. 'I will commence the full examination once the parents have been in, as it's never nice for them to see the body after I have cut her open and removed different organs.'

Vincent forced down the bile forming in the back of his throat, and turned to head for the exit door.

'Thank you, doctor,' he called out without turning back. He needed fresh air and a large cup of strong, black coffee.

23

Neil Barrett turned to look at his wife across the breakfast table. She was absent-mindedly staring out of the window, into the wet back garden. She had been doing a lot of staring into space in the last week, Neil observed. It felt as if she was hiding from the reality of what they were facing. Their little girl, their beautiful, clever, little girl was missing and for all they knew, dead. Sure, she had cried a lot, an indication of the emotional stress she was under, but she had yet to speak to him about it.

They had been wheeled out, like a prize exhibit, in front of the gathered journalists on Tuesday evening, to plead for the life of their little girl. Neil knew the press conference was unlikely to make any difference to the outcome of this abduction case. It was naïve to think that the person or persons who had taken Natalie would be sat at home watching the news, see the press conference, and decide that actually they had done the wrong thing and would return her. That sort of thing just didn't happen. Still, it had been at Detective Inspector Vincent's bequest that they attend the press conference and say the necessary things expected of concerned parents; someone watching just might have seen something, however, it had seemed so false to Neil. The statement that he and his wife had read out had been written by a duty solicitor, so it wasn't even their own words. He had felt like a poor actor, as he had read the speech, and had half expected to see a review slating his performance in the paper the following day.

Neil poured himself a fresh cup of tea from the pot that had been sat beneath the woollen Southampton FC tea cosy. He raised the pot towards his wife, to try and get her attention, to see if she wanted a top up, but he couldn't make eye contact with her. In fairness, she still hadn't touched the cup that he had poured her earlier, which was probably only warm, at best, now. He took three spoonfuls of sugar from the open packet on the table and stirred them into his mug. Still she continued to stare out of the window. Was she grieving, even though the whereabouts of Natalie had yet to be confirmed? Was she imagining a life where this terrible thing hadn't happened? Why wouldn't she just speak to him? He was hurting too!

Vincent had phoned late the previous evening, while Neil had been dozing on the sofa. It was incredible how tired he had felt all week, even though he hadn't been to work since her disappearance. Vincent had told him that the body of a young girl had been discovered somewhere near Dibden golf course. Neil had listened in stunned silence while Vincent had explained that they would need to come and confirm if the body was indeed that of Natalie. Neil had merely answered 'Yes,' when Vincent had asked if they could be at Southampton's General Hospital by midday today. It hadn't been until an hour after he had disconnected that the reality of what Vincent had said had sunk in. Both parents had spent the whole week clinging to the hope that their little girl would suddenly burst into the house, apologetic at running away for so long, with the promise that she would never be so naughty again. In Neil's imagined vision, he would clasp her up in his arms and kiss her all over, telling her not to worry about it and that he forgave her. But now it seemed that that vision would remain merely imaginary.

Neil had drunk half a bottle of vodka when he had finished crying and had woken Melanie, who had been asleep upstairs, courtesy of some pills the G.P. had given her. He had calmly told her what Vincent had said but she hadn't really responded, before closing her eyes and returning to sleep. It was as if she had thought she was still asleep and having a bad dream. Neil had decided not to try and wake her again, instead choosing to seek solace in the bottle of cheap, supermarket-brand vodka.

It wasn't just the fear for his daughter's safety that was causing his restlessness. It was also the guilt that he had not been at the school to collect Natalie on Friday. He had known there was a chance Melanie's last appointment would overrun, but, rather than doing his fatherly duty, he had driven out to Cadnam to meet his contact. So far, the police had bought the cover story of a broken down vehicle, but if they continued to dig, it wouldn't be long until the truth came out.

He had woken a little after seven this morning, and fixed himself several cups of coffee before switching to tea when Melanie had surfaced. She looked like a panda, with big, black bags under her eyes, despite the sleep. They had been sat at the breakfast table for the last half an hour, neither really eating, more like machines just going through the motions of breakfast chores. It was nearly eleven a.m. and they would have to leave in twenty minutes to get across town to the hospital. Vincent had said something about getting cleared by security before they would be admitted to the morgue, where the identification would take place.

He wasn't sure what he should wear to the appointment. What was the protocol for such events? A shirt and tie? Was that too formal? Jeans and a t-shirt? Was that too casual? Ultimately, it mattered not what he chose to wear to go to the hospital, but at least it preoccupied his mind and stopped him thinking about the prospect of formally identifying his little girl.

*

Jack Vincent knocked back the final dregs of the coffee in the cardboard cup and grimaced at the luke-warm sensation: the coffee had gone cold while he had been waiting and he despised the taste of warm coffee. He couldn't believe they still hadn't arrived yet.

Vincent had been stood outside the pathologist's office for the last half-hour as he had agreed to be present with the Barretts to identify the body if it was indeed that of Natalie Barrett. Having already seen several photographs of Natalie, Vincent *knew* it was her, but procedure was procedure and a living relative was required to formally identify the body. Having never been in the position of having to provide such confirmation himself, Vincent couldn't really begin to appreciate the stress and strain that Neil and Melanie Barrett were currently going through.

The morgue at Southampton's General Hospital was located in what could be considered the basement of the building. It could only be reached through a special entrance, and all visitors had to be formally identified through on-site security. Vincent looked at his watch for the umpteenth time and tutted when he saw how long he had been waiting.

He heard the ping of a lift arriving, down the corridor and, a moment later, in walked a visibly-upset Melanie Barrett, being led tenderly by her husband. Melanie burst into another wave of tears when she saw Vincent stood waiting at the door with a manila folder and a cardboard cup in his hand.

'Mr and Mrs Barrett,' he began, sounding as calm as he could. 'Thank you for coming down. There are a few details that I need to cover with you before we go in.'

Vincent waited for an acknowledgement, and when none seemed to be coming he decided to proceed. He opened the manila folder, in which he had hidden a checklist of points he needed to cover with them. When he had completed his reading, he raised his head to look at them and he could see that Neil Barrett was trying to hold back the tears in his eyes, and that Melanie's head was still buried in her husband's shoulder.

'There is a chance that the body behind the curtain is not Natalie,' he said cautiously, knowing that he was causing false hope. 'Also, I only need one of you to confirm identity if either of you would prefer not to go into the room?'

'We'll both be going in,' replied Neil, still forcing back the tears.

'Okay,' said Vincent, turning so that he could open the door to the room and lead them through. The room itself looked like something out of a Soho peep show. It was small, with a couple of wooden chairs and a glass window at the front, which had curtains drawn behind the glass. There was an intercom next to the glass where Vincent would talk to the attendant when they were seated and ready to view the body.

'Are there any distinguishing marks on Natalie that would help us confirm identity?' Vincent asked, once they were seated on the chairs.

'She has a small red mark, in the shape of a triangle, on the back of her left leg, just above the knee,' replied Melanie, wiping tears from her eyes with the back of her hand. It seemed that she had found a new inner-strength since they had entered the room.

'Vincent pressed the button on the intercom and relayed the information to the attendant. The dark curtains parted slightly, revealing a metal stretcher with a large sheet draped over the small body beneath it. A gloved hand appeared from behind the curtain and lifted part of the cream sheet up to reveal a small leg. The gloved hand manoeuvred the limb so that the back of the leg was visible. Melanie Barrett burst into a new sob as a red, triangular shape was revealed.

Vincent gave a little cough before saying, 'Can you confirm that you recognise the birth mark?'

'I want to see her face!' Neil Barrett demanded bluntly.

'That's not necessary, Mr Barrett,' Vincent began, but he was cut off by Barrett repeating the statement.

Vincent reluctantly pressed the button on the intercom once again, and advised the attendant that a full examination was required. The curtains opened wider, to reveal the rest of the stretcher along with the owner of the gloved hand, a bespectacled man in his early twenties, probably a student. The attendant pulled the sheet back from the cadaver's head to reveal the pretty, but now lifeless, face of a young, blond-haired girl.

This time it was Neil Barrett who let out a gasp as he collapsed to his knees and wailed, 'No!' at the top of his voice. Vincent signalled to the attendant that the curtains could be closed once more, and he dutifully obliged. He had all the confirmation he required.

24

Sarah turned the key in the lock to her front door and pushed it open. The first thing she noticed was the absence of Erin. She had, of course, returned home several times alone before, when Erin had been at work, so an empty house shouldn't have been so unfamiliar to her, but today the absence of Erin seemed all the more apparent. For the first time, however, she didn't feel the urge to cry, as her heart panged for the loss of Erin.

There were a couple of envelopes on the door mat, which she casually scooped up and placed on the small table, near the door, where she tended to leave her house keys when at home. She decided she would look at the mail later as all she really wanted to do right now, was jump into a hot shower, and wash off the dirt and stress of the last couple of days. She was planning to pop into the school and see Peggy McGregor later, to request some time off to grieve and she knew she couldn't go in with her hair in its current state.

Sarah noticed a red light flashing on the home phone, indicating a missed call. She checked the answer-phone but no messages had been left. The number that had phoned didn't look familiar but had called six or seven times since yesterday afternoon. If the call was so important, why hadn't the person left a message, she wondered. She decided not to return the calls and instead headed for the shower.

Twenty minutes later, she emerged, feeling as close to a new woman, as circumstances would allow. She went through her wardrobe, looking for something she could wear that reflected her mood: grieving widow, determined to continue with her life. The trip home had been good for Sarah; reconnecting with her father at a time when she needed it most. She was still worried about the re-emergence of Ryan Moss. Was it really possible that he could have kept feelings of hatred towards her buried for more than a decade, until he had had such time as to convince the authorities of his rehabilitation, to then return and seek his revenge? The more she thought about it, the more she believed it possible. A niggling doubt remained; Sarah still believed that Erin's death was related to Natalie's disappearance, but she couldn't fathom how Erin would have found out about Moss. She decided to push that last thought from her mind, as her suspicions made more sense without it.

Not finding anything adequate to wear, she ventured over to Erin's wardrobe. As she opened the doors tentatively, she was greeted by Erin's unmistakeable scent and for a moment it was like she was in the room with Sarah. It gave her a warm feeling. She idly ran her hand through some of Erin's trouser suits that she had worn each day to work. She had always looked so smart and sexy when she was wearing them, giving off an air of confidence that was infectious. It was this feeling that Sarah was looking for so she selected a black ensemble with a bright turquoise-coloured, satin blouse. She had never worn Erin's clothes before, and questioned whether her decision to borrow the clothes now was a bit depraved. But as she tried the trousers and blouse on and slipped the jacket over her shoulders, she knew she was doing the right thing. In a strange way it made her feel like Erin was there with her, shielding her from danger. She admired herself in the long mirror, in the corner of the room, and was pleased with the results; it was fortunate they had been of similar build.

Sarah's attention was caught by the sound of her home telephone ringing in the other room. She wondered whether it was the mysterious caller again. As she did, a terrible thought struck her: what if the mystery caller was Ryan Moss, phoning to taunt her? It would make sense for him not to leave a message, to avoid incriminating himself. She stopped still, not wanting to go near the phone. The phone number was again unfamiliar, but it wasn't the same number that had phoned earlier. She eventually picked up the receiver when she realised how ridiculous her behaviour was.

'Hello?' she said quietly into the phone.

'Sarah? Thank God I got hold of you,' replied a male voice.

'Dad?'

'Yes love, it's me,' replied Alan Jenson.

'What number are you phoning from?' Sarah enquired. 'I didn't recognise it.'

'My new mobile phone,' he replied. 'I've been meaning to get up to speed with modern technology for a while, and seeing you yesterday inspired me to nip to Weymouth to buy one.'

Sarah smiled with admiration, her father, who had been a technophobe most of his life had just bought a mobile phone!

'Anyway,' he continued, 'That's not why I am ringing. I have some news about Ryan Moss that I thought you should hear.'

'What is it?' she asked, unable to hide the trace of panic from her voice.

'I decided to speak to James and Pat, before tonight's catch up, so I phoned them both, just after you left.'

'And?'

'They suggested I speak to the current prison warden, chap by the name of Doug Barnes. He offered to speak with Moss' former cell mate, to see if he had said where he might head upon release. The cell mate gave quite a candid statement.'

'What did he say, dad?'

'Well,' continued her father, 'He didn't know where Moss was headed exactly but he did say that he had a message to deliver to a former girlfriend. Apparently he didn't mention anyone by name, but he did say he hadn't seen this girlfriend since he had been locked up. I'm sorry, love, but it looks like you might be right. He's coming for you.'

Sarah nearly dropped the phone and stood there open-mouthed as the reality hit her.

'Listen to me, love,' her father said. 'He was released two months ago but you've not heard from him, so there is still a chance that he wasn't referring to you, but I think you need to be on the look out. Did Erin have any friends in the force that you could perhaps stay with or at least speak to, to advise what is going on?'

Sarah tried to think about Erin's colleagues. Erin had never liked to mix business with pleasure, and although Erin had referred to some of them by name, Sarah had never really been formally introduced to any of them.

'Sarah? Are you still there?' her father asked, when she hadn't replied.

'Yes, dad, I'm here. Sorry, I was trying to think of someone.'

'Do you want me to come up and stay with you for a bit? You know, as added protection?'

Sarah nearly laughed out loud. 'Dad, I hardly think you're in any position to be my bodyguard,' she teased gently. 'Not with a heart condition like yours.'

'Okay,' he conceded. 'Is there anyone you can call?'

'I suppose I can speak with Erin's old boss, Jack Vincent,' said Sarah, thinking out loud. 'He's a bit of a chauvinist, but if he thinks it is linked to Natalie Barrett's disappearance, he might be prepared to listen.'

'Good,' said her father. 'Speak to him now. See if he can arrange any protection for you. I'll give you a call back tonight and see how you got on.'

'Thanks, dad,' she said. 'By the way, do you know which country uses the dialling code '+32'?'

'Not sure. How come?'

'I've missed several calls from a strange telephone number. The number begins with a '+32' so I wondered whether you recognised it?' she replied.

'Can't say I do, to be honest. Maybe Germany or France?'

'Never mind,' she replied. 'I'll look it up on the internet later.'

Sarah and Alan Jenson said their good byes and she then returned to her bedroom, to apply some make-up to her face. Once she was satisfied with the results, she sat down and dialled the number she had for Jack Vincent.

25

Vincent was back in his office at the Central Headquarters when Sarah's phone call came through. Against his better judgement, he had remained with the Barretts for an hour after the identification, doing his best, but failing miserably, to calm them down. He had seen many relatives confirm the identity of victims, but today was the first time he had seen two parents, so young, grieving for their child. Vincent believed he was a man of the world, but, as much as he hated it, he had to admit that today had affected him more than he had anticipated. The way Neil Barrett had dropped to his knees and broken into loud, unhinged sobbing, was a memory that would stay with him forever. Barrett had looked and sounded a broken man and if that could happen to him, then potentially it could also happen to Vincent; this was a thought that sent a shudder down his spine.

As he had made his way up to the Major Incident room he had hoped to be bombarded by his team, with new leads that had been uncovered in his absence or maybe even a crack in the case: he was disappointed. He had managed to freely navigate his way from the entrance to the station, up the stairs, through the incident room and into the solace of his private office with fewer than two 'Hellos'. In fairness, there weren't many of his team around. Again, the optimist in him, hoped that meant they were out on the streets, shaking down suspects, and not hidden in the nearby McDonald's, fearful to return to the office without an update.

Those officers he had spotted had been pouring over old child abduction cases, looking for links and similarities between those cases and the on-going investigation. Their glum faces, as he had made eye-contact, had been enough to tell him how well progress was going. He really wasn't in the mood for any kind of argument or confrontation, so he had opted not to engage with any of them, instead marching onwards to the little room that had become his home, in more ways than one.

There were still some thin shards of broken glass on his desk, but the larger parts that he had been handling the evening before were safely stashed in the waste bin in the corner. It showed that the office cleaner hadn't been in, but this was more cause for celebration than complaint. The last thing he needed now was for somebody to raise questions over his possible mental state. Last night had been a bump in the road, he told himself. He was fine! At least, he hoped so.

He had sat down at the desk and forced the memory of the night's drunken antics from his mind: repression was a kind of exorcism, he figured. He had been replaying what he knew about Natalie's disappearance in his mind when the phone on the desk had started to ring. The display revealed it to be a local number, so he answered it, unaware who it might be. When he heard Sarah's voice at the other end, he didn't know whether he was pleased or disheartened.

'Detective Inspector?' her voice had enquired, eagerly. 'It's Sarah Jenson, Erin's other half,' but her voice trailed off as she remembered that she was no longer anybody's significant other. 'It's Sarah Jenson,' she had reaffirmed.

'Yes,' he had replied, unsure what to say. Vincent had never been one for small talk, and he was even worse at talking to people in difficult circumstances, particularly when they had lost someone close.

'Am I disturbing you?' she had asked, the enthusiasm once more returning to her voice.

'No,' he replied before adding, 'That's fine.'

'Good,' she said. 'How is the case going?'

Vincent wasn't sure if she was referring to the disappearance of Natalie or her belief that a case should be opened into what had happened to Cookie.

'I can't really discuss an open investigation,' he said, choosing to bluff his way out of potentially awkward questions. 'It's policy,' he added in a pointless effort to shift responsibility for his avoidance of the question.

'I have an idea who took Natalie,' Sarah stated, matter-of-factly.

'I see,' said Vincent, opting to humour her rather than telling her to get her nose out of his business.

'Does the name Ryan Moss mean anything to you?' she asked, hoping to bait him into asking her questions about what she knew.

'No,' he replied.

Annoyed, Sarah added, 'You might want to look him up.'

'I see,' said Vincent, leaning back in his chair and lifting his legs so that he could stretch them out across his desk. 'And why might I like to do that?'

Vincent didn't like to be told how to do his job, and he had a sneaking suspicion that it had been

Sarah's interfering that had led Erin into proposing Jimmy Barrett as a possible suspect at Tuesday's briefing.

On the other end of the line, Sarah was weighing up in her mind whether to blurt out everything she knew about Ryan Moss, and what she had learned in the last day, or whether to feed Vincent just enough and hope he went away to investigate himself. She chose the latter option.

'Ryan Moss is a convicted child abductor who attempted to murder his last victim,' she began, keen not to trivialise the story in an attempt to give it credence. 'He has just been released.'

'And how do you know of this man?' Vincent asked, not particularly interested in her response.

'I used to date him,' she answered.

'I see,' he replied in a condescending tone. 'Did he break your heart?'

The question caught Sarah off guard. 'What?' was the best she could muster.

'Do you want us to investigate all your ex-boyfriends as well? You know, just in case they could be guilty?'

Sarah didn't like Vincent's tone and wondered why he was being so mean, particularly in light of what she was going through, emotionally.

'You no longer think Jimmy Barrett did it then?' Vincent asked, knowing he was taking a risk mentioning Jimmy Barrett's name, in case Sarah had no idea about Erin's suggestion.

'What?' asked Sarah, thrown once again by Vincent's question and manner. 'Yes. No. Maybe. I don't know,' she blurted.

'Listen, Miss Jenson,' Vincent said, suddenly

growing bored of the conversation. 'I appreciate that you are grieving for the loss of Erin, and I sympathise with your situation, I really do. And I know you are upset by the disappearance of one of your pupils, I am sure the stress you are feeling is significant.' He paused, expecting a rebuttal, but when one wasn't forthcoming, he concluded. 'It is my job to investigate wrongdoing, not yours. I am now heading up a murder investigation, and I don't have time for some amateur sleuth's theories on who might be culpable. This isn't a game of *Cluedo*, Miss Jenson!'

Vincent smiled to himself, pleased with how well he had delivered his condemnation of Sarah's suggestion.

'I beg your pardon?'

'I know it's been tough, but you need to let me do my job and just focus on the grieving process!' he added in an effort to prevent any further theories.

Sarah was livid at the other end of the line. There were so many names and abusive phrases she wanted to throw his way, to express how angry she was at the way he was speaking to her. Erin had always said he was a bit of an arse, but this was going beyond the pale!

'You should know,' he added as an afterthought, 'The body found at the golf course last night was Natalie's.'

Sarah didn't shout out or burst into tears, the reaction she would have anticipated at hearing such news.

'Ryan Moss is in Southampton,' she said evenly. 'He is looking to settle a score with me. Yes, we used to date, but that is *his* motivation, not mine. He was released from prison two months ago, vowing to get even with me and now one of my pupils has been snatched and my partner killed.' Sarah could hear her voice cracking as she said the words, but there was a determination in her not to break into tears. 'If you want to catch the man who took Natalie, who is the same person who killed Erin, you need to find Ryan Moss!'

Vincent was, himself, taken aback by Sarah's rant and scribbled the name 'Ryan Moss' onto a scrap of paper, to look into later.

'Okay, Miss Jenson,' Vincent conceded. 'We will look into this man for you. Can I ask: what makes you think he is in Southampton?'

'He wants to make me suffer,' she replied, before disconnecting the call.

She knew she should have asked for a police presence to be placed at her door, to protect her from Moss' evil intentions but she wasn't convinced that Vincent would take her seriously. It was clear that he still believed Erin's death was self-inflicted, and not the result of some twisted bastard's murderous revenge.

26

Sarah was still shaking, as she returned the telephone to its stand. Her worst fears had been confirmed: Natalie was dead. It seemed unreal. Only six days before, she had been praising Natalie for her outstanding imaginative story and well-conceived painting, and now she was gone. It just isn't right, she thought to herself: children aren't supposed to die; they are supposed to grow up and turn into brilliant adults and live long, meaningful lives.

Sarah pulled a scrunched-up piece of tissue from her pocket and dabbed at her eyes. It was hard to believe that there were any tears left! She had always considered herself such a strong woman. She nearly jumped out of her skin, when the phone started to ring again. She had to take a moment to steady her breathing. Maybe it was Vincent, phoning back to apologise for the abrupt way he had broken the news of Natalie's discovery.

Sarah took another deep breath and picked up the telephone, placing it to her ear, she said, 'Hello?'

'Sarah?' said a recognisable, Scottish brogue. 'It's Peggy McGregor here. How are you, dear?'

'Peggy, hi,' Sarah replied, 'I've been better, to be honest. I'll be okay.'

'So you've heard the news about Natalie, then?'

'I was just told,' Sarah replied, wiping her nose. 'It's so hard to believe.'

'I know, dear,' answered Mrs McGregor. 'Sarah,

listen, would it be possible for you to come in and see me? There is something I want to discuss with you.'

'Sure. Yes,' replied Sarah. 'I was planning to pop in anyway. I'll come in straight away.'

'That's great, see you soon.'

Sarah hung up the call and looked at her reflection in the nearest mirror. Big, black stains dissected her cheeks, like a jigsaw puzzle, where her make-up had run.

'What a mess!' she said to herself, and then added, 'I suppose you think this is all quite amusing, don't you?' She was looking up as she spoke, picturing Erin stood nearby; and smiling, shaking her head in that teasing way she always did. 'I wish you were here with me,' she added and the imaginary-Erin blew her a kiss and mouthed the words, 'I love you.'

Sarah re-applied her make-up before jumping into the car, and driving to St Monica's School. She didn't hear the telephone ringing as she had walked from the apartment to the car. What she wouldn't see until later that evening was that the number dialling started with '+32'.

*

Sarah arrived at the school a little after three, aware that most of the children would be on their way home. Mrs McGregor was sat in her office, waiting for her.

'Sarah, come in,' said Mrs McGregor when she saw the young teacher's head pop around the door.

'Hi, Peggy,' Sarah said, and then quickly checked to make sure that there were no errant pupils stood nearby who could have overheard.

'It's okay, dear,' Mrs McGregor replied. 'We closed the school just after two today, so there is nobody else around.

'How come the school closed so early?' asked Sarah, taking a seat opposite the Headmistress.

'That's what I wanted to talk to you about,' she replied, removing her glasses and allowing them to hang around her neck by the cord. 'Detective Inspector Vincent telephoned me, and had some very troubling words of advice that he wished to share.'

The look on Mrs McGregor's face said it all: it was ashen.

'What's wrong, Peggy?' asked Sarah, suddenly concerned about the Headmistress.

Peggy paused while she considered how best to share her concerns. 'Detective Inspector Vincent has advised me to close the school for a week, allowing him time to fully investigate Natalie's murder and hopefully find the horrible person who committed this crime.'

Sarah was pleased that the suggestion had been made, especially if Ryan Moss was watching the school; the children would be safer if they weren't near Sarah. She wondered why Vincent had not told her of this when she had phoned him earlier.

'The Detective and I spoke with the Board of Governors and they have agreed with the proposal. Mr Jackson, from the Board phoned me about half an hour ago to confirm the decision.'

'I see,' said Sarah, not sure why Mrs McGregor had felt the need to call her in, rather than speaking over the phone.

'What is it, Peggy?' asked Sarah after a pause. 'What *else* is troubling you? Why did you want to see me?'

Mrs McGregor, with a troubled look on her face, rose and started to move around her desk. She stopped when she was stood directly behind Sarah, and she placed her hands on the young teacher's shoulders.

'I'm worried about you, Sarah,' she said. 'You've been through a lot in the last week and I am concerned that you may be struggling with all the stress.'

Sarah was taken aback, but also rather cross with the suggestion that she was not coping. She attempted to stand up and brush Mrs McGregor's hands away but the Headmistress' grasp was stronger than she had anticipated and she remained where she was sat.

'It is understandable, dear,' Mrs McGregor continued. 'The grieving process is difficult for everyone, and the way people deal with it is different. You shouldn't feel afraid to take some time to properly grieve for your loss.'

'What makes you think I'm not coping?' asked Sarah, through slightly gritted teeth.

Mrs McGregor released her grip slightly. 'Inspector Vincent mentioned to me that you believe you know who might have taken Natalie.'

Sarah was angry that Vincent had told Mrs McGregor about their earlier conversation.

'He also said that this is the second man you have accused of taking Natalie since the incident, and that you have been making allegations that Erin's death was something other than a tragic accident.'

Sarah could contain her anger no longer, 'What are you saying, Peggy?'

'Your behaviour is very erratic at the moment,

Sarah. You lost Erin on Tuesday night but you were back in here yesterday taking part in the filming of a reconstruction of Natalie's abduction. You then tell me you are heading off to spend some time with your dad in Weymouth but now you are back, spouting conspiracy theories. I'm worried about you.'

Sarah stood quickly, and in doing so, caused Mrs McGregor's hands to fall. The Headmistress took a cautionary step backwards.

'I'm not crazy, Peggy,' said Sarah, turning to face her accuser.

Mrs McGregor held her hands up defensively, stating, 'I'm not saying you are, dear, but even you must admit that your behaviour is out of character.'

Sarah's face turned a shade of crimson as her anger continued to rise.

'Natalie was abducted and killed after leaving *my* classroom on Friday afternoon,' she said, trying to keep her voice even, but not succeeding. 'Then somebody drove *my* girlfriend's car off the road, almost killing her. A man I used to know who was prosecuted for abducting and nearly killing a young girl is free, and has threatened revenge on *me*. I am not being irrational, Peggy.'

Mrs McGregor's arms remained in the air, keeping a safe distance between herself and Sarah.

'I don't mean to upset you, Sarah. I only have your best interests at heart.'

Sarah regained her composure and moved to the other side of the office to cool down.

'The school will be closed for at least a week, Sarah. Detective Vincent doesn't want to see any more children harmed and is taking your suggestion about the revenge-motive into consideration. Take some time, Sarah. Go away. Grieve for Erin. I am sure I can arrange for a supply teacher to take your place this term and then you can come back, fully refreshed and focused in the new school year.'

'I'm not going to run away from this, Peggy,' said Sarah determinedly.

'No-one will see it as running away, dear. I am offering you a chance to get your head together. I am not questioning your ability as a teacher but the children in your class need someone strong to help them through what will be an understandably difficult time for them.'

'They need me!' shouted Sarah. 'How is it going to look to them if I just disappear?'

'We will explain why you have gone away. It will be okay.'

'No,' said Sarah. 'My children need me. I let harm come to one of them, I won't allow harm to come to the rest.'

'What happened to Natalie was not *your* fault, Sarah,' pleaded Mrs McGregor. 'There is nothing you could have done. There are some sick people in this world, Sarah. You mustn't blame yourself.'

'I should have been there for her, Peggy,' said Sarah, staring out of the Headmistresses' office window at an empty playground. 'If her mother hadn't arrived to collect her, she should have come back into the school. Why didn't she? She must have been able to see me in my classroom from where she was stood. Why didn't she come to *me*?'

'We will never know why she stayed out there, Sarah. You cannot blame yourself.'

'Who else is to blame, Peggy?' Sarah countered. 'She should have trusted me enough to come back in.'

'Sarah, stop this!' ordered Mrs McGregor.

'And why did she get into some strange man's car? She was smarter than that, Peggy. I made sure all my children knew not to speak to strangers; I drilled that into them. Why did she go?'

Sarah could feel her voice cracking again. Mrs McGregor must have noticed it too as she moved across the room to Sarah and put her arms around her.

'It's not your fault, Sarah. It's not your fault,' repeated Mrs McGregor over and over. The embrace was the last straw and Sarah found herself wrapping her own arms around the Headmistress and burying her head in the older woman's welcoming shoulder. It felt for a moment, to Sarah, like having her mum back. The two women remained in embrace for the next ten minutes.

Sarah eventually managed to re-compose herself and told Mrs McGregor that she felt better.

'So will you take some time off, to get things together?' Mrs McGregor persisted.

'It's not that I'm not grateful, Peggy. I am. I'll think about your offer.'

'Okay, okay,' said the Headmistress, accepting that she wouldn't get an immediate answer. 'Let me know as soon as you can, dear.'

'I will, Peggy,' said Sarah, excusing herself. 'I'm going to go to my classroom and collect some bits and pieces. I'll give you a call at the weekend.'

'Okay, Sarah,' said Mrs McGregor, smiling, pleased that she had managed to have the conversation with the young teacher.

Sarah said 'Good bye,' and headed for her classroom. There were chairs pulled out from the tables as well as various bits of paper and colouring pencils strewn across the floor. Clearly, the teacher who was currently covering for Sarah, didn't share her sense of order. Sarah began picking up the various items of litter and didn't see the classroom door open behind her. Nor did she see the man who walked in through it. Sarah froze when she recognised a voice that she hadn't heard in several years.

'Hello, Sarah,' said Ryan Moss.

27

'What the fuck are you doing here?' asked Sarah, before she could stop herself.

'Easy, Sarah,' replied Moss, holding up his hands defensively. 'How about a 'hello' or 'how are you?' first? Jesus, I know it's been a few years, but swearing? Is that what I deserve?'

'Keep the fuck away from me, you sick son of a bitch,' Sarah said, moving as far from the man as she could, eager to keep distance between them.

'Sarah, what's wrong?' asked Moss, unsure why his one-time girlfriend seemed so unhappy to see him. 'Don't be silly, I won't hurt you.'

'How the fuck did you get in here, Ryan?' demanded Sarah.

'I walked in through the front door. Why are you being so strange?'

'So strange?' countered Sarah. 'A child abductor and attempted murderer turns up at my school and I am being *weird*?'

'Look,' began Moss, trying to move closer, to decrease the distance between them. 'I know it must seem strange, my turning up after so long, but I needed to see you.'

'Why not phone?' retorted Sarah, suddenly fearful for her life. If this bastard had abducted and killed Natalie and murdered Erin, what was to stop him killing her here in her classroom?

'Sarah, I don't understand why you look so

scared. It's me, Ryan. Come on, stop being silly.'

'Silly? You think I'm being silly? Keep the fuck away from me, you sick son of a bitch.'

'Sarah, I'm sorry,' replied Moss. 'I didn't mean to upset you. I came here to make amends, not to frighten you.'

Sarah watched her former boyfriend pick up a nearby chair and sit on it.

'What the fuck are you doing here, Ryan?' she managed to sputter, although there were a dozen other questions she wished to ask.

Moss looked at his palms, in a manner that he had rehearsed to keep himself calm over the years. 'Look,' he said. 'I know that the last time we saw each other, it wasn't easy. I was in a different place back then. I did some things, which…I am not proud of. I was going through a lot, it's not an excuse, but I was a different man. I did some things, which…were inexcusable.'

Sarah stared back at the man who had once been a good friend, but whom recently had become the object of her hatred, since she had begun to suspect him of being responsible for Natalie's disappearance.

'I'm calling the police,' she said, unsure what else she could do.

'The police? Why? I haven't done anything wrong. I only came to speak to you. I never imagined that you would react like this. I mean, I had expected a little animosity, but nothing like this. Why are you so upset?'

'You really need me to spell it out for you? Is that how you get your kicks?'

'Get my kicks? Sarah, I really don't know what you are talking about,' Moss said looking confused.

Sarah considered her options. Her mobile phone was in her handbag, over by the classroom door. The school was virtually empty and she had no idea what other teachers may have hung around once the children had been sent home early. Mrs McGregor was in her office but not even Sarah's loudest scream would reach that far. If she ran, would Moss go for her? At least he seemed passive at the moment. Maybe all he did want to do was talk? After all, she was a bit older than his usual type. She chastised herself silently for that last thought.

'Natalie Barrett,' she said after a while.

'Oh, the little girl,' replied Moss, looking unhappy. 'Such a shame.'

Sarah waited for more and when he noticed her glaring at him, the penny dropped and he realised what she was implying.

'Oh God, you think I had something to do with that?'

'Well, didn't you?' she challenged.

'Good God, no,' he countered disgustedly.

'She goes missing on Friday afternoon, and you just happen to turn up at the school to see me a week later? Come on, Ryan, I'm not a fool!'

'Sarah, do you really think I'm still that kind of person?'

'Why not? Once a killer, always a killer,' she shouted, spit flying from her lips as she did.

'I have nothing to do with that little girl's disappearance,' he protested.

'How do you know about her then?' Sarah countered, thinking she had trapped him in a lie.

'I watch the news, Sarah. I saw yesterday that she had been abducted from a school in Southampton. I had no idea she was from your school.'

Sensing, he was trying to use delaying tactics, she decided to push him again.

'I suppose you have an alibi for your whereabouts on Friday afternoon, as well?' she said flippantly.

Moss paused for a moment, while he thought about the question. After a moment he smiled a broad grin. 'I have the perfect alibi,' he said. 'I can tell you exactly where I was on Friday afternoon: I was with Chloe Green.'

Sarah blinked several times while the name danced around in her mind's eye.

'Chloe Green?' Sarah repeated.

'That's right. I was with her for the same reason I am here with you now, Sarah: to make amends.'

'You expect me to believe you were visiting your old friend Chloe Green?' Sarah asked sarcastically.

'Well I wouldn't describe her as my 'old friend', but, yes, I was with her. If you calm down and let me explain why I am here, I will tell you why.'

Sarah was still wary of the man sat uncomfortably on a plastic chair. She was no closer to her mobile phone, and there was every chance that Mrs McGregor had packed up for the day and gone home herself.

Seeing Sarah's eyes darting around the room, Moss offered, 'Do you have a mobile phone, Sarah?'

'What?' she questioned, thrown by the question.

'I can see you are worried by my presence here, and whilst I can guarantee I mean you no harm, you may feel more at ease with your phone in your hand.'

It was an interesting offer, Sarah had to admit. Moss put his own hand in his trouser pocket and fished a small item out.

'Here,' he said holding up the small mobile phone he had just removed from his pocket. 'Take mine, if you wish. If you genuinely fear me, after I have explained myself, then you can phone the police or a friend or the talking clock, for all I care. Please Sarah? There is something I need to say to you and I have travelled a long way to be with you today. The least you can do is hear me out.'

'My phone is in my handbag,' Sarah eventually responded. 'I would feel better if I had it near me.'

'Okay,' he responded warmly. 'I'll go and fetch your handbag. I mean you no harm, Sarah.'

'And I want us to sit nearer the door,' she added as he rose from the small seat.

'If it will make you feel better, we can sit wherever you like. Just please, hear me out.'

'Okay, Ryan,' she said, the confidence returning to her voice. 'My handbag is over by the door. You can sit on the chair behind the teacher's desk, over there,' she pointed at the large desk towards the front of the classroom. 'I'll perch on that desk nearest the door,' she added.

'Very well,' Moss replied, pleased that she was finally being reasonable but still surprised at how scared she seemed to be. He couldn't believe that she thought he had anything to do with the disappearance of Natalie Barrett.

Once they were both seated in their new places, Moss removed his anorak and placed it over the back of the chair. Sarah had her mobile phone gripped tightly in her hand, so Moss began his explanation.

'I've rehearsed this speech a dozen times, hoping that I would have a chance to speak to you, one day and make peace with you,' he began.

'I heard you told a former cellmate that you had a message to deliver to me. What is it?' Sarah challenged.

'That's true, Sarah. If you let me continue, I will tell you what I have come to say,' Moss responded, angry that she continued to interrupt his trail of thought.

'What happened all those years ago was very strange. When I try and recall that period when I did...what I did to Chloe...it is like a bad dream...or a bad movie, watched late one night. It's as if it wasn't me. I decided, when inside that I would tell you everything, so here goes: I'm gay, Sarah.'

He waited for some kind of reaction: shock, surprise or recognition, but Sarah's face remained impassive.

'Anyway,' he continued, 'I knew back then that I was different. In fact, I suspected I was gay, back when I was fifteen, but I was in denial. I used to watch some of the other boys when I was in the showers at school and then I would go home and beat myself up about it. I told myself that all *normal* boys went through the same thing, and that it didn't mean anything. That's probably why I was so intent on dating as many girls as I could, to prove to everyone, myself included, that I was straight. Sorry, Sarah, that included you.'

He paused again, hoping for some kind of acceptance, or absolution, from Sarah but she remained silent.

'I had a fight with my dad on...that day...he accused me of being soft, because I had gotten upset over something or other. I think I left the house, hoping to prove to him that he was wrong and that I was all man. I must have met Chloe at some point along the road…and…well…you know the rest.' He paused to wipe a small tear from his eye. 'I didn't accept what I had done, for a long time. Even when I arrived at the Verne, I just thought it was God's way of punishing me for being gay. I didn't want to think it was because I had done something…something so bad. Thankfully, there was a chaplain in the prison who persisted with me, until eventually, he got me talking. He told me that what I had done was wrong, but that God would forgive me, if I was truly repentant. I was worried that I would be capable of doing the same thing all over again. The chaplain explained that I was ill and that, with treatment, I would be better.'

'So what, he prescribed you with some antibiotics and then released you?' Sarah said with an unbelieving frown.

Moss smiled at the jibe; at least she wasn't accusing him anymore.

'There isn't any medication that can control the urges I was experiencing. It helped when I eventually accepted my homosexuality but that wasn't the answer. I began to do research on the internet while inside, and came across a procedure that would help curb those urges.'

'What kind of procedure?'

'Two years ago, I underwent voluntary castration,' he fired back.

Sarah couldn't help it, but her eyes darted down to Moss' crotch. What she had expected to see, she didn't know; perhaps a gravestone? Moss smiled at her reaction, it was one he experienced every time he told somebody what he had done. Chloe had reacted the same way last week.

'A little extreme,' he laughed, 'but it has definitely made things easier.'

'Is this a joke?' Sarah asked, unsure what else she could say.

'I have them pickled in a jar if you'd like to see them,' he said.

'Oh God! That's disgusting,' Sarah replied, fighting down the urge to retch.

'That was a joke, Sarah,' Moss replied, laughing at his own twisted sense of humour. 'I'm not sure what the hospital does with them, to be honest. Anyway, I continued to see the chaplain, and he showed me that the only way I would be able to move on with my life, would be to seek out those that I had hurt, and offer my sincerest regret. That is what I meant when I said I would deliver a message. My message is my heartfelt apology to you. I treated you poorly and I want you to forgive my indecent behaviour.'

Sarah was stunned by the frankness of what Moss had told her. She was torn in how to respond. Part of her wanted to tell him of her own denial when they had been dating, and she wondered if that was what had drawn them together to begin with. Part of her wanted to shout at him and say he was a liar, that he had killed Natalie and Erin and that she was going to phone the police, but in truth, she didn't really believe that anymore. Instead, she said, 'I don't think I'm the one you should be apologising to, Ryan.'

'I have made my peace with Chloe,' he replied. 'It took me a while to find her, after I was released, but the internet is an amazing tool and I tracked her down in Darlington, up North. She is working as a nail technician in a local salon, there. She is very happy and making a decent living.'

Sarah didn't know whether to believe him or whether to dial Jack Vincent for help.

'She didn't recognise me at first, and when I told her who I was, she was angry and refused to speak to me. It took me several weeks to convince her to meet with me, so that I could say sorry, but she eventually relented and agreed to see me on Friday afternoon. We met in a quiet bar in Spennymoor and she brought a friend with her. It was all very awkward,' he admitted, 'but she listened to what I had to say and said she accepted my apology. She told me she could never forgive me for what I had done to her but she accepted that I was sorry, and was satisfied with the actions I had taken to prevent any kind of repetition. I left her at the bar just after five, and returned to my hotel room on the edge of the town, and caught a train early Saturday morning down to Southampton to look you up.'

'It's Thursday, Ryan, what have you been doing since Saturday?' Sarah challenged, but almost immediately felt guilty, after she had said it.

'You weren't so easy to find,' he said, smiling, trying to crack her frosty exterior. 'I found out you were a teacher and managed to narrow down which school you worked in, but you've not been here for a couple of days. Today was the first day I saw your car in the car park, so I decided to come in and see you.'

Sarah looked him straight in the eye. Was he telling the truth? She felt so confused. After all that had happened in the last week, she didn't know what to believe. Moss fished in his trouser pocket again and pulled out a small piece of paper. He stood and moved to where Sarah was perched, and handed the note over.

'What's this?' she asked, seeing numbers scrawled on it.

'That's Chloe's telephone number. You can call her if you want. She will verify what I have said.'

He seemed so sure of himself that she found it hard not to believe him.

'Phone her, Sarah. It's okay,' he said.

'I may do,' she replied, folding up the piece of paper and placing it in her pocket. 'I have listened to what you have said, is there anymore?'

'No,' he said, shaking his head. 'That was it. I want you to know that I am sorry about what happened, and I am sorry with how I treated you. Maybe, if I had admitted what I knew to be true, none of this would have happened.'

He returned to where he had been seated, and removed his anorak from the back of the chair.

'Thank you for listening to me, Sarah,' Moss said, zipping up the anorak.

'What happens next?' she asked, more out of politeness than curiosity.

'Hopefully you will find it in your heart to forgive me. You won't see me again, Sarah. I have made my peace with you and my future looks brighter.'

'What are your plans?' she asked, jealous that his future seemed so certain when hers was in such disarray.

'I have a long journey ahead of me, this weekend,' he said. 'I have a train to catch.'

As quietly as he had walked in; he left, leaving Sarah stunned and more confused about who had taken Natalie as ever. Her gut was telling her that

Ryan Moss was truthful, and if that was the case then he had nothing to do with Natalie's disappearance, or Erin's murder. If that was true, then that left only Jimmy Barrett as the likely suspect, but the police didn't seem to think he was guilty. There was only one other possibility: the killer was someone she had yet to encounter and the thought that some stranger was responsible frightened her more than anything.

FRIDAY

28

'What the bloody hell am I doing here?' asked an angry Jimmy Barrett. It was early morning, by his standards, although to the rest of the world it was nearly ten. Usually at this time of the day he would be about to get up, throw on some clothes and head to *The Swan*.

'There are just a few questions I have for you,' replied Jack Vincent.

'Questions about what exactly?' demanded Barrett.

'About the disappearance and murder of your niece, Mr Barrett,' replied Vincent, in an even tone.

'I've already spoken to your lot about where I was on Friday afternoon,' he shouted back. 'In the pub!'

'I'm aware of your conversation with Detective Constable Cooke,' Vincent began, 'however I have some further questions for you.'

Barrett paused for a moment and sat back in the hard, plastic chair they had provided him with. He folded his arms and chewed on his lip, thinking.

'Okay,' he said, after a while. 'Ask away.'

'How are things at home, Jimmy?'

'Fine,' replied Barrett, adopting the approach of giving as little information as he could.

'No disagreements with Neil? Or Melanie?'

'Nothing more than usual,' he replied.

'Officers have been called to the house by worried neighbours a couple of times in the last few months. Any idea why?' asked Vincent, trying to keep his tone relaxed.

'Nothing to do with me,' replied Barrett, shrugging his shoulders.

'So, your brother and his wife haven't been having heated arguments about your moving in with them?' Vincent was hoping to provoke a reaction from Barrett, something that would give him a clue about whether he could have had something to do with what had happened to Cookie. That was the real reason he had dragged Jimmy Barrett in this morning, and why he had kept him waiting for over an hour before commencing the informal interview. He wanted to see Barrett angry, to see if the wrong question would provoke a violent reaction. Vincent had already received verification that Barrett had been in the bookies before he had headed to *The Swan* on Friday afternoon, so couldn't have taken Natalie. However, that didn't mean he had nothing to do with her disappearance and it didn't mean that he couldn't have been involved in the death of D.C. Cooke.

'You'd have to ask them about that,' Barrett replied nonchalantly.

'We have,' Vincent mused. 'Melanie told us she can't stand having you around in the house. She says there isn't enough room for all of you under the same roof, and that you're not paying your way. What do you have to say to that?'

'Everyone's entitled to their opinion,' he replied, and then grinned at Vincent, as he sensed what the policeman was trying to do.

'She doesn't like you much, your sister-in-law, does she, Jimmy?'

'As I said, detective, she's entitled to her opinion.'

'Must be difficult though,' replied Vincent sucking

air in through his teeth, 'your brother having to choose sides. I mean, who would he side with, you, his brother, or the woman he chose to marry? It can't be easy.'

'I don't see what this has to do with what happened to Natalie,' Barrett fired back.

'I just want to understand the background, Jimmy. I want to know what kind of atmosphere little Natalie would have been living with. You know? Was there anything to make her feel like she would want to run away from home?'

'You're unbelievable! Do you know that?' shouted Barrett, angry at the suggestion that his arrival could have caused Natalie to disappear. 'Neil and Melanie are good parents. Do you hear me? She was well-loved and had a happy upbringing. She wouldn't have run away!'

'Wouldn't she? When the going gets tough, that's what you Barretts do, isn't it, Jimmy?'

'What the hell is that supposed to mean?' shouted Barrett again.

'Well that's what you did in the army isn't it? Ran away when the going got tough?'

Barrett launched across the table towards Vincent, sending the plastic chair crashing to the floor.

'You son of a bitch!' he shouted, unable to control his temper. Luckily for Vincent, his chair was far enough away that Barrett's grasp missed him. P.C. Capshaw, who was also sat in the room, leapt from his chair and restrained Barrett.

'Temper, temper, Jimmy,' Vincent goaded. 'Is this how you always are when you're angry? Violent? Is that the real reason the police have been called several times this year? Ever been violent with your brother?

Or your sister-in-law? Or your niece?'

Vincent knew he shouldn't be pressing Barrett like this, but he was sure there was something Barrett was holding back. Capshaw struggled to keep Barrett in place when Vincent suggested he might have hit Natalie.

'You son of a bitch!' Barrett yelled again with a snarl.

'Easy, easy!' said Vincent, raising his voice in an effort to regain control of the exchange. 'Sit down and calm down, Jimmy or I'll have you locked up for assault on an officer. You want to spend the night banged up?'

Jimmy snarled again in a final effort to get at Vincent and when he couldn't break Capshaw's hold, he relaxed his muscles and said he would retake his seat. Capshaw looked at Vincent for confirmation that he could release Barrett, and when Vincent nodded, Capshaw allowed him to pick up the chair.

'You really do have a temper on you, don't you, Jimmy?' said Vincent when they were all seated again.

'You were pushing me,' Barrett retorted.

'True,' said Vincent, 'but it didn't take much, did it?'

Vincent paused to allow this to sink in before he said, 'We know you weren't the one to take Natalie, Jimmy. We've had your whereabouts verified by CCTV and witness accounts. But what puzzles me is Natalie's teacher's statement that Natalie was scared of a monster of some sort. Who do you think she could have meant?'

'Look,' said Jimmy, 'Neil and Mel have had arguments about me living with them. That much is true. The police were called when the shouting got too much, I'll admit, but Natalie wasn't unhappy. And she wasn't scared of me,' he added for good measure.

'If not you, then who?' Vincent fired back.

'I don't know,' replied Barrett, exasperated.

'What are you hiding, Jimmy?' Vincent asked.

'I'm not hiding anything.'

'Yes you are,' continued Vincent. 'I've sat here and accused you of being involved in Natalie's disappearance and beating her. You have reacted angrily, but there has been no regret expressed at her disappearance. Something doesn't sit right.'

'I don't know what you're talking about,' replied Barrett sheepishly, turning his head to avoid Vincent's stare. It was the tell-tale sign Vincent had been waiting for.

'Yes you do,' accused Vincent, pointing a finger at him. 'Come on, Jimmy, what are you hiding? What haven't you told us?'

'I've told you everything,' stated Barrett, looking away for a second time.

'There it is again,' beamed Vincent, this time standing, while pointing his finger. 'Tell me what you know, Jimmy.'

Barrett looked from Vincent to Capshaw, and back again.

'Come on, Jimmy,' continued Vincent. 'Do you really want me to charge you with wasting police time? I can if that will help?'

'No,' interrupted Jimmy. 'Okay, okay,' he conceded, 'Look, there is something else. It might be totally unrelated, but I just don't know.'

'What, Jimmy? What is it?' demanded Vincent, retaking his seat, pleased his instinct had been right.

'There was this weird guy who phoned the house

on Wednesday morning. Spoke with an accent. He was asking questions about Natalie. About what she looked like, where she went to school and that sort of thing. Claimed he was a reporter.'

'And?' asked Vincent, surprised by the nature of this apparent confession.

'Well, Neil and Mel were out so I answered the phone. He said he would give me money for the information. So...I answered his questions, told him what he wanted to know. It was only after he had hung up that I started to think about what he was asking? The questions were odd.'

'In what way odd?' Vincent enquired.

'I don't know, really...they just weren't what I would have expected a reporter to ask.'

'Can you give me an example?' Vincent persevered.

'He wanted me to describe what she looked like, whether she was popular at school, whether she was pretty, stuff like that. After he had hung up, I started to wonder whether his questions were a bit...you know...perverted.'

'Did you take his name?' Vincent asked.

'No.'

'Did he say what newspaper he worked for?' Vincent asked.

'No.'

'Jesus Christ, Jimmy!' exclaimed Vincent. 'Did he even say how he would pay you?'

Barrett's head dropped forward as he uttered, 'No.'

'Have you told anyone else about this?' Vincent asked, standing up.

'No,' replied Barrett, head still drooped.

'Capshaw,' Vincent said. 'Get on to your contact at the phone company, see if they can find the number that called the Barrett's house on Wednesday. It may be, that this moron, here, spoke with the killer.'

Capshaw stood and left the room. Vincent looked back at Barrett and shook his head.

'You fucking idiot!' he said.

29

One thing Sarah learnt whilst at university was the tell-tale symptoms of a hangover. For her, a sore head, a dull ache behind the eyes and a gravelly voice, from too much shouting the previous evening, were the signs that she had consumed too much alcohol the night before. Once she got out of bed, dizziness, nausea and a sour taste in the mouth would soon develop also. Friday morning brought each of these feelings to her. Not that she should have been surprised, not given the two bottles of cheap wine that she had consumed, when she had returned from school yesterday.

The meeting with Ryan Moss had affected her more than she had first realised. She had been shocked to come face-to-face with him, at first, and the edginess she had felt had stayed with her since; it had been like seeing a ghost. She had gone in search of him in Portland, and had been disappointed not to find him. Finally catching up with him had failed to bring the feeling of satisfaction she had been looking for.

She had been surprised when Moss had admitted to being homosexual, and she had actually empathised with him, when he had explained how difficult he had found it to be a young, homosexual man in Portland. Sarah could still remember Ryan's father: a stern and gruff fisherman, not afraid to use his fists to settle an argument. Ryan had never openly told her, but she was pretty sure that he had been on the receiving end of an occasional beating from Moss Snr. She could understand why he had found it impossible to come out in front of his father. From memory, Moss Snr had passed away shortly after Ryan's conviction, so there was every chance he had never found out.

Moss' struggle with his homosexuality had made her think long and hard about her own. She knew, almost too well, how hard it was to tell your parents that you are gay, but at least her father seemed to have accepted it now. She wondered whether she should phone her father, and tell him that she had caught up with Moss, but she decided she would leave it until the weekend and then give him a call. Sarah had nearly told Moss of her own sexual journey, but as she had still been uncertain about whether or not he was responsible for Natalie's disappearance, she had decided not to give him the satisfaction that they might be more similar than he ever realised.

The way Moss had explained his time behind bars had been captivating and she had found herself believing him, in spite of herself. It angered her that she may have got it so wrong in telling Jack Vincent that Moss was the guilty man. The correct thing she should have done, upon leaving the school, was to tell Vincent that she had been mistaken. Instead, she had driven to an off licence, around the corner from her apartment and had bought two bottles of rosé wine for ten pounds on a special offer. She had also paid for a bag of *Kettle Chips*, as she knew she was in no mood to cook. These were the first two mistakes she had made last night, and boy, was she feeling the consequences now.

Sarah had opened the front door and dumped her

shopping bags on the floor. She removed the two bottles of wine and the crisps and headed for the living room sofa. She decided she needed cheering up, and in an effort to achieve this, she put on her *Pretty Woman* DVD on. She made every effort to watch the film but her mind kept wandering back to Natalie's disappearance and possible suspects. One large glass of wine soon became two and before she knew it the first bottle was drained. She already felt drunk and should have gone straight to bed. Her third mistake of the night was to ignore the voice in her head, and to open the second bottle. The more she drank, the more maudlin she became. She started to think about Erin, and the tears soon flowed again, but this time she welcomed them. She was disappointed that she had managed to go more than an hour without thinking about Erin, and it scared her. She knew that as the days, weeks, months and years passed she would think about Erin less and less, and she dreaded it happening. At the start of the week, she had imagined spending the rest of her life with Erin, and now she was facing the prospect of spending the rest of her life without her. She wanted to force herself to remember Erin and opted for a second movie. This was her final mistake of the evening: watching *Ghost*. She had always found it an uplifting movie by the final credits, but on this occasion, it didn't bring her any respite. She cried herself to sleep, but at least she was thinking about Erin. Sleep during the night had been restless; the alcohol knocked her out, but she wasn't properly asleep.

Sarah ran her tongue around her mouth: it felt dry. She stumbled from her bedroom to the kitchen, deliberately avoiding the two mirrors en route. She could imagine the state of her hair and yesterday's make up, and didn't need to see the evidence. She was relieved to make it to the kitchen sink before she threw up the bile that had previously settled in her stomach. The cupboard where glasses were stored was at the opposite end of the kitchen, and, fearing a repeat bout of vomiting, she opted to drink water directly from the tap. It had been a while since she had felt *this* drunk. 'Never again,' she told herself, already knowing it was a lie.

Sarah stayed rooted to the spot for half an hour, before she managed to drag herself to the bathroom and into a warm shower. It did nothing for her aching head, but it did wake her up a little bit. She couldn't decide what to wear, so she remained in her towelling robe, waiting for inspiration. She slumped down on the bed and looked at her clothes, through the open cupboard doors. 'What to wear, what to wear?' she thought.

Her attention was caught by the sound of her home telephone ringing. She idly left her bedroom, moved to the hallway and lifted the receiver.

'Hello?' she said.

'Sarah Jenson?' asked a French-accented, deep voice.

'Yes?' she replied, a surprised look on her face.

'Bonjour, mademoiselle,' replied the voice. 'My name is Claude Rêmet. Are you free to speak?'

Sarah's hungover-mind was struggling to keep up. Why was a Frenchman phoning her? The penny dropped as she looked at the telephone number on the phone's display and saw it began with '+32'.

'Who are you?' Sarah asked, trying not to sound confrontational.

'I am a journalist, Miss Jenson,' he replied.

'Why is a French journalist phoning me?' she thought to herself. The only response she could muster was that he worked for a British newspaper but was French-born. He must have been trying to write a piece about Natalie's disappearance. Maybe he worked for a tabloid and was after salacious details of her relationship with Erin.

'Miss Jenson? Are you still there?' he enquired.

'Sorry, yes,' she replied, having not realised it had been several seconds since she had last spoken. 'How can I help you, exactly?'

'I need to speak with you urgently, Miss Jenson,' came the response. 'Can you meet with me?'

'What? No,' she replied. 'What do you want from me? Why do you want to meet with me? What story are you chasing?'

'I do not understand what you are asking, Miss Jenson,' he replied gruffly. 'Will you meet with me?'

'Why should I meet with you?' she retorted and was unprepared for his response.

'I have some information about the disappearance of Natalie Barrett,' he replied. 'I know who killed her.'

Sarah nearly dropped the phone, as her mouth widened.

'Who? What? Why?' she blurted.

'Meet me later today and I will tell you everything I know.'

'Why tell me?' she asked, without thinking. 'Have you told the police?'

'Not yet,' he said quietly, as if he was trying to stop somebody overhear him.

'Tell the police!' she demanded. I can give you the number for the lead detective. His name is…'

'No police, Miss Jenson,' he interrupted. 'Not yet.'

'You need to tell them, Mr, Mr, Mr…what is your name again?'

'Claude Rêmet,' he replied.

'Well, Monsieur Rêmet, you need to tell the police, so that they can go and arrest whoever it is.'

'In time, Miss Jenson,' he said, calmly. 'If I told them now they would not believe me. Meet me today and I will tell you what I know. After that, if you still want me to go to the police, you can take me to your detective.'

Sarah considered this for a moment. The man on the other end of the line could be a lunatic, or a crank-caller of some kind. On the other hand, if she ignored him, she might never find out what had happened to Natalie and Erin.

'Where do you want to meet?' she said reluctantly.

'I can be in Southampton in about six hours. Where should I meet you?' he answered.

'Six hours?' she replied. 'Where are you travelling from?'

'I live in Brussels, Miss Jenson.'

It was not the answer Sarah had expected, but at least it explained the vaguely Gallic-accent.

'Right, okay,' said Sarah, feeling suddenly flustered. 'There is an Italian coffee bar, near the train station in Southampton.' She checked her watch. 'I can meet you there at five.'

'Very well, Miss Jenson,' he replied. 'I will see you there.'

'Wait,' she said, sensing he was about to hang up. 'How will I know what you look like?'

'Don't worry,' he replied, 'I will find you.'

With that, the line went dead. Sarah returned the

handset and realised her hands were shaking. Little did she realise that the phone call would alter the course of her life completely.

30

P.C. Kyle Davies parked the unmarked squad car by the side of the road, and switched the engine off. It was nearly lunchtime, and this was the second time he'd parked in this spot today. He had originally arrived at seven that morning, but had been called away to support the pursuit of a serial mugger who had popped up on the radar. By the time he had arrived on scene, the mugger had already been nabbed, and D.I. Vincent had been mightily annoyed that Davies had left his post. He had apologised to his boss and promised he would head straight back, but had taken an unconventional detour past *KFC* to pick up some boneless chicken. He had used the Drive-thru to speed up his return, as he didn't feel it unreasonable to be allowed to refuel, especially as he had missed breakfast to attend this stakeout.

Davies hated this area with a passion. Filled with high-rise towers and council-owned property, Thornhill really was a scar on the face of the city. It was the fifth time this week he had come looking for Miles Heath, a registered sex offender, who lived in the house opposite where Davies was parked. It wasn't a lot to look at: a one-bedroom, terraced property with a small concrete garden at the front, and a couple of ceramic plant pots, void of any life. Davies had never met Heath and the photograph on file was quite dated, so he wasn't certain whom he was looking for.

Miles Heath had come from money. He had attended private school in West London somewhere, and it was probably his early sexual experiences in the shower rooms of the school that had set him on the unsteady course his life would take. Davies had asked a couple of his colleagues what Heath was like, and they had described him as openly-camp with a flair for indiscretion. One officer had described him as 'a bit of a Dick Emery,' but Davies wasn't sure what that had meant.

There was still a bottle of milk on the doorstep, which suggested that Heath had yet to return to the property. At least that was good news, as Davies knew Vincent would probably kick him off the team if he found that they had missed their target because he had left his post.

Davies unbuckled his seatbelt and moved the cardboard bucket of chicken onto his lap. He wound his window down to help release some of the smell, and then began to tuck into his lunch. It was still hot, thankfully.

'Any sign yet?' squawked the radio unit in the car.

Davies quickly swallowed what he was chewing, pressed the talk button and replied, 'Not yet, Guv. Milk is on the door step so doesn't look like he is back yet, over.'

Davies knew that Vincent was struggling to come up with a name, for the D.C.I., to confirm who had taken and killed Natalie Barrett. With Jimmy Barrett now out of the frame as well, they were virtually back to square one. Vincent had described the case as 'vital for justice,' but in Davies' opinion what he had meant was 'vital for Vincent's career.' It was the sort of case that would bring Vincent the kind of glory he always seemed to crave. Similarly, failure to crack the case, and Vincent would be hung out to dry.

Davies finished his box of chicken and wiped his hands and face with a paper napkin. As he did, he spotted a dark green, VW camper van pull up two cars in front. The driver clambered out of the van and started walking towards him. In a panic, Davies began to wind his window back up and desperately looked for something to do, so that it wouldn't be obvious he was a police officer. The driver stopped outside the car and tapped on the window. Davies looked up and saw a tall man with light grey hair staring back at him. The man was wearing brown, leather driving gloves and his lips were pulled tight in a thin smile. Davies knew it was Heath the moment he spotted the eye liner and crimson blusher on his face.

'Are you planning on stopping long?' Heath asked in a friendly manner.

'Err…I…err…what…err…no,' Davies stammered.

'Are you alright, love?' replied Heath, 'You look like you've seen a ghoul.'

There was no doubting the camp twang belonged to Miles Heath, but he didn't seem to realise who Davies was or why he might be here.

'It's just,' continued Heath, 'you're parked in my space and if you're not going to be here long, could you move so I can have it? Sorry to be a nuisance. I've been away on a trip, you see, and the van's in a bit of a state. If I leave it parked where it is, the cable from my vacuum won't reach, whereas if I'm here, it will.'

Davies wasn't really listening. He was having an argument with himself in his head over whether to arrest Heath now, or to wait and see what he did.

'Hello? Anyone there?' Heath sang camply.

Davies reached a decision, opened his door and climbed out of the car. 'Miles Heath?' he asked.

'Yes,' came the drawn-out response.

'I am Police Constable Kyle Davies. I wonder if you wouldn't mind accompanying me down to the station to answer some questions?'

'Questions? What about?'

'About the disappearance of a local school girl.'

'Am I under arrest?' asked Heath.

'Not yet,' replied Davies, as he opened the back door of the car and ushered him into the car.

*

'Perhaps you can start by telling us where you went on Friday morning?' asked Vincent, when he had Davies and Heath sat in an interview room.

'I've been up to Blackpool, to visit some friends,' Heath replied as sternly as he could.

'And can these friends verify that?'

'Of course they bloody can. Do you need them to?' Heath challenged back.

'It would be good if somebody could confirm where you were for the last week, yes.'

'Fine,' replied Heath. 'Give me a flaming pen and paper and I'll write their numbers down.'

'Have you lived in Thornhill for long?'

'Three years, since I was released from prison. I'm assuming you knew that, so what was the point of the question?'

'Three years you say? So you are pretty familiar with the area then?' asked Vincent calmly.

'You could say that,' replied Heath, rolling his eyes.

'And your release order, what does it say about where you can and can't live?' continued Vincent.

'It says I am not to go within a two mile radius of a school, and that if I do, I am liable to further prosecution. Look, I know where you are going with this, but it wasn't my choice to move into that poxy house in Thornhill, it was the council's. They put me there. I raised it with my Community Support Liaison Officer but she said that it would have to make do.'

'So you know where St Monica's School is then?' asked Vincent.

'Yes I do, but I've never been there. I didn't like being locked up, darlin' and I don't intend to go back inside. I wouldn't set foot near that school.'

'You mentioned to my colleague that there was a bit of a mess in the back of your van. What kind of mess are we talking about?' Vincent asked. 'I have a team of forensics specialists looking at the van at the moment, so it's in your best interests to tell me.'

'Probably a mixture of semen and breadcrumbs, darlin',' replied Heath, smirking.

'What about blood?'

'I've been to Blackpool, love, not a flamin' pagan festival. I've been sleeping in that van for the last week, so there are bound to be some tell-tale stains. Know what I mean? That's why I wanted to get it cleaned up.'

'What do you know about the murdered school girl?' Davies asked.

'Only what I've read in the papers. Tragic story.'

'So you have nothing to do with her disappearance? You didn't load your van up with supplies last Friday morning, drive to the school and wait for a little girl to appear, so you could take her away and satisfy your perverse desires?'

'Did you not read my file, love?' questioned Heath, folding his arms. 'Girls don't do it for me.'

'What?' asked Vincent, looking across to Davies for not pointing out this salient fact.

'That's right, love,' replied Heath, starting to smile. 'It was young lads that did it for me. I've got as much interest in a young girl as you would, a dog. Besides, there are places men like me can go, when we wish to *satisfy our desires*, as you put it.'

Vincent shot a glare at Davies, which told him they would be having serious words later.

'Look,' continued Heath, unfolding his arms and leaning in. 'If you still don't believe me, fetch my phone and call Bobby. His will be the first name on the redial list. Call him and ask what time I arrived in Blackpool. There is no way I could have abducted that little girl, as I was hundreds of miles away.'

Vincent stood up angrily and left the room, slamming the door behind him. Heath stood up and smiled at Davies.

'What did you mean when you said there were places you could go to... ?'

'Satisfy my urges?' finished Heath. He pulled a paper card out of his wallet, and placed it on the table in front of them. 'This place, here,' he said pointing to the card. 'Everyone is over the legal age, but they get them to dress younger, for those of us who like something...fresher. You should come by some time. I'm sure we could find something for you.'

Davies stood quickly and left the room, he too, slamming the door behind him. Heath gathered up his few belongings and put the paper card back in his wallet. He laughed, as he did so, at how sensitive some modern policemen could be.

31

Sarah rolled her sleeve up and glanced at her watch. It was nearly five, but she had been sat waiting for her guest for ten minutes already. She had driven from her flat to the coffee bar and had given herself plenty of time to allow for possible rush-hour traffic. She hadn't expected to be so punctual but at least it gave her the opportunity to try and spot who might be the journalist. She had spent most of the afternoon replaying the conversation with Rêmet in her head. He had sounded so confident that he knew who had killed Natalie. He hadn't mentioned Erin's name, but Sarah was still hopeful that whoever had taken Natalie had also caused Erin's death, and that what Rêmet was due to reveal this afternoon would bring her closer to the truth.

The coffee bar was run by a friendly Italian family and, even though this was her first visit to the establishment, they had welcomed her with open arms and broad smiles. She had opted for a table in the corner, giving her a good view of the street and the entrance to the bar. She had tried to find an image of Rêmet on the internet, when she had been at home but, although she had found several references to him, from various articles, there had been no image attached to any of the internet pages. From his voice, she imagined him to look like *Clouseau* from the Peter Sellers' films, but, so far, nobody fitting that description had approached the café.

There was another couple, a man and a woman, sat in the opposite corner to her, but they looked young and in love, so she was pretty confident neither of those was Rêmet. Otherwise, the café was empty, save for the young owner, stood behind the counter, preparing her drink. She had ordered a fruit smoothie, as she was bored of the taste of coffee, having drunk nothing but all afternoon.

The whirring of the food processor came to a halt. She could then see the young Italian pouring the contents into a tall glass, before he moved across to her table and presented the beverage. She thanked him and he disappeared back off behind the counter. There was another thought troubling Sarah: what if Rêmet was in fact Natalie's abductor, relishing the chance to see the pain his destruction had caused? It was unlikely, but it was odd how he was adamant not to involve the police. It was also odd that he had approached her, and that's what worried Sarah the most: She had agreed to meet a total stranger who had managed to identify her as Natalie's teacher. Why approach her? How did he know that she was trying to discover who had taken Natalie? She tried to push the thoughts to the back of her mind, and took a slurp of drink through the brightly-coloured straw that it had come with.

A bell pinged above the door to the café, indicating the arrival of a new customer. It caused Sarah to glance up and she knew instinctively that the man at the door was Rêmet. He was a short, portly man with light grey hair, rectangular-shaped glasses, and wearing a yellow mac. He wasn't *Clouseau* but was maybe what *Clouseau* would have looked like if he grew old and put on a lot of weight. Rêmet's round belly could be distinctly seen beneath his jacket. He had a small, brown satchel bag over his shoulder and was holding a black, leather briefcase.

Rêmet looked around the café until he spotted Sarah, and then he waved. She waved back, before she could stop herself, and he made his way over to the table.

'Mademoiselle Jenson?' he enquired in his deep, Gallic tone.

'Yes…yes,' she stuttered, unsure whether she should stand and shake his hand, or kiss him on the cheek; what was the correct etiquette for this kind of situation? Before she could decide, he had swivelled his back to her and beckoned for the Italian to bring him over a large espresso. He then turned back to face Sarah, and took the seat opposite her.

'I apologise for being late, mademoiselle,' he began, shrugging his shoulders, and placing the satchel bag on the floor. 'The train was unavoidably delayed.'

Sarah was surprised at how well he spoke her language. She smiled kindly, and told him it was okay. The Italian brought the large coffee mug to the table and returned to his previous perch again. Rêmet took a long gulp of coffee and then opened the briefcase he had been carrying. He removed several plastic wallets, full of paper, and placed them on the table before Sarah. He then closed the briefcase and put it on the floor by his feet.

'Thank you for meeting with me,' he said. 'I am not sure where to begin.'

'Well,' replied Sarah. 'Perhaps you could start with who you are, where you are from, and how you came to contact me.'

Rêmet seemed surprised by the directness of her questions and took another gulp of coffee before saying, 'My name is Claude Rêmet and I am a journalist working freelance across Europe.'

'Freelance?'

'Oui,' he said. 'I go where there are big news stories; I investigate and sell my findings to the national newspapers of whatever country I am in.'

'I see,' she replied. 'And how did you come across me?'

'I spend a lot of time reading the internet, and I read that a little girl had been abducted from a school in England. I looked up the school and found you were the teacher of the missing girl.'

'I'm confused,' Sarah interrupted. 'What makes you think you know who took the little girl?'

Rêmet paused and picked up one of the plastic wallets of paper. He began to flick through pages, until he found what he was looking for. He placed the chosen page on the table in front of him. To Sarah, it looked like some scribbled notes that weren't legible.

'Let me tell you what I know and that might answer your questions,' he said. When Sarah didn't respond, he took it as his cue to continue. 'Five years ago, I was working in Baden on a story about drug trafficking, when I came across a news item about a girl who had gone missing during a school trip. Her class had been camping in tents, in a local nature reserve, but when they had woken up in the morning, the little girl could not be located. She was seven years old, pretty and very popular with her classmates. The teachers raised the alarm, and the nature reserve was scoured by police and dogs, but she still could not be found. A week or so later, her body had been discovered badly beaten and abused. The police were investigating the matter, when I came across the story. After some investigation, I thought I had identified the perpetrator, but the police were not interested in my conclusion. I persisted and when they eventually spoke with my suspect, his friends gave him a cast-iron alibi. I tried to sell my story to a newspaper, but they laughed me out of their office. But I knew; I knew it was *him*. I remained in the town for another three months, doing more investigative work, but it was no use, I could not find the piece of evidence that would confirm my suspicions.'

Rêmet paused to take another gulp of coffee and Sarah sipped from her smoothie, transfixed by what Rêmet had to say.

'I moved on with my life, but I could not forget what happened, so once in a while I would search for *him* and see what he was up to.'

'That's all very interesting, but what does that have to do with me?' Sarah questioned.

'Well,' said Rêmet. 'The man I suspected of taking and killing the girl is now living in Southampton. He moved here two years ago, so when I saw the story about your missing girl, and the way she disappeared, I just knew it had to be *him* again.'

'Who?' said Sarah.

Instead of answering, Rêmet opened one of the plastic wallets and pulled out an A4 black and white photograph and placed it in front of Sarah.

'Do you recognise any of the men in this photograph?' Rêmet asked.

Sarah studied the picture carefully, and a chill went down her spine when she realised exactly who he was referring to.

<u>32</u>

'Wait a second,' said Sarah, staring more intently at the photograph in her hands. 'This is…no…it can't be.'

The photograph was of about a dozen men, stood in two lines, half of them were on their knees, stood in front of the remaining men. They appeared to be in some kind of field, though it was hard to tell, due to the age of the picture.

'So you recognise him?' asked Rêmet rhetorically.

She continued to look at the man in the photo. It sent a further shiver through her. Sarah's eyes darted to the faces of the other men in the photograph, desperate for any kind of additional recognition that might indicate that Rêmet was referring to somebody other than the man she knew all too well. No other faces looked familiar, even in the slightest.

'But this is…'

'Yes, mademoiselle,' said Rêmet, 'It is Johan Boller; the football player.'

'Wait…you don't really think Johan Boller took Natalie?'

'No, I don't think it; I know it!' Rêmet responded authoritatively.

Sarah burst into a fit of giggles, convinced that this was some kind of practical joke. When Rêmet remained silent, staring at the strange reaction, her giggles stopped.

'You cannot be serious, Mr Rêmet?' she said. 'You

think Premiership footballer Johan Boller is some kind of paedophile? He plays international football for Switzerland. He is a fucking hero in this city, for Christ's sake!'

'Lower your voice, mademoiselle,' Rêmet said, placing his finger to his lips in the same way Sarah had done more than a hundred times with noisy children in her class.

Sarah leaned forward so that her whisper would still be audible to the journalist, 'You're crazy, Rêmet. No wonder the police didn't want to know. It's madness!'

'I'm sorry, you think so, mademoiselle, but I think you'll find you are the one who is mistaken.'

His reaction was so calm, so passive. He didn't look like he was crazy, a little dishevelled, maybe, but that was to be expected given his profession.

'I have evidence that will prove my theory to you,' he continued in hushed tones, concerned about who might overhear their conversation. 'It is not with me, now, but I can show it to you tomorrow.'

'Oh, well that's convenient,' Sarah said sarcastically.

'Please, mademoiselle, keep your voice down. I don't want people to know what we are talking about. It is a sensitive topic.'

'You mean you don't want people to hear what a nutcase you are?'

'I assure you, I am quite sane, mademoiselle, and I will prove to you I am right.'

Sarah looked back at the photograph again, disbelieving. At the bottom of the image was some kind of placard that read, 'Baden sous les 21: Champions de foot.'

'The photograph was taken one week before the little girl went missing in Switzerland,' said Rêmet, aware that Sarah was starting to consider what he was saying. 'The local football team in Baden had just won the under-21 football league. Boller had been a key figure in the side, helping them to their first ever championship.'

'Okay, Rêmet,' Sarah whispered. 'I'll humour you, what makes you believe Johan is responsible?'

Rêmet fished through one of the other plastic wallets, still scattered on the table before them, and retrieved a printed copy of a map. The label at the top revealed it was of Baden and its surrounding towns. There were several markings on the map as well as Rêmet's scribbled notes. He placed the map down so that Sarah could see what he was going to point to.

'This area, here,' said Rêmet, pointing at the left edge of the image, 'is where the children were camping. It is a well-known nature reserve, and the school held the same trip to the area every year. The nature reserve spans about eight kilometres in diameter, and there is only one road into it from the Baden town centre.'

Sarah glanced up at the journalist and saw him lick his lips, showing the passion he had for this topic of conversation; it made her wonder how many other people had been bombarded with this speculative nonsense.

'The trip was on May twenty six, two thousand and seven,' Rêmet continued, catching Sarah watching him. When Sarah saw that he had seen her, her eyes darted back down to the image and her cheeks flushed slightly. 'The school arrived at the site, just before midday on the Saturday, and spent the first hour constructing all the tents, where the children and teachers would sleep. The tents could each house two students. Nichole, the girl who went missing, was in a tent with another girl called Arielle. They were best friends and did everything together. The girl's teacher, later told me, that they were inseparable, like sisters.'

Rêmet paused, long enough to signal the Italian behind the bar, to order another large espresso.

'A little after five in the evening, the teachers built a small fire to cook some fish and pasta. All the children ate the small meal together, at six o'clock, and then they all sang songs and toasted marshmallows on the fire until the children were told to enter their tents at seven o'clock. Two of the teachers took it in turns to patrol the site, until nine o'clock, when they were satisfied that the children were asleep. There was a small concrete building next to where the tents had been placed that the children were to use as a toilet and washroom. The children were aware that they could use the facilities, in the event that they needed to, during the night.'

The Italian brought Rêmet's cup of espresso over, along with a small paper receipt. He placed both items on the table before Rêmet looked up, angry at the disruption.

'Where was I?' he asked rhetorically, before continuing. 'There were no lights at the site, so each child had been given a torch they could use, to help them find their way in the darkness. It had been a warm day, and according to meteorologists, there was very little cloud that night, so it would have been relatively light outside of the tents, but the torches were there for extra precaution. Arielle said she and Nichole fell asleep just before nine o'clock, and that she could vaguely remember hearing the zip on the tent being opened during the night and she thinks Nichole said she was going to the toilet. Arielle admitted that she was half-asleep, and did not make a note of the time. The teachers came to wake the children up just before eight o'clock in the morning, and that is when it was discovered that Nichole was missing. The teachers searched all over the site, but there was no trace of her. The Baden police were called, as were Nichole's parents, but she could not be located. As I said earlier, her badly beaten body was discovered five days later, a mile from the camp site in a shallow grave. The coroner confirmed that Nichole had been sexually assaulted.'

'I still don't see the connection to Johan,' Sarah said, glancing from the photograph to the map and back again. Rêmet took the photograph of the Baden youth team from her to study it himself.

'The football team clinched their title one week before the school's camping trip, but they did not hold a party to celebrate, until the weekend of May twenty six.'

Rêmet placed the photograph back on the table and then pointed a stubby finger back on the map that Sarah was still holding.

'This is where the club held their celebration.'

Sarah saw that the dot he was pointing to was only half a centimetre away from the nature reserve.

'L'hotel Bien Voyagé is half a kilometre from the nature reserve. The team hired out the hotel for the night so that the players could drink and run riot.'

'Okay, so he was in the area, that doesn't mean he did it. What was his motive?' Sarah challenged.

Rêmet ignored the comment and continued, 'I

spoke with several members of the team myself, after I began to investigate. One of the players, a goalkeeper, I believe, told me that things got a little out of control at the party and a couple of the players had come to blows over something silly. One of the players was Boller and according to my source, he left the hotel between midnight and one a.m. to cool off. The goalkeeper said that he and two others went after Boller, to try and calm him down. My source said they didn't really know where they were, but Boller was looking for somewhere he could either get a drink, or pick up a girl. They weren't to know that there were no bars in the area. My source told me that they stumbled into a field, and found what looked like a small outdoor concrete cellar. Boller went in, looking for wine, but it turned out the small building was some kind of toilet and washroom facility. It was at this point that the group realised they were at a campsite, and that there were several tents nearby.'

Rêmet took a large sip of coffee, psyching himself to continue with the part of the story that always made his stomach turn.

'The goalkeeper told me that Boller and one other ran into a little girl who was coming out of the toilet. My source was stood a little way back with the remaining player so they couldn't really see what was going on. He told me that he thought the girl had blonde hair, but it was difficult to see in the dim light.' Rêmet paused again and blinked several times, as he looked for the words to describe what happened next. 'My source said he saw Boller grab the girl and place his hand over her mouth and then Boller and the other player took the little girl back into the concrete building. My source said he and the other player moved in closer, to find out what was going on. They were concerned about the girl's safety. They were not prepared for what they saw when they looked through the window of the building. The little girl was being held to the floor by the second player, his hand cruelly over her mouth, while Boller…was rocking back and forth on top of her.'

33

Rêmet removed a soiled handkerchief from his pocket and grubbily wiped beads of sweat from his forehead.

'My source told me he wanted to burst into the room and stop what was happening, but he was scared stiff, frozen to the spot. Boller had always been a bit of a bully in the dressing room, and my source did not want to cross him. You must bear in mind that Boller was twenty, but my source was only seventeen, and his physical presence was tiny compared to Boller's.'

Sarah felt sick to her stomach, as she listened to the story Rêmet was weaving. As he spoke, she could picture in her mind the scene as if she was watching a film, but rather than seeing a little French girl, being held captive, all she could see in her mind, was Natalie's face, crying out for Sarah to help.

'Oh, God!' she exclaimed under her breath,

'My source had a mobile phone with a camera on it, but you must remember that this was five years ago; technology has come a long way since then; it was no smart phone. However, he used the phone to take a picture of what was happening in the facility. The room was dark and the camera did not have a flash but there is enough light to make out the back of Boller on top of the captive girl,' Rêmet added.

'You have a photograph of what happened?' said Sarah

'Yes I do, but it is not with me now. It was too big a risk to bring all of my evidence with me today. If you will agree to meet with me tomorrow morning, I will produce the photograph then.'

'Did your source give you the photograph?' said Sarah, ignoring his question.

'No, I received it anonymously in the post, a week after I spoke to the goalkeeper.'

'Why didn't you take it to the police? Surely that would back up the theory you had presented to them?'

'I did,' replied Rêmet, defensively. 'I gave them the photograph to look at, but they claimed it was too grainy, to make a positive identification of the man with his back to the photographer. Alas, the image shows the back of his head, but not his face.'

'But what about the little girl?' she asked, desperately.

Rêmet shook his head, 'It is clear there is a girl in the photo with blonde hair, but because there is a hand over her mouth and the room was dim, it could not be confirmed that it was indeed Nichole. There are no other distinguishing details in the image to even confirm where it was taken,' Rêmet added glumly.

'If all of that is true, Rêmet, how can *you* be sure it is Johan in the photograph?'

'My source told me he had taken a photograph, and the image I received in the post, matched what he had told me.'

'Well surely, with your source's statement and the photograph, the police would have to listen?' asked Sarah exasperated that the Swiss police had seemingly turned a blind eye, and indirectly allowed the incident to be repeated with Natalie.

'You have to understand, mademoiselle, Baden is a small town in Switzerland. The youth team winning their championship was unprecedented and turned those players into local heroes, particularly Boller. I took my accusation all the way to the head of the force, but he told me the evidence was circumstantial at best, and was insufficient to investigate further. He warned me that, if I persisted with my accusations, he would make life difficult for me.'

'What did he mean by that?'

'I think he was planning to arrest me for harassment,' Rêmet said, rolling his eyes.

'I don't understand why they wouldn't investigate. Surely the statement would corroborate what was in the photograph.'

'I am sure it would have…if…my source had not retracted his statement.'

'He did what?'

'A week after he had spoken with me, I approached him to ask some more questions. He looked scared but told me that he had lied to me and had made up the accusation against Boller out of jealousy.'

'What?' Sarah practically shouted.

'I know,' Rêmet acknowledged. 'Boller must have threatened him, after he had told me what he knew. I cannot think of any other reason for him to change his mind. Remember, I told you, Boller's frame was considerably larger than my source's. Boller was a bully, everybody knew it, but he was now a hero; nobody would speak out against him.'

'So what happened?' she asked.

'I took the photograph to the police, with what he

had told me, but when they asked me to reveal my source; I had to tell them that he had retracted his statement. That's why the newspaper I went to wouldn't print the story either.' Rêmet drained the rest of his coffee, before adding, 'I know it was *him*!'

Sarah didn't know what to think. Rêmet's story had been compelling, and she had found herself wanting to believe what he was telling her. He clearly believed what he was saying. She thought about the Johan Boller she had met last Friday, and then again earlier this week: he had seemed so gentle and sweet. He didn't sound like the man that Rêmet had described.

'Are you sure we are referring to the same Johan Boller?' she asked. 'Is there no chance there is another Swiss footballer, with the same name?'

'I am certain, mademoiselle,' he replied removing a picture of Boller on the day he signed for Southampton Football Club. Sarah compared the new image to the first photograph Rêmet had presented, and although he looked a little older, it was the same man.

'I am just struggling to believe that he would be capable of something…so…sick. I've met him several times, and he is not as you described.'

'The devil can be a convincing salesman,' Rêmet replied matter-of-factly.

'But he just doesn't strike me as a…'

'Paedophile? Why is that? Do you assume they have to be old men?'

Sarah had to admit it was a fair point and when, she thought back to how young Ryan Moss had been when he had taken Chloe, she couldn't argue against what Rêmet was saying.

'I read yesterday that Boller was supposedly the last

person to see your little girl at the school? That is convenient,' he continued.

'That doesn't necessarily mean he took her,' Sarah countered.

'According to the internet, the local police are looking for a red car, n'est pas?'

'That's right…' she replied, trailing off.

Rêmet fished for a further A4 image in his plastic wallet and presented a newspaper article that he had clearly printed from the internet. It showed Boller stood shaking the hand of a very happy-looking car salesman. They were stood in front of a Red Ferrari.

'Boller drives a very fancy red car,' said Rêmet, so that Sarah understood what he was saying.

'Yes…but…'

Rêmet removed another piece of paper from the plastic wallet. It was another map, but this one was of the county of Hampshire and the New Forest. Rêmet had drawn two circles on the map in bright pen.

'This is where the body was discovered,' said Rêmet pointing at one of the circles. Sarah saw it was Dibden golf course 'This is where Boller lives,' he added, pointing at the second circle, which indicated Hythe Marina. There was only a small distance between the marks.

'Surely he wouldn't be stupid enough to dump the body so close to his own house? That could make him a possible suspect.'

'Really? Think about it, mademoiselle, did you think he could have been a suspect, before you spoke to me? Why would the police? He is a local celebrity here, isn't he? Like when he was in Baden; people just don't expect that he could also be a monster.'

Sarah stared back at him in stunned silence.

'Let me put it this way,' said Rêmet continuing, 'Have the police started to investigate him yet? They know he was at the school. They have probably seen him driving in his red car. A little digging would reveal where he lives but I don't imagine he is the only Southampton football player living in that area. They have clues pointing at his involvement, but they subconsciously choose to ignore them because of his status.'

'I'm still not convinced by all this, Rêmet,' Sarah said, frowning.

The Frenchman looked perturbed by her admission. 'What is preventing you from seeing the truth, Sarah?' he said, using her name for the first time that day. It did the trick and got her attention.

Sarah weighed up whether she should share her own theory about the link between Natalie's disappearance, and Erin's suspicious death. It was almost ironic that Vincent had laughed at her crazy thought processes, and here she was, doing the same to Rêmet.

'Okay,' she said after a moment. 'My girlfriend was one of the police officers investigating Natalie's disappearance.' Sarah paused for breath as she willed herself to utter the next words, 'She was involved in a serious car accident on Tuesday night and passed away. The police claim she was drunk behind the wheel and that caused the accident, but I don't believe it. She was a recovering alcoholic and had been clean for nearly two years, I know she wouldn't have given in to temptation.'

'I am sorry for your loss,' said Rêmet, quietly. 'What do *you* think happened to her?'

'The police told me that she had said she needed to

investigate something on her way home to see me, but she never arrived.'

'Did they say what she was going to investigate?'

'No,' replied Sarah glumly. 'Apparently she didn't say. She had been speaking to Natalie's uncle in the afternoon so I can only assume that she went back to speak with him. I believe that she must have been close to finding out what had happened and the person responsible for taking Natalie, killed Erin too.'

'Why do the police think she was drunk?'

'They did a blood test when she was found and it said she was over the limit,' replied Sarah.

'How would the killer have gotten the alcohol into her bloodstream, if you believe she wouldn't have voluntarily accepted it?'

'I don't know,' said Sarah, letting out a sigh and cupping her face in her hands. 'Maybe...maybe...whoever it was drugged her and forced it in? I don't know.'

'Is it possible that she could have figured something out about Boller?'

'I don't think so,' replied Sarah, 'and that's why I'm struggling to accept that Johan did this thing to Natalie.'

Rêmet glanced at the watch under his sleeve and said, 'It's nearly six o'clock and I need to eat. Let us go our separate ways for now, Sarah, and we will meet again in the morning, so I can show you the photograph of Boller and Nichole. Maybe a night's rest will help us both think clearer tomorrow.'

Rêmet stood up and started to place the plastic wallets and papers back in his briefcase. 'I am sure he is the man, Sarah. And...maybe...he was also responsible for the death of your girlfriend. We'll meet here in the morning and put a plan together of what we can say to the police. Do you have the name of someone at the police we can speak to?'

'Yes,' she replied. 'What time shall we meet?'

'I'll phone you in the morning, when I am ready, and then we will meet. Okay?'

Sarah nodded, 'Do you have a place to stay tonight?'

Rêmet said he hadn't, and so Sarah gave him directions to the West Quay Retail Park, which had a couple of hotels nearby. Rêmet thanked her, spun on his heel, placed the satchel bag over his shoulder and headed out of the door. She had no idea whether he would find a room, but she imagined in his line of work, he had become resourceful and would be okay. Sarah drank the remains of her smoothie and left payment on the table to cover Rêmet's drinks, before strolling towards the car park and, ultimately, home.

<u>SATURDAY</u>

34

Something stirred Claude Rêmet from his sleep. He rubbed his eyes and blinked several times to try and help his eyes adjust to the darkness of the room, but it was still no good; he couldn't see a thing. He reached out and found the glass of water he had left on the bedside table, and took a sip from it. He grimaced at the taste of the hard, British water. He put the glass back down and tried to remember the events of the night before.

Following his brief, yet worthwhile, meeting with Sarah Jenson, Claude Rêmet had followed her directions and had headed over the railway bridge, above the train tracks, through the *Toys 'R' Us* car park and then turned right, in the direction of *McDonald's* and a couple of inexpensive tower blocks that advertised themselves as hotels. The first had claimed to be full for the night, as there was a wedding booked the following day, and several guests had checked in a day early, to avoid getting stuck in traffic on the big day. Rêmet had casually glanced around the hotel's lobby, and silently pitied the couple who had decided that this would be the venue for their dream wedding. He didn't pity their lack of money or religious consideration; he pitied their lack of taste.

He had swiftly turned on his heel and headed to the next tower. This one advertised cheap rooms Monday to Thursday and as he rightly presumed, the room rate was double over a weekend. That didn't matter, however. As far as Rêmet was concerned, when he finally proved that Boller was guilty of the abduction and murder of two children, newspapers globally would be queuing up for his story. He might even sell the movie rights!

Thankfully, the young lady behind reception said there was one room still available for the night, although it was going to cost £100 and wouldn't include breakfast. This suited Rêmet fine, as he despised the British idea of breakfast: lots of meat fried up in a pan, dripping in fat. It made his stomach turn just thinking about it. The pretty receptionist told him the room could either be accessed from the lobby, though it was quite a walk, or it could be accessed from street level, which was probably the most direct route he could take. She jotted down a small map and he headed for his room.

During his varied stays in different countries, over the years, following the big stories, he had had the pleasure of staying in some luxurious hotel rooms. He had also had the displeasure of staying in some of the grubbiest hotels that Eastern Europe had to offer. As he surveyed the room that would be his resting place for the night, he thought it certainly wasn't the worst place he had ever stayed in: it had a double bed, small television set and an en suite housing a small shower cubicle, basin and a toilet. But he had expected more for the £100 it had cost him. Still, beggars couldn't be choosers and it would serve its purpose.

Rêmet had dropped his small satchel bag, containing a change of underwear and some toiletries, on the bed, along with the briefcase that contained the various maps and photographs he had shared with

Sarah earlier. He had then quickly and efficiently stripped off and jumped in the shower. Once he was dry, and felt more awake, he put his clothes back on with the change of underwear and looked at himself in the mirror. He hadn't shaved in a couple of days and he had a healthy amount of hair forming on his chin and cheeks. He would have described himself as rugged, while any other casual observer probably would have used the word, "scruffy".

The hotel didn't offer much by the way of dining facilities, but a quick conversation with the pretty receptionist had told him that there were a couple of bars and restaurants two minutes up the road at the industrial estate-cum-entertainment park known as *Leisure World*. Rêmet had thanked her for her help and had walked the short distance, until he found where she meant. The park housed a casino, a couple of night clubs, a cinema, a gentlemen's club and a couple of restaurant-bars, one an American-Italian place and the other a pizza restaurant; so much for variety! Rêmet headed for the American-Italian restaurant, and was grateful to get a table by the window. He ordered himself a large glass of Rioja as a starter and a dish referred to as 'Italian Chicken' as his main. When the meal arrived, he was disappointed to find it was a bread-crumb covered chicken breast dripping in an overly-sweet, red, tomato sauce. He ate as much as he could, but it really wasn't to his taste. He ordered a second glass of Rioja to clean his palette.

When he was halfway through drinking the second glass of wine, he spotted something out of the window that made him do a double-take. Johan Boller was strolling down the road, with a couple of other tall men, broad smiles on their faces. For a moment, he thought he had fallen asleep and was dreaming, such was his surprise at seeing the face that had haunted his dreams for the last five years, but sure enough it was Boller, looking as arrogant as ever. Rêmet continued to watch him from the restaurant window and saw him turn in somewhere further along the strip. Rêmet downed the contents of his glass, and signalled for a passing waiter to bring over his bill. Rather than waiting for the waiter to return, he dropped thirty pounds on the table and hurried out the door. He was sure it would be enough to cover his bill, and would probably leave the waiter with a healthy tip.

As Rêmet hit the cool night air, it didn't take him long to work out where Boller must have headed, as the gentlemen's club was the last building on the strip and was the right distance from the restaurant. Rêmet took a couple of deep breaths, while he tried to work out what to do next. Part of him wanted to approach the young striker and demand the truth, but he knew that was madness. He still needed to convince Sarah first, and then they would approach the police and catch the killer the right way. The sensible thing that he should have done was to turn around and head back to his hotel room. Instead, he decided to go and observe the Swiss and headed for the club.

There was no queue to get in the bar and although the bouncer gave him a suspicious look, he was allowed to pay his entrance fee and head in. The club was almost pitch black, the only light coming from the occasional small red neon lights hanging from the walls. It took a moment for Rêmet's eyes to adjust to the light, but once they had he headed to the bar and ordered a shot of vodka. He found a small table to the edge of the bar and took a seat. It was too dark to really see any of the other patrons in the club, and Rêmet assumed this was how the management wanted it to be. He figured that the only way he would be able to find out where Boller was, would be to go from table to table; staring at each man in the place, and this would certainly blow his cover. Rêmet decided to remain at his table, by the bar, and wait until he saw Boller approach and order a drink, then Rêmet would be able to follow him back to wherever he was sat, unnoticed, and take a new seat of his own nearby, so he could continue to observe Boller, without him becoming aware. In truth, the best light in the club was around the bar, probably so that the woman behind it could see what change she was giving the punters.

Directly opposite, but a good thirty feet away, was the main stage. It was empty at the moment, but it was only nine o'clock, and Rêmet imagined that the show probably wouldn't start much before ten. There were a couple of scantily-clad waitresses moving from table to table offering drinks and private dances, and whilst Rêmet was tempted, when he was approached, he declined the offer and remained in his covert position.

Nearly an hour had passed, before he finally saw Boller approach the bar. Rêmet felt his pulse quicken, as he laid eyes on the man he hated more than any other in the world. By this point he was on his fifth shot of vodka and most of his inhibitions had disappeared for the night. Rather than quietly observing the Swiss flirting with the barmaid, he decided to confront him. Rêmet stood and moved to the bar so that he was only five feet from where

Boller was stood. At first, Rêmet didn't say anything; he just glared at the tall striker, until eventually Boller turned and saw Rêmet. Boller didn't seem to recognise him at first, but within ten seconds, he was glancing back at Rêmet as the penny dropped and he made the connection. The look of terror in Boller's eyes, gave Rêmet a satisfying feeling of triumph. Rêmet raised his glass in a mock toast to the footballer.

'Bonjour,' mouthed Rêmet.

The music in the club was loud enough to drown out most conversations and when Boller started speaking, Rêmet couldn't make out what the footballer was saying and remained stood in his spot, smiling back at him, oblivious to the obscenities being screeched at him. Boller seemed to realise that his message was falling on deaf ears and moved in closer to Rêmet.

'What the hell are you doing here, Rêmet?' Boller shouted in the journalist's ear.

'I am here to finally prove what you did to young Nichole in Baden,' he shouted back. 'I have all the proof I need, you understand?'

Boller tried to exude confidence, but it was undermined by the look of fear in his eyes.

'You couldn't prove it five years ago, Rêmet, and you have nothing on me now!'

'I know you abducted and killed Natalie Barrett as well, Boller! Your time of freedom is nearly up,' beamed Rêmet, pleased that his confrontation was clearly unnerving his nemesis.

Unable to think of what to say, Boller pushed out at Rêmet, who responded with a shove back of his own. This was followed by a couple of further shoves from each man, until the barmaid signalled for the bouncers to come and break up the scuffle. When the bouncers saw that it was local celebrity Johan Boller, they decided to ask him what was going on. Rêmet couldn't hear what he whispered to the bouncers but he guessed it was something like, Rêmet was an obsessed fan who was causing trouble and could they turf him out. In fairness, it's what he would have said in Boller's position. During the scuffle Rêmet's wallet had fallen out of his pocket and once he had been thrown out, to add to the embarrassment of the situation, he had had to ask the bouncer to go back in and fetch it for him. Satisfied with his evening's work, he had casually strolled back to his hotel room but found that his room key was not in his pocket. Thankfully, the receptionist recognised him and gave him a spare. He had watched some late night chat show on the television in his room, and had then fallen asleep.

Something moved near the foot of the bed that caught Rêmet's attention and brought his mind back to the room. There was somebody sat in a chair.

<u>35</u>

Rêmet sat up, so that his back was against the headboard, with his pillows serving as filling to this unorthodox sandwich. He pulled his knees up to his chest, instinct taking over. Only one, chilling, thought raced through his mind; *why was someone in his room?*

In the same way, as some have described in the past, where a person's life flashes before their eyes in their final living moment, so a thousand thoughts were whizzing through Claude Rêmet's mind as he tried to make out the figure at the foot of the bed; *Did he even realise that Rêmet could see him?*

As if to answer the Frenchman's question, the figure rose and moved closer to the bed. Rêmet imagined the figure pulling out a blade, and ending his life there and then. Instead, the figure reached out an arm and turned on the bedside light. The face and torso of Johan Boller stood before him. It made Rêmet shudder; *how had Boller got in his room?*

'Boller,' he uttered hoarsely under his breath.

'Bonsoir, Monsieur Rêmet,' Boller hummed back, before returning to the seat at the foot of the bed. Rêmet could see it was the lone, stationary chair provided by the hotel for those more discerning guests who refused to watch television from their bed.

'Wh-wh-what are you doing here?' he stammered, unable to hide the fear from his voice.

'I decided we should talk. You've been shouting your mouth off about me for too long and I've come to ask you to stop. I am happy here in Southampton; settled. Go home, Rêmet, you are not wanted around here.'

'How did you get in?'

'I was the one who handed your wallet to the bouncers. I guess your key must have fallen out.'

Was it fear? Was that why Boller had come here tonight? Had Rêmet said something earlier that had caught him off guard? Yes, that was it.

'You don't scare me, Boller,' Rêmet challenged, growing in confidence.

'Don't I?' Boller challenged back, leaning forward in the chair. Rêmet responded by shrinking back closer to the pillows, causing Boller to let out a laugh.

'I know what you did. Doesn't that bother you? I know what you did to little Nichole in Baden. I have seen the photograph of you...raping her.'

'Shut your fucking mouth!' bellowed Boller, his eyes tightening.

'Why should I?' replied Rêmet, eager to see how far he could push the young Swiss. 'What you did to that little girl was monstrous! She was innocent, and you...you destroyed that innocence!'

Boller launched across the bed and grabbed Rêmet by the neck. 'You shut your fucking mouth! You know nothing!'

Rêmet was worried. His attacker's grip was strong, and Rêmet wasn't certain that he wouldn't keep squeezing and end it all. Rêmet tried to loosen one of his arms, which were both being pinned down by Boller's sheer weight. He continued to wriggle beneath him until he managed to wrench his right arm free. It took all his might but he managed to swing the limb around and catch Boller in the ear. It was a pathetic attempt to overpower his assailant but it was enough as Boller leapt from the bed, clutching his ear, howling. Rêmet took the opportunity to scramble from the bed and make a move for the bedroom door. Exiting in just his underwear would hardly be dignified, but it didn't matter; survival was more important.

Boller could see Rêmet heading for the door and chased after him. The benefit of being an athlete was his speed, and he reached the fleeing journalist just as he reached the door. Rêmet swung his flabby arms around as Boller wrapped his strong arms around Rêmet's midriff and dragged him back to the bed.

'You sit down!' demanded Boller as he flung Rêmet onto the mattress. 'I came here to talk with you, not to fight.'

Boller moved the chair he had been sat in earlier, so that it was between Rêmet on the corner of the bed, and the door behind them.

Rêmet sat up and allowed Boller to sit in the chair, meaning they were fewer than two feet apart. Even though the bed was several centimetres above the seat, Boller's frame dominated Rêmet's vision. The two men sat in silence for five minutes trying to suss each other out. Eventually, Rêmet spoke, 'What do you want, Boller? Why are you here?'

'I want you to leave Southampton. You tried to drag my name through the mud the last time we met. I have a good life here and I don't want you to take that away.'

'You have a good life? What about Nichole? What about her life?'

'What happened in Baden is…is…in the past. What I did…'

'What you did was to brutally rape her, then kill her and dump the body, like a piece of rubbish. You deserve to spend the rest of your life in prison, and I will see that it happens. You might have frightened the goalkeeper all those years ago, but I will not be so easily intimidated.'

'You have no proof. It will be your word against mine, and you will lose. Why even bother? You should just forget about what you know and move on with your life.'

'You think it's that easy? I have seen the photograph of you fucking her. I see it every night when I close my eyes. I swore I would avenge her death. I will see justice served.'

'Don't be stupid! You couldn't prove anything five years ago, you will fail again now.'

'We'll see,' replied Rêmet, letting out a sigh. He knew deep down that it would be tough to prove Boller was responsible for Nichole's death. He was more confident about proving that Boller had something to do with Natalie Barrett's death.

'If you go now and forget about what you have seen, I can make it worth your while. I've seen your clothes; I know you don't earn much. I can give you some money, to make things more comfortable.'

Rêmet burst out laughing; it was so typical of today's world, thinking money could solve everything.

'I don't want your money, Boller. I want to see you put away for life.'

'That won't happen, old man. You have no proof.'

'If that's what you want to believe, then so be it,' replied Rêmet. 'Why don't you just tell the truth? Confession is good for the soul.'

Boller stood and walked towards the bedroom

door, as if he was going to leave. When he reached the door, he turned back to face Rêmet. He smiled when he saw that Rêmet was sweating.

'Okay,' said Boller, still smiling. 'You want to hear my confession? Here it is. My friends and I left the hotel after an argument and started walking along what we thought was the main road. We eventually came across what looked like a barn or a shed and I went in, looking for something to drink. It soon became clear that we had stumbled upon a campsite and as we turned to leave, a pretty, little girl walked in. She looked half asleep, but she recognised me. She said her father was a big fan of mine and he reckoned that I would make a great Swiss international one day.'

Rêmet moved uncomfortably on the bed. He desperately didn't want to hear Boller's version of events, but at the same time he wanted the vindication that his theory had been right all these years. A pain in his side, made him adjust his positioning again.

'There was an innocence about her,' continued Boller, moving back into the room. 'She wasn't like the girls I was used to seeing, so willing to sleep with me, just because I was becoming famous. This girl didn't seem interested at all...and...it made me want her more. I asked her if she would stay to talk with me, but she said she would have to get back to her tent. I signalled for my friend to grab her hands and hold her down. It was like I wasn't me, something took over my body. The more she struggled, the more turned on I became, and the more I had to have her.'

Rêmet felt sick to the stomach, and he had broken out in a cold sweat that he couldn't explain.

'It was the most exhilarating night of my life,' Boller continued. 'But when I was finished, she was bleeding badly and weeping. I knew that what I had done was wrong and I couldn't allow her to tell anyone else what had happened. I sent my friend to find some sheets that we could wrap her in. While he was out looking for them, I picked up a nearby stone and brought it down on the back of her head. It took half a dozen swings, until she stopped making any noise and I knew that she would not cause me anymore bother. I told my friend that we needed to bury the body and he helped me dig a hole. He was scared of me, so I knew he wouldn't say anything. At that point I didn't realise the other two guys with us knew what had happened. One of them approached me, a couple of days later, to say he was going to tell the police what had happened. I told him that if he did, I would tell the world the truth about his sexuality and his football career would be over. He knew I knew he was gay, and that if his secret was revealed, he would be shunned by the football community. He put in a transfer request shortly after, and I haven't spoken to him since.'

Rêmet had to fight the gag reflex pulling at the back of his throat.

'I have slept with dozens of women since that night, but none of them gave me the thrill that Nichole had. Not until...Friday night.'

Rêmet could feel his chest tightening and he knew what Boller was about to say. He wanted to stop him, as he had heard enough, but the words refused to leave his mouth.

'I saw the same look that Nichole had given me, in the eyes of Natalie Barrett. She seemed impressed by me, but not in the same way as the usual girls I sleep with. I offered to give her a lift home, but instead I took her to my house. She was very impressed with how big it was, and how I had a television in every room, including the bathroom. She kept telling me she should phone her parents and tell them where she was. I told her I would do it and I would say that I would drop her home later that night. She seemed so happy and so glad that I was taking an interest in her.'

Rêmet felt a second stabbing pain in his lower back and thought if he didn't throw up soon, he might actually pass out.

Boller glanced at the watch on his wrist and then continued, 'I slipped something into her drink that would help rid her of her inhibitions and would stop her remembering anything in the morning. And then…I made love to her.'

Rêmet doubled over and fell to the floor. A numb feeling was rapidly rising from the pit of his stomach and up his body.

'Like Nichole, she bled heavily and when I was finished, she wouldn't wake up. I left her overnight and in the morning, I realised she was dead. I panicked and knew that I would have to dump the body.'

Boller moved closer to Rêmet and crouched down so that he was only feet away from the journalist's face.

'So you see, Rêmet, you were right all along. I am a monster, and now you know the truth, you know my story. Tell me, what are you going to do about it?'

Rêmet wanted to say he was going to write it down, word for word, as he had committed most of the passages to memory. He wanted to say that he was going to tell Sarah Jenson everything, and that when the sun came up, he was going to go to the police and tell them everything too. He wanted to finish by saying that he would then sell the sensational story to every media outlet across the globe. All Rêmet managed to do was gurgle as he lay on the floor, frozen still.

'Oh, that's right,' whispered Boller, 'you won't be able to do anything about it, because you're nearly dead. That poison I put in your glass of water when I first entered your room seems to be working perfectly. The label on the bottle said I only needed a small drop, but I poured half the contents in to make sure they did the trick.'

Rêmet remembered the sour taste of the water when he had woken earlier and the feeling of nausea, as Boller said, had probably been caused by the toxin and not the description of what he had been told. The last thing Claude Rêmet thought about before his brain shut down was a feeling of anger that the truth about Johan Boller would die with him and that he had failed to deliver justice for Nichole and Natalie.

<u>36</u>

Sarah had been pacing the living room floor for an hour, waiting to hear back from Rêmet. She had been chewing at her nails, as well, an old habit from when she was a child. She hadn't slept particularly well during the night. She had been trying to picture Johan Boller taking Natalie from outside of the school, but the image just didn't seem to stick. She barely knew Johan but, on the occasions when they had met, he had seemed nice, certainly not the sort of person she would imagine capable of raping and murdering a small child. Eventually she had given up on trying to sleep and had headed for the kitchen to make a strong coffee. She had drunk a further four cups since that initial one and the amount of caffeine in her blood was not helping the nervousness she was feeling.

Rêmet had claimed he had photographic proof of Johan with the girl from Switzerland and she wondered whether that would be the final piece of the puzzle that would allow her to picture him as the perpetrator. What she had found even more difficult to believe was that he could have had anything to do with Erin's death. There seemed to be nothing to connect the two of them.

Unless…

The telephone's ring cut her growing thought in two and she had already forgotten what was building by the time she had lifted the receiver.

'Hello?' she breathed into the phone, expecting to hear Claude Rêmet's unmistakeable drawl on the other end.

'Sarah? It's Detective Inspector Jack Vincent. How are you?' came the reply.

'Oh,' said Sarah, surprised and disappointed that it wasn't Rêmet. 'I am okay, I suppose.'

'Good, good,' said Vincent before pausing. 'There's something I feel I should share with you, even though you may not be pleased to hear it.'

'I see,' said Sarah cautiously.

'We've interviewed Natalie's uncle, Jimmy Barrett, and we are ruling him out of our enquiries, as a possible suspect in her disappearance. After extensive questioning and verifying his story through several witnesses, we have released him without charge.'

'Okay,' replied Sarah, matter-of-factly.

'Is that it? Okay? I thought you would be angry, Sarah,' replied Vincent, unable to disguise the anger in his own voice. 'After all it was you who seemed so convinced that he was guilty.'

Sarah's mind was elsewhere, she was wondering why Rêmet had still not called her. Maybe he had been lying about the photograph and had been mistaken about Johan's involvement. However, if Rêmet were right, then it would only have been a matter of time before the police did release Jimmy Barrett. On the other hand, if Rêmet were wrong about Johan, and Jimmy was also innocent, she would be back to square one.

'I am sure you've done your job fine, Detective Inspector,' replied Sarah, trying to sound re-assuring but coming across as condescending.

'Well, we do have a further potential lead,'

Vincent continued, ignoring Sarah's remark. 'Jimmy took a phone call from a foreign-sounding man, claiming to be a journalist and asking all sorts of strange questions about Natalie's disappearance. We've managed to trace the call to Brussels, and have been liaising with our colleagues there, to try and identify who placed the call...'

'Claude Rêmet?' Sarah interrupted.

'Umm...yes...how did...how did you know that?' stammered Vincent, thrown by Sarah's foresight.

'I met the man yesterday,' Sarah continued. 'He thinks he knows who may have taken Natalie. He claims he has proof.'

While Sarah spoke, Vincent was eagerly hunting for a pen and paper to write on.

'You met him yesterday? Where? In Belgium?'

'No, don't be ridiculous,' admonished Sarah, the school teacher in her, coming to the fore. 'I met him in Southampton. He is here, now.'

'He's with you now? In your flat?' Vincent's excited voice shouted back.

'No. Not with me here, I meant, here in Southampton. He's staying in a hotel in the city somewhere.'

'Really? That's fantastic news. I don't suppose you happen to know which hotel?'

'I'm afraid not,' replied Sarah grimly. 'He was headed towards the retail park, when I last saw him. You could phone and check in those hotels first.'

'We will, we will,' replied Vincent eagerly. 'Did he tell you whom he suspects?'

'No,' lied Sarah. 'He was supposed to be meeting me today to reveal all, but I've yet to hear from him.'

Vincent thanked Sarah for her time and promised

he would be in touch when he knew more. Sarah replaced the handset on the receiver and returned to the living room. She took a large gulp of coffee from her mug and tried to remember what she had been thinking about, before the interruption.

Sarah had been replaying the week's events over and over in her mind, since meeting with Rêmet; every conversation with Erin that she could remember. Johan's name had never come up in conversation as a possible suspect, largely in part, because Sarah had not even considered him, until she had met Rêmet the evening before.

There was only one instance where his name had come up.

It was on the night of Erin's accident.

It was right before she went to file her report with Vincent, which was the last account of anybody seeing her.

Surely not...

Sarah stopped still, as a connection gradually formed in her mind's eye. It was circumstantial at best. But...

Sarah fished the mobile phone out of her pocket. Erin's passing was still so raw that she had not yet deleted any of the messages they had sent one another, over the last few weeks. The last message she had sent to Erin was at a quarter to six on Tuesday evening. She re-read the message now and a small tingle of nervous excitement rattled down her spine; she had told Erin that Johan had come into the school, out of the blue and made a pass at her.

She had meant the message as a light-hearted moment, shared between lovers, but what if this had triggered something in Erin's mind? It had always amazed Sarah, how Erin's brain could piece clues together, to reach accurate conclusions. It was the reason why Sarah refused to watch crime-dramas on the television with her; she always guessed the villain halfway into the story.

Sarah sat down on the sofa, and grabbed a nearby scrap of paper and a pen. She started scrawling down a brief timeline for Erin on one side and then on the back, the known whereabouts of Johan during the same period. She read what she had written on both sides and then grabbed a second scrap of paper and jotted the points together.

Erin knew that Johan was at the school on Friday afternoon. She knew that he had claimed to leave at about quarter past three, when Natalie would have been stood near the school gates. But what if he were lying? Nobody had come forward to verify the exact time he had left, other than after three. If he had actually left later, he would be a definite suspect.

She continued to jot her notes.

The lady across the street had claimed to see a red car pulled up outside of the school, but couldn't identify the make. Rêmet had shown Sarah a newspaper cutting of Johan taking ownership of a red Ferrari.

Another memory chilled Sarah's nervous system.

On the day of the reconstruction, Johan had watched the filming of the scene. Why hadn't he offered to be part of the reconstruction? What if he had been worried that somebody would recognise his red Ferrari?

Sarah re-read her notes. She knew she was forcing the facts to fit Rêmet's theory, but it was all plausible. Johan's sudden, unscheduled appearance at the school on Tuesday had seemed a bit off, but she had dismissed the thought when he had made a pass at her. What if he had been checking that he was in the clear? Playing the part of concerned citizen?

She knew it was weak, but it was just the sort of trail that Erin would follow. Vincent had told Sarah that Erin said she was going to check one more thing before returning home. What if she had made the connection and had gone to pay Johan a visit? Maybe she had spotted his car and asked some difficult questions he couldn't answer? What if the only way out of it had been for him to kill her, and make it look like an accident?

Sarah nearly laughed out loud. She was being ridiculous. Johan Boller was a nice man. He wasn't a serial killer. He was a Premiership footballer, for God's sake!

She picked up her empty mug of coffee, and headed to the kitchen to rinse it out. As she stood at the kitchen sink, she laughed to herself again. Rêmet had been so sincere the night before that he had almost convinced her. She felt embarrassed that she had got so carried away. Part of her felt guilty, about letting Vincent know where Rêmet could be found. He had said yesterday that he didn't want to go to the police, until he had her on-side, but if there were any truth in what he was saying, it was better to leave it to the professionals to resolve.

As she wiped the wet sponge around the rim of the mug, one question continued to bother her; why hadn't he called?

37

An hour later, Sarah was pacing around the living room again. There had still been no word from Rêmet and it was nearly lunchtime. There was every chance that he was a late-sleeper, but he had given the impression that he would call in the morning. She had certainly expected an update by now. There had been no further word from Vincent either, but then she didn't really expect him to call every hour with updates. In fairness, she was surprised that he had been in touch as much as he had. Maybe he was just feeling guilty about Erin.

It was highly possible that Vincent had tracked down Rêmet at the hotel and had hauled him in for questioning. Sarah thought it a bit unpleasant that Rêmet had phoned Natalie's home, fishing for details about her. Ultimately, Sarah understood why he had done it, but couldn't imagine doing a job like that where the moral compass is so skewed. If Vincent had collared Rêmet then he would probably be quite angry with her for disrupting his plan, but then ultimately the police would have been involved at some point so why not sooner?

The reason Sarah was pacing was the uncertainty of the situation. She had convinced herself that suspecting Johan Boller of being the killer and rapist was ludicrous; he was a celebrity for God's sake! Yet, she couldn't shake the tangible facts that suggested it could be him. She needed to know; she needed closure and justice. She couldn't help feeling anger and hatred towards the man who may have been responsible for killing Erin. There was only one way she was going to get it and that was to confront Johan herself.

She barely knew him so walking up and accusing him of abducting, raping and killing Natalie was not an option. He would be just as likely to have her committed as he was to tell her anything. She needed to be smarter; to think like Erin would; she wished Erin was with her now.

Sarah forced herself to sit down on the sofa, if, for no other reason than to save the carpet from wearing away. She looked back at the scraps of paper she had jotted notes on. There was every chance that Johan could explain the links she had found and at least that would give her peace of mind. She just needed to find a way to raise the subject with him. There was no chance she would casually bump into him in the street as he lived out in Hythe Marina, and it might look suspicious if she were to just turn up on his doorstep out of the blue.

After much soul-searching she eventually opted to phone him on the ruse that she needed to discuss some school-based sports activity. He had been quite pleased to be approached to come to the school originally, and she still had the copy of his telephone number that Mrs McGregor had given to her on Friday morning. Sarah picked up the phone and input his number.

She could feel butterflies floating around in her stomach and it reminded her of being a teenager again, phoning a boy to ask him out on a date: nervous excitement.

He answered after three rings.

'Hello, Johan?' she began nervously. 'It's Sarah Jenson from St Monica's…'

'Hello, Sarah,' he said, cutting her off mid-sentence. 'How are you?'

He sounded relaxed and jovial and Sarah assumed he was smiling as he spoke. She knew a little harmless flirting would go a long way to securing the meeting.

'I am well, Johan, thank you. Is it a good time for you to speak? You're not in the middle of anything important?'

'No, it's okay. I was just watching some TV. What can I do for you?'

'Peggy McGregor asked me to give you a call,' Sarah lied. 'She wanted you and I to work together on organising the children's Olympics-themed sports day at the end of term. I believe she's spoken to you about this before?'

'Yes. Sure.'

'Great. Would you be able to come and meet me so we can sort out the various bits and pieces? It shouldn't take too long. About an hour or so?'

'Oh,' he replied reluctantly. 'I'm due at the training ground for a physio session in an hour.'

'That's okay; it doesn't have to be right now. Are you free later on?'

'I can have a look at tomorrow or next week?' he offered.

'No!' said Sarah defiantly. 'Sorry. What I mean is, would it be possible to meet today? I appreciate it's short notice, but Peggy is keen that we sort this out sooner rather than later.'

Boller paused as if considering what she was asking and then said, 'How about dinner tonight?'

Sarah didn't answer at first. She wondered whether he still fancied his chances with her even though she had rebuffed his last advance. On the one hand she didn't want to encourage him, but on the other hand it would give her the time to gently ease out the information she needed.

'Okay,' she eventually replied. 'Where were you thinking?'

'I was thinking my place. We could order some takeaway.'

Sarah was about to accept when she remembered the potential repercussions of the meeting.

'No,' she said quickly, and then tried to reassure him that it wasn't that she didn't want to see his house, but actually him coming to her house would be better, as she could then cook him a meal. She added that all the school paperwork for the Sports Day event was at her place, so it would be easier than her transporting it to him. He seemed to accept this story and agreed to meet her. She gave him the address and said she would see him at half past seven.

That gave her enough time to head into town and pick up some recording equipment. She didn't want to rely on a small Dictaphone in her handbag to pick up the conversation. There would be a danger that the handbag wouldn't be nearby at the appropriate time. No. What she had in mind for tonight would require the ultimate in spyware.

Sarah strapped on a pair of sandals and headed to town. Covert technology was more Erin's interest but Sarah had heard her talk often enough about various different listening devices and what they could be used for. Sarah also knew the best place to go for guidance. A former colleague of Erin's worked in a specialist shop in the city centre. Sarah was sure she could rely on him to hook her up with what she needed. It would be expensive, Sarah accepted that, but at worst it would only serve to prove Johan's innocence and get Rêmet off his case. At best, it might record the confession of the man who abducted and killed Natalie Barrett; the same man who was responsible for the death of Erin.

*

Johan Boller had been sat at home playing computer games with a couple of reserve team players, who were the closest thing he had to friends in Southampton. They had been playing the recently released Fifa football game and Boller had not been winning. When the phone had rung he had been pleased with the distraction, and had allowed one of the others to take his place in the mini tournament.

He had been both surprised and pleased to discover it was that primary school teacher phoning him. When he had asked her out on Tuesday, and she had turned him down, he had been sure that he had seen a glint of excitement in her eye but he couldn't be sure. Her phoning him now to ask if he would come over and help with a school project was clearly a ruse to see him again and so he was now sure that actually she might be interested in him. She had claimed to be a lesbian but for all he knew she might also be attracted to men and the thinly-veiled story about the Sports Day was obviously her attempt to show she was keen.

He had lied about the fact he had a physio session later on, the truth was he didn't need to go to the training ground at Staplewood today and was planning to just relax with his friends. He didn't want to see her yet, though. A meeting over dinner would suit him better. He had told the other two players about the primary school teacher so they had been egging him on in the background, telling him to get her round for dinner. As far as they were concerned, once she saw Boller's house, she would be his for the taking. It was a sentiment he shared.

Unfortunately she had declined the chance to come to him but had instead insisted he come to her flat. Maybe she was a bit shy, he thought. That didn't mean she wouldn't still be his tonight though. Boller was used to getting his own way; when there was something he wanted, he generally got it.

Boller told his friends he was just going to go to the bathroom to shower but they could continue to play in his absence. They had teased him about spending the next six hours in the bathroom to prepare himself for the big date. Rather than heading straight for the bathroom, Boller took a detour via the safe in his bedroom and then headed to the kitchen. He selected a bottle of white wine and a bottle of red, which he planned to take around with him. He stood the two bottles, which were sealed with a cork and plastic wrapping, on the kitchen table and removed from his pocket, what he had collected from the safe. It was a small syringe filled with a colourless liquid. He pushed the syringe through the top of the bottle of white wine and squeezed half the contents into the bottle. He then pushed the syringe through the top of the red bottle and emptied the rest of the colourless liquid into it. He then removed the syringe and put it back in his pocket, ready to return to the safe, after his shower. He shook the two bottles up and then placed them back on the table.

The colourless liquid in the syringe was flunitrazepam, a drug that specialised in relaxing muscles, lowering blood pressure and causing bouts of memory loss. Its street name was rohypnol but he had it in its purest form. Boller had used it several times in the past, and it had worked perfectly in the toffees he had offered Natalie Barrett on Friday night. He was determined that he would have Sarah Jenson, willing participant or not. One glass of wine would probably be enough to make her his and then it would all be a distant memory when she woke up. But he would remember. He always remembered.

38

It hadn't taken Jack Vincent's team long to locate the journalist, Claude Rêmet. Rather than phoning the various hotels near the West Quay retail park, he had arranged for a couple of uniformed officers to visit each hotel with a crude image of Rêmet provided by their Belgian colleagues. They found him at the first hotel they had gone to. The stern-looking woman behind the reception desk, had explained that she hadn't been on duty the evening before, so had not seen Rêmet. However, there was a guest of the same name, registered in one of their rooms. She confirmed there had been no contact from the room that day, but she had only started her shift at eleven o'clock, so there was every chance he had already left for the day. Regardless, she gave the officers directions to the room and they went on their way.

The smell, as they reached the door, hit them first. When one of the officers banged on the door and called out Rêmet's name, they had not been surprised to receive no answer. The 'Do Not Disturb' sign clung to the door handle, suggesting the hotel's maid had not been in the room this morning. The second officer jogged back to the reception desk and asked for a skeleton key.

The odour grew stronger still, as the first officer turned the door handle and prised the door open. At first, it was difficult to make out any shapes in the room, as the curtains were drawn tight, so they turned the room's lights on. Even though both officers were experienced and had seen dead bodies before, neither was prepared for what they saw, and for one, it was too much, as he dashed for the bathroom to vomit up his breakfast.

*

By the time Vincent was allowed to enter the crime scene, the corridor had been cordoned off with blue and white tape, and officers had been posted at all entry points. Vincent had ordered the entire hotel to be vacated and closed, while the forensics team did their job, but the hotel's manager had protested and eventually they had compromised on just shutting off the corridor in question.

Vincent climbed into the white polythene suit, provided by the forensics team, and stretched the blue latex gloves over his hairy fingers. He hated this part of the job, but he wasn't one to go against the protocols of the SOCO team. The room's windows had been opened, to try and disperse some of the rotten stench, but it still caused Vincent's nostril hairs to twitch and he fought the urge to retch. He was not prepared for the scene before him.

The body of Claude Rêmet hung from tight black ropes that were attached to each of the bed's four posts. Each piece of rope was carefully tied tightly around either a wrist or ankle, leaving him hovering about ten inches above the mattress. The body was naked, save for a black, studded dog collar around the victim's throat and a cheap-looking black, latex thong that had been pulled down. A used condom could be seen poking out of Rêmet's anus. A small vial was open on the bedside table, which Vincent went over to view. The label on the bottle indicated that it had contained amyl nitrite, more commonly known as 'poppers' amongst the gay community.

'Sexual endeavour gone wrong?' said a voice over Vincent's shoulder. He turned to see Dr Neil Spinks observing the suspended cadaver.

'Looks like it,' Vincent concurred. 'I take it a suicide note hasn't been found?'

'Apparently not,' replied Spinks, fascinated by what he was looking at.

'And no forced entry, is that right?'

'So I'm told,' mused Spinks.

'So what are we thinking, Doc?' continued Vincent. 'Our visitor here decided to get some local action last night and brought his guest back to this room? They decided to get better acquainted, and then what?'

'By the surprised look on the victim's face,' replied Spinks, moving to the head-end of the bed, 'I'd say heart attack, I suppose. He's clearly not in good shape; maybe the mixture of alcohol and amyl nitrite was too much for his system, and he just passed away.'

Vincent considered the theory. It was all guess work, but it sounded plausible.

'It's a bit crude, though,' said Vincent pointing to Rêmet's backside. 'Leaving the condom still in.'

'My guess is, the guest panicked and scarpered, without thinking twice. Most minds don't think straight where sudden death is involved.'

'Well whoever his friend was, hopefully we'll be able to find a DNA profile from inside the condom. In the meantime, I'll send a couple of uniforms to the local gay-friendly bars and clubs to wave Rêmet's picture around.'

'Good idea: see if anybody remembers seeing him hanging around last night,' concluded Spinks, before smiling and adding, 'Forgive the pun.'

Vincent surveyed the room for a second time, but there was nothing obvious to indicate the identity of who had been in the room with Rêmet last night. He would speak to the hotel manager, to obtain a copy of any CCTV that may have captured Rêmet and his acquaintance returning to the room. That might at least give some indication of the time of death, until Spinks was able to give a conclusive answer. He would also send a couple of officers to the local taxi companies, to see if any of the drivers had escorted Rêmet last night. Most of the gay-friendly haunts in the town were some distance from the hotel, and Vincent doubted the tubby Rêmet would have walked there and back.

It was unfortunate timing for Rêmet to pass away. Sarah Jenson had mentioned that the journalist knew who had taken and killed Natalie Barrett, and if that was true, then Vincent had just lost another potential lead. He decided he would personally review Rêmet's career, to see if there were any hints as to whom he had suspected. Was it possible that Rêmet had been killed by whoever he suspected? Vincent doubted it. After all, the person they were looking for was interested in innocent, young girls; not overweight French journalists.

Vincent decided he would give Sarah Jenson a call, to let her know that Rêmet was dead, so at least she wouldn't continue to sit and wait for him to phone her. He would ask her again whether Rêmet had revealed the identity of the likely culprit, in case she had been covering earlier on. If they had spoken, as she had indicated, then maybe she had heard something that she didn't realise was significant, but that a canny detective's mind like his would thrive on.

As Vincent walked back to his squad car he pulled out his mobile phone and dialled Sarah's flat. The line rang and rang before the answer-phone eventually cut in. He decided not to leave a message, as he didn't want to freak her out. Besides it would be better to speak with her face to face so that he could tell if she were lying, when he asked if Rêmet had identified the killer to her. That could wait until tomorrow morning. It was more important for him to try and identify the owner of the used condom first.

39

Sarah still had butterflies in her stomach, as she sat waiting for her guest to arrive.

Her trip to town earlier that afternoon had proved successful. She had headed to the electrical store, and thankfully Erin's former colleague, Dudley, had recognised her when she had entered the shop, and had been happy to explain what she would require to bug her own house. He had looked quizzically at her, as he tried to understand why she was looking to carry out such a devious mission, but she had just shrugged her shoulders and asked him not to worry about her motives. Out of respect for Erin, he had agreed to it. He told her that he had heard about Erin's passing, through the grapevine, and enquired when the funeral was planned for. The question should not have surprised her, but it had caused her to nearly faint.

The truth was, although she had told herself that she had come to terms with Erin's passing, she hadn't really, and hadn't even considered the requirement of organising a funeral, which inevitably would be necessary in the coming days. Dudley had made her a hot cup of tea, for the shock and then they had sat together and worked out what she would need in the property. She had handed over her credit card and the transaction was complete. As a favour, Dudley even agreed to come round and help set up the equipment.

Dudley had finished the job half an hour ago, which had given her just enough time to change into something more akin to a dinner date and to apply some make up, to hide her tired eyes. The equipment Dudley had installed was voice-activated, so she wouldn't need to worry about pressing any concealed buttons to start it recording. Dudley had also said that the system could cope with twenty-four hours' worth of recording, and she had said that would be more than enough. As he had completed the job, he had again enquired what she needed the equipment for, and she had lied, saying there had been several break-ins in the area, and this just seemed a good way of catching the culprits, should they strike her flat. He had frowned, but seemed to accept the reasoning.

Johan was late. It was nearly eight o'clock and there was no sign of him. Sarah started to wonder whether he had changed his mind, or worse, that he might be on to the real reason she had invited him around. This thought, was of course crazy, as there was no reason for him to suspect her true motives; it didn't stop the thought going through her mind, however.

In concentrating on setting up all the recording equipment, she had totally forgotten that they were supposed to be discussing the school Sports Day. She had no paperwork with her that she could produce, and so had phoned Peggy McGregor and asked her to email the plans over. Peggy had been unhappy that Sarah was even considering the Sports Day, but Sarah had told her what she needed right now was a project to focus her mind. Peggy had forwarded the minutes from the preliminary planning meeting, but had reiterated that Sarah should be grieving and not working. Sarah had told her that she was coping and wouldn't allow the project to stop her grieving.

As soon as she had received Peggy's minutes, she had printed them out and headed to the kitchen to start preparing something edible for Johan to eat. She was not a natural cook and had been relieved to find a packet of chicken kievs in the freezer, along with a portion of roast potatoes and a small container of cauliflower cheese. It was hardly sophisticated, but then she wasn't trying to sweep him off his feet, so the food would have to do. She threw the items in the oven, aiming for them to be ready by eight o'clock. Ironically, if he didn't arrive soon, dinner would be ruined!

Sarah looked down at her phone. He hadn't called to say he was running late. She had received three missed calls, while she had been out in town. The first had been from Jack Vincent's mobile number, but he hadn't left a message, and she had not had time to return his call. The other two had been from her dad's mobile. On the second call he had left a message, asking her to give him a call and let him know that she was okay. It was a nice feeling, knowing that he wanted to be part of her life again, and she chastised herself for not returning his call straight away, particularly as she had blamed him for not keeping in touch.

Sarah was weighing up whether to call her dad back, when she heard a car pull up in the street, followed by the sound of a car door closing. She moved to the window, looked out, and saw Johan moving towards the communal front door. He buzzed at the intercom and she pressed the button and told him where to find her flat. Two minutes later, she was letting him in.

He was dressed in a pair of tight-fitting dark

trousers and a slim-fit shirt that seemed to cling to his muscular torso. She wondered whether he had deliberately chosen the outfit, to show off his assets. He had leaned in and pecked her cheek, sending a shudder down her spine. It wasn't a shudder of excitement; it was one of anxiety.

Johan passed her two bottles, wrapped in brown paper, suggesting he had picked them up on his way over. He explained that he didn't know what her preference was and so had brought a red and a white.

'Can I pour you a glass?' she asked.

'I cannot drink tonight,' he replied. 'I have training tomorrow, and so I have to have water only.'

Sarah felt sorry for him in that instance, having his diet carefully monitored and not being able to splurge out whenever the urge took him. She was glad that there was nothing to stop her from drinking and she led him into the kitchen. She fished around in the cutlery drawer until she located the cork-screw and then proceeded to work on extracting the cork from the bottle. Clearly, Johan had gone to some expense to purchase this wine, as it was rare to find a bottle plugged by a cork these days; was this really the thinking of a killer? She thought not. She poured herself a large glass of white; she needed something for her nerves!

She filled him a glass of water from the tap and they headed through to the living room. They chatted casually for a couple of minutes about his career. He came across as quite humble, explaining that he liked living in Southampton, and would be happy to play on at the club for as long as they wanted him. It was not what she expected, and deep-down she got the impression he was lying; not that it mattered.

Sarah started to feel a little light-headed and put it down to the lack of lunch. She had been so busy with Dudley that the thought of grabbing an afternoon snack had slipped from her mind. She excused herself whilst she went to check on the food. The kievs were bubbling in their bath of garlic butter, the potatoes looked brown and crisp, and the cauliflower cheese was golden brown at its outer edge. The smell of the garlic was overpowering, and she quickly served up the various items on plates and placed them down on the table in the kitchen. As she did, she had to grab at the corner of the table to stop herself from falling over. It was the second time that day she had nearly fainted. Johan entered the kitchen at this point and coiled his long fingers around her wrist to steady her.

'Are you okay?' he enquired.

'I think my blood sugar must be a bit low,' she said before adding, 'I missed lunch.'

'Sit down, sit down,' he ushered and she did as she was told. 'Let's eat,' he added, once he had taken his seat across from her.

Sarah didn't need telling twice and she happily cut into her kiev and potatoes, and began to shovel the food into her mouth eagerly. It tasted so good, but in fairness, anything would have tasted amazing at that point, such was her hunger.

'I'm sorry it's not more extravagant,' she said after a time.

'It's delicious,' lied Johan. He had never been a fan of garlic and it made him glad he had stopped, en route, for a burger.

'Are you sure I can't get you something else to drink?' Sarah asked taking a large gulp from her glass. 'I have other soft drinks, besides water.'

Johan smiled and said he was fine.

'My girlfriend doesn't…sorry…didn't drink alcohol, so there are various flavoured waters and tonics about the place.' It was her attempt to empathise with his situation, but in the end, it just made her feel sad for her loss.

'Are you not together anymore?' Johan asked.

'No,' said Sarah, taking a larger gulp of wine. 'She passed away earlier in the week.'

'Oh God,' said Johan, with a concerned look on his face. 'I'm so sorry. What happened?'

'I'd rather not talk about it,' she said.

'I understand,' replied Johan, taking a sip from his water, to try and deflect the awkwardness of the situation. 'Were you together long?'

'Seven years,' said Sarah, draining the rest of her glass.

Johan leaned over and poured her another glass from the open bottle on the table.

'Would you like me to go?' he offered. 'You should be grieving, not meeting with me.'

'It's okay,' she said, reaching out and touching his hand. 'I wanted to meet tonight, remember?'

She pulled her hand back quickly. What was she doing? That was so unlike her. Maybe this wine was going to her head, she thought.

'Let's go through to the other room,' suggested Johan, hopeful he could leave the plate of food behind him.

Sarah nodded, stood and moved to the living room. Johan, noticing she had left her wine behind, picked up the glass and followed her through. He found her sat on one of the sofas. He passed her the glass and sat down beside her. They remained sat in silence for several minutes, before Sarah became aware of the silence and snapped her attention back to reality. What was wrong with her?

'Sorry,' she said, 'I was off in my own little world, there, for a minute.'

'That is okay,' said Johan. 'I was looking at the photographs on the mantelpiece. Is that your girlfriend?' he asked indicating to a small framed image.

Sarah stood and moved across the room, to look closer at the photos. She felt a little uneasy on her feet, but told herself that her blood sugar was bound to rise shortly, following the meal. She picked up the framed photograph of her and Erin, taken on a trip to Euro Disney. They had only gone for a weekend, but it had been a great trip. The photograph had been taken outside the castle in the Magic Kingdom. She moved back to the sofa and handed the frame to Johan.

'Yeah, that's her. Her name was Erin.'

Boller began coughing, as if something had caught in his airway.

'Are you okay?' Sarah asked, wondering what had brought on his spluttering.

'Yes, fine,' he said, quickly handing the frame back. 'Can I use your bathroom?'

Sarah gave him directions to the bathroom and he excused himself.

40

Boller entered the en-suite bathroom and moved straight for the basin. He turned the cold water tap on, began to scoop up water in his hands, and splashed it on his face. This couldn't be happening; the woman in the photograph was the policewoman who had come to his house on Tuesday night, asking difficult questions!

He had been in his house, scrubbing the floor with bleach, when there had been a knock at the door. He had not been expecting visitors, and he had panicked that it would be one of his team mates, popping by for a late drinking session. He didn't want to let anybody in, particularly in the kitchen where blood had congealed on the floor; Natalie's blood. He had already taken the stained bed sheets out to an incinerator in his back yard and burned them. But on Saturday, he had left her lifeless body on the laminated kitchen floor, whilst he had gone to find something to carry her body in, to dump it. When he had returned, a dark crimson pool of blood had formed around her body and had seeped between the thin cracks in the flooring. He knew that bleaching the floor would only hide the blood from the naked-eye, but would be no challenge for a forensics team to find. He had decided to scrub the floor for now, and would look to replace the flooring as soon as possible.

As he went to open his front door, he had decided that he would just steer whichever team mate it was, to the living room and say that the kitchen was out of bounds. He had been surprised to see a pretty woman, dressed in a business suit, stood at his door. There was a small drizzle falling in the background, which was illuminated by his security light. At first, he thought she was a passing stranger whose car had broken down, but she held up a warrant card and said she was a Detective Constable. His eyes had widened. There was no way they could have connected him to Natalie's disappearance, or so he thought.

The policewoman had asked to come in as she had some questions she wished to ask him about the last time he had seen Natalie. She told him that as he had been the last person to see her alive, his perspective on things might help steer them to the person who had abducted her. He was sweating heavily at the thought that she could read his mind, but he tried to play it cool and welcomed her in.

She asked him to describe what he had seen, what Natalie had been wearing, whether she had seemed happy or upset, whether he had noticed anybody else around. He pleaded ignorance to all of her questions, claiming that he hadn't really been paying attention and how he wished he could have been more help. He thought she was about to leave when she started asking more pertinent questions: What time did he finish meeting with Mr Stanley, the head of Year-5? What time did he get in his car? Where was Natalie stood when he saw her? What route did he drive home? What was traffic like? The questions came thick and fast and then she would repeat questions, but using different words, as if she was trying to trip him up. It made him feel quite jumpy.

Just when he thought he had answered all of her

questions, she had asked if she could have a look at his car. He didn't want to show her the car, as he hadn't finished cleaning up the boot and if she happened to ask to look inside, he would be caught. As he went upstairs to fetch his keys, he left her in the living room, waiting. When he returned, he noticed that she was chewing on something. He looked quizzically at her and she apologised, saying she had helped herself to one of the toffees from the paper bag on the coffee table. At this point, he knew he was in trouble, as it was one of the drugged toffees he had given to Natalie on Friday night. If the policewoman became aware that the sweet was drugged, she was sure to arrest him, pending further enquiries. He had quickly said he did not mind and offered her a second toffee. She gratefully accepted, making the excuse that she had not been home for her dinner yet.

She was half asleep when they reached the car but by the time she realised what had happened, she had passed out and banged her head on the floor. There was nothing he could do, apart from finish the job and dispose of her body. Nobody would believe that he had accidentally drugged a policewoman. He had put her in her car, in the passenger seat and drove out into the dark night. He had brought a shovel and a bottle of whiskey with him, his intention to crack her skull with one and drown his sorrows with the other. His mind raced as he drove. He wasn't paying attention to what he was doing and nearly hit a startled deer that ran in front of the car. It was the inspiration he needed, and at that moment, he decided he would make out like she had been involved in a car accident. He pulled the car over, placed her in the driving seat and poured half the bottle of whiskey down her throat, the rest he splashed liberally over her suit. He made sure her seat belt was unfastened and then placed a large rock on the accelerator pedal. The car tore off down the road and soon left the road, winding up in a ditch. When he wandered down the road to survey the scene, he wasn't surprised to see her bloody head poking through the cracked windscreen.

He disposed of the large rock and jogged back home. He made it within thirty minutes, where he then made an anonymous telephone call to the police, taking care to withhold his number, to explain he had seen what looked like a drunk driver careering off the road.

There had been several nights of uneasy sleep since that moment, but he had all but forgotten about it, after last night's rendezvous with Rêmet. The image of the policewoman, looking so happy with Sarah, had made his stomach turn; the grim truth crashing down around him. He took several deep breaths and looked at his reflection in the mirror. *It isn't your fault*, he told himself; *it isn't your fault. She had it coming; it was her fault for asking the wrong questions. She had it coming.* The face in the mirror smiled back at him and he regained his composure. He could hear Sarah singing gently in the other room, as if she hadn't a care in the world. Her voice sounded almost-angelic and he felt it calling to him. He splashed more water on his face, wiped it with a towel and returned to the living room.

Sarah was slouched on the sofa, the effects of the flunitrazepam taking their toll.

'Johan, hey,' Sarah slurred, trying and failing to sit up. 'Dance with me?'

Johan smiled down at her intoxicated state. She

would be his, he thought to himself. He reached his arms out and took her hands in his own. He pulled her up towards him and she collapsed into his arms.

'I think I'm a bit drunk,' she mused, not quite able to keep her eyes open.

'That's okay, Cherie,' he replied. 'I'll take care of you.'

Sarah felt weightless, as Boller scooped her up in his arms and carried her through to the bedroom. She felt like she was dreaming, as he laid her down on the bed and began to pull at her dress.

41

Sarah thrashed about in her dream-like state. It felt like she was in a sail boat, in the middle of a torrential storm, and she was alone. It was taking all her strength to batten down the hatches, and keep the boat afloat. She could feel the waves splashing against her face, and the force of the wind, knocking her from side to side, pulling her down then pushing her up again. She felt something hard scraping against her thighs and then a sharp pain just above.

She came to, to find herself lying flat on her bed, her dress ripped open and Johan aggressively grinding himself up and down, on top of her. Her drug-addled mind was struggling to process what was happening. Why was he on top of her? Why was he hurting her? Her flailing arms tried to push him off, but it was no good, his upper body strength was more than she could cope with.

Her eyes rolled back in her head, and she briefly passed out again. She fought hard to regain control of her mind, and forced her eyes to open again. She could feel Boller's hand between her legs, roughly pushing against her, whilst his other hand was reaching down, trying to undo his trousers.

'Wh-what?' she tried to say but her mouth wouldn't allow her to pronounce the words. It was as if her lips were sewn shut.

Boller mumbled something in French that she didn't understand, but then she felt him push harder between her legs, and the grim reality, that she was being raped, hit her like a locomotive.

Thoughts raced through her mind, but she was unable to finish one and link them together to find a solution to the problem. Why was he doing this?

She yelped out in pain, as he thrust against her semi-naked flesh. She yelped again, but it just seemed to spur him on.

She needed to get him to stop.

Yes, that was it! She needed him to stop. But how?

He continued to force himself, deeper between her legs, feeling the excitement of having her, against her will. He began to moan too.

'Stop!' she tried to shout, but it was barely a whisper.

Something wet rolled down her cheeks, and she realised she was crying. She chastised herself for being so weak. Crying wasn't the answer! She had to be strong, to think of a way out of this. God, how she wished Erin was here right now.

Boller moaned louder, as he felt her tensing up around him. It meant she was regaining consciousness. It made him look down towards her. He could see her crying and the expression of hopelessness on her face.

Sarah saw his eyes look at her, and she felt sickened by the animalistic-look they had. He pushed harder and faster. Sarah raised her eyes to the ceiling and brought them around in an arc, looking for anything she might use as a weapon, or at least leverage, to get this hulk off of her. But there was nothing obvious she could use. The alarm clock sat on the bedside table but like the lamp, was wired to the wall, so there was no way it would stretch. The only other things in reach were her pillows and she knew they wouldn't do him any harm.

Unless…

She grabbed at the nearest pillow and put it over her face to help her position her hands, in such a way, as she had a hand on each edge of the pillow. Then, with one, quick motion, she thrust the pillow up and into the face of her attacker with all the strength she could muster. She pushed with all her might and felt his body lift slightly from her.

Boller began to focus his weight on pushing back against the pillow. Her decision to use it as leverage had surprised him, but he knew he was stronger than her.

Sarah continued to push up, despite the weight of Boller forcing her arms to bend. She just needed to position him so that…

There.

She thrust her right knee up, as hard and as fast as she could, and landed the blow somewhere between his buttocks and testicles. He yelped out in pain and it caused him to topple over the side of the bed, his penis roughly expelled from her, sending a shooting pain up through her groin.

Sarah knew she didn't have time to think about the pain, and she pushed herself so that she rolled down and off the end of the bed. Boller was bent over with his hand between his legs, protecting it from further damage. She could feel a warm sensation between her own legs and saw blood dripping onto the carpet. There was an even bigger pool of blood forming on the bed where she had been only moments earlier.

Sarah got to her feet and stumbled into the hallway. She realised that Boller must have drugged her in some way, and she tried to regain her balance, before her legs buckled beneath her, and she crashed into the table that the phone sat on. There was a loud crash, as the plastic phone clattered to the floor. She could see her front door and knew that if she could just get to it, she would be out and could get help.

Her whole body was aching, in particular her groin, and it took all her will power to crawl to the front door on her hands and knees. The bristly spikes of the door mat rubbed against her legs and she knew that if she could just stand and reach the door knob...

But it was too late. Boller had recovered from the attack and was stood right behind her. He placed his hands around her waist and dragged her back from the door. She cried out as she sensed what would happen next.

Satisfied that they were now far enough from the door, Boller placed her back down and pushed her head to the floor, causing her buttocks to rise as a result.

'You will be mine,' he spat in her direction and knelt down behind her.

Sarah felt his grubby hands reaching between her legs, ready to finish the job off.

'Please,' she begged between sobs.

'It will be over soon enough, Cherie,' he replied.

'People know where I am,' she continued, desperate to say anything to frighten him into stopping. 'They will come for me. They will come for you.'

Boller withdrew his hand and moved around, so that he was speaking into her ear.

'Nobody will come for you, bitch. This time, they won't even find the body.'

Sarah's head whipped around so that she was facing him.

'What do you mean?' she said, forcing the tears to stop.

'Your bitch of a girlfriend thought she was on to me as well,' he said between gritted teeth, 'but I dealt with her. I will deal with you as well, once I am finished.'

'You killed Erin?' Sarah said in a cracked whisper. 'Why?'

'If she hadn't come to see me on Tuesday, she would still be alive today,' he retorted, as if it was Erin's own fault. 'That stupid bitch should have just left it alone!'

'Oh God,' Sarah said, as she realised the truth. 'Rêmet was right; you killed Natalie.'

Sarah's statement caught his attention, 'You knew Claude Rêmet?'

'What do you mean, 'knew'?' she replied as it became evident why the journalist had failed to call her that morning.

'Rêmet was another one who should have kept his nose out of my business,' Boller shouted before shuffling, so that he was back behind her.

'You won't get away with this,' Sarah shouted again and screamed as he thrust himself between her legs again.

'You sick son of a bitch!' she cried between his thrusts.

'Keep crying, bitch,' he retorted. 'It makes it so much better.'

Sarah closed her eyes and willed the newly-forming memories from her mind, trying anything to repress what was happening. She thought about little Natalie, an innocent girl in the wrong place at the wrong time, when this monster came calling. She thought about Erin, a good and kind officer, following her hunch and winding up a victim. She thought about Claude Rêmet, a crusader who would never see justice served. The pain continued, as he thrust harder and harder. She felt a wave of relief, as he began to moan and she sensed he was near climax; at least it would be over soon enough.

'Are you ready, bitch?' she heard him moan, before a sudden, loud clatter caused her to pass out again.

42

Alan Jenson hated mobile telephones. In his opinion, no phone call could ever be so important that it couldn't wait until one had returned home. It bothered him to see young people wandering around, wired into their ever-shrinking mobile phones. These days, mobile phone devices were music players, internet devices and game machines. People seemed to spend more time using a mobile phone device than they actually spent physically interacting with other people.

In spite of his opinion, he had succumbed to purchasing a mobile phone himself. Whilst he despised the thought of carrying a phone on his person all day, he could see the advantage of being able to contact someone in an emergency, should the situation require it. It had been Veronica's suggestion that he buy the phone.

Veronica was a sixty year old spinster that Alan Jenson had known for over thirty years. Never married, she always claimed that she was waiting for the right man to come along; nobody could argue that she hadn't dipped her toe in the water, as her string of lovers would testify to. However, none had seemed worth committing to, in her opinion. Despite her age, Veronica was still a bit of a looker and she knew that most of the widowed men in Fortuneswell fancied her. She used it to her full advantage and she couldn't even remember the last time she had bought herself a drink when she had been at the local club.

Alan had taken quite a shine to Veronica, since his wife had passed away and they had unofficially become an item, not that he had told Sarah about her yet. Veronica had her own house in the town, and they would generally take it in turns to cook and stay around at each other's houses on alternate nights. The love-making had given Alan a new lease of life, a new reason for living, and that was why he had now improved his diet, to include several portions of fruit and vegetables each day. It was also helping him to increase his stamina.

Veronica liked to think she was still relatively in-touch with the world, and had bought herself a mobile phone that allowed her to check her emails while she was out shopping. She had told Alan he must invest in a phone so that she could get hold of him whenever required, and so he had relented.

It had been an awkward scene when he had walked into the mobile phone shop in Weymouth. A young, confident-looking man with his hair slicked back, had approached him and asked how he could help.

'I want a phone,' Alan had replied.

'Okay,' the young man had said. 'Do you require 3G, Wi-Fi, HD video capabilities?'

Alan had looked at him, as if he were speaking another language, before repeating, 'I want a phone.'

The young man had asked him if there was a particular handset he was interested in, if he wanted free minutes and text messages and how much data he would be downloading per month. Alan was bemused and had turned around and left the shop. When he explained what had happened to Veronica, she had dragged him back to the shop and had thankfully explained that he needed a basic phone, with no fancy trimmings. He had no idea what make of phone he had ended up with, but Veronica had showed him how to make a call on the device and had pre-programmed it with several telephone numbers, so that he wouldn't need to commit them to memory.

Alan Jenson was worried about how Sarah would react, when she discovered that there was a new woman in his life. He missed his wife every day, but he needed companionship, and that is exactly what Veronica gave him. He desperately hoped that Sarah would understand, and not be too put out. It was for this reason he had attempted to call her, earlier that afternoon. He had spent an hour working out what he would say, before looking her number up on the mobile phone and pressing the green phone symbol. He had been disappointed when the phone had gone unanswered, and had transferred to the answer-phone. He had hung up, without leaving a message, as what he had to say, needed to be said person to person, and not via recorded message.

Later on in the afternoon he had been talking to James Dale at the club and James had asked whether Ryan Moss had made contact with Sarah yet. Alan had panicked at the question, because he was unable to answer it. A feeling of dread had enveloped him and he began to fear for his daughter's safety. He excused himself from the table and tried to phone her again. It was a little after four o'clock, and he had been surprised that the phone had gone to the answer-phone again. This time he did leave a message, just explaining that he hadn't heard from her and just wanted to check she was okay. When he returned to the table, the look on his face said it all and James tried to reassure him that Sarah was probably just out. But the thought stayed with him, and he made the snap decision to pay his daughter a visit. It had been several years since he had last caught a train to Southampton, so James gave him a lift to the train station in Weymouth and helped him buy a ticket.

The train was packed full of people and he was lucky to find a seat. Earlier that day, a man had jumped in front of the Weymouth-bound train from Southampton, which had caused massive delays to the service. Thankfully the line had been cleared and services had resumed, but it meant that all those passengers who had been booked on trains that had not run, were crammed in wherever they could get. It angered him that some people could be so selfish, as to commit suicide in that manner. It caused untold disruption to so many others!

Alan had tried to phone his daughter twice before the train arrived at Southampton Central, but this time it told him the line was disconnected. This only served to fuel his fears more. As he exited the train station, he hailed a waiting taxi and gave his daughter's address. Ten minutes later, the taxi pulled up outside her Ocean Village apartment block. He gave the taxi driver ten pounds and didn't wait for his change. He ploughed up the steps to the front door of the building, and was grateful that another resident was leaving the building as he arrived. He ran, almost breathlessly up the two flights of stairs to her floor and then banged on the door. He could hear groaning on the other side of the door, and, imagining Ryan Moss throttling his little girl, he shoulder barged the door open.

The door swung inwards and crashed into the wall behind it. What he saw shocked him to the core. There was a trail of fresh blood leading from the door mat, along the hallway. It came to an abrupt stop where he saw his daughter bent over, head down against the floor, passed out. Behind her and clearly enjoying himself was an athletic-looking man, having rough sex with her.

43

The front door crashing open, had been so unexpected. Boller had been unsure of what he would see in the doorway, but the sweaty, old man struggling for breath had not been it.

Boller had been close to climax, when the old man had appeared and it had been enough to stop the urge. As he knelt there, astride Sarah, he was torn with what to do next. On the one hand, he was suitably aroused to continue, but he didn't really like the thought of the old man as an audience. There was also the fact that he didn't, as yet, know how the old man was going to react or who he even was. It was like a Mexican stand-off, neither knowing quite what the other would do.

Sarah wasn't struggling like she had been. In fact, as Boller moved his hands around her waist, she wasn't moving at all. Her back was arching up and down, ever so slightly, to indicate that she was still breathing, leading Boller to the conclusion that she must have passed out again from the drugs in her system.

The old man didn't seem to know what to say either, and he remained stood there in the door-way framed, like a still photograph. Boller knew one of them would have to react sooner or later, and was about to say something when the old man let out a horrendous bellow and charged towards him, rucksack still in hand.

'Get off her!' screamed the old man, as he hurtled down the corridor.

Boller was worried and withdrew himself from Sarah, pushing her towards the oncoming maniac, desperate to obstruct the path between them. The old man had his hands out in front of him, ready to wrap the dry, bony fingers around Boller's neck, when the opportunity presented itself. Boller was naked and vulnerable, and needed distance. He launched himself back and to the side, so that he was flying through the air and into Sarah's blood-stained bedroom. He landed on his back, but was agile enough to raise his legs above his head, and bring them crashing back down into the bedroom door, causing it to slam shut, preventing the old man from getting to him. A bang on the other side confirmed that old man had crashed into the door, but this time, he had not been strong enough to open it.

Boller's eyes darted around the bedroom, as he looked for something he could use to barricade the bedroom door, while he gathered his thoughts and tried to figure a way out of this ever-worsening predicament. In the end, he sat up and pushed his back against the door, to keep it from being opened.

He had originally planned to have sex with Sarah and then if she seemed to recall what had happened, once the drugs had worn off, he would have disposed of her body, as he had Natalie's. Whilst the police undoubtedly would have linked the two murders, there was no reason they would have tied it back to him. But now, the old man's arrival had scuppered that plan. Something inside would not allow him to kill the old man and dump two bodies; where would the bloodshed end?

But what was the alternative? The old man had seen him with Sarah, and even the best defence barrister in the world would not have been able to defend his actions as consensual. So, should he hand himself in? Accept a plea of sexual assault but deny the murder charges? It was possible that Sarah wouldn't remember him confessing to Natalie's, Rêmet's and the policewoman's murders and if she didn't, then he would be in the clear. Of course, if she did remember any of it, there was no guarantee the police would buy her story. Ultimately, it would come down to his word against hers, but then given that he would have just admitted to raping her, his word would not be worth a lot. At the very least, any claims she made about his involvement in the deaths of the three, would lead to the police sniffing about his place, and in his life, more than he desired.

Boller remained sat with his back to the door while he contemplated his options. All the time, he was listening out for the old man's voice, to understand who he was and what he was doing here.

44

Alan Jenson cradled his daughter's head in his hands. After the cowardly man had shut himself inside the room, he had scooped Sarah's exhausted body, into his arms and rested her back and head on his legs. From the amount of red smeared into the carpet, she had clearly lost a lot of blood, and it wasn't clear how long she had left before she would be in a critical condition. There were bruises forming on her front and side, suggesting that whatever that brute had done to her, it had been going on a while. Whilst every urge in his body was telling him to get up and kill the monster on the other side of the door, he knew his priority had to be taking care of Sarah and getting her some help. He reached into his pocket and fished out the mobile phone. Never had he been so grateful to have bought the device. On the floor, near the living room, he could see Sarah's home telephone. It was smashed into several pieces and the cable from the wall had been ripped out. At least that explained why he had been unable to get hold of her.

But who was the man behind the door? He certainly wasn't Ryan Moss. Just how many sexual predators did his daughter know? He had to admit, the rapist's face did look familiar, but he couldn't place where he had seen it before and wondered whether he was another of Sarah's former school mates. Whoever he was, he deserved to be behind bars and Alan Jenson vowed he would see that day.

He dialled '999' and advised the voice he required an ambulance urgently but would also need the police. The voice told him he could either be connected with the medical team or the police but not both. Alan looked down at his daughter's dwindling body and asked for the ambulance team. When he was connected, Alan quickly gave the address and told the woman on the phone that he had come to his daughter's house to find she was being sexually assaulted. When he told the woman the predator was still in the house, the woman obliged and said she would contact the local police to arrange for a patrol car to come to the property. The woman also suggested that Alan carry Sarah away from the property, and out of harm's way.

Sarah groggily began to come round, though she could not open her eyes. She was subconsciously aware that she had recently suffered a trauma, but her subconscious would not tell her what it was until she was ready.

'It's okay, sweetie,' Alan whispered to her. 'Daddy's here. Everything is going to be okay.'

45

So, the old man was Sarah's father, Boller thought to himself. It might make sense. Until he had heard the old man say that everything would be okay, he had assumed the old man was an elderly neighbour, sticking his nose in, where it was not wanted. That he was Sarah's father made things more complicated.

Whilst he had been sat in the bedroom, listening to the old man phoning for an ambulance, he had come up with two further options available to him. The first had been to offer Sarah and the old man a significant amount of money to keep their mouths shut about what had happened. That was what he had done in Baden, all those years ago with the two team mates who had watched him kill Nichole. He had managed to threaten the third into keeping quiet, but he didn't think his threats would work on Sarah and the old man. Now that he knew the old man was in fact Sarah's father, he knew no man in his right mind would idly sit by and accept hush money from the man who had raped his daughter. Not even a million pounds would buy his silence. Had he been a neighbour, maybe things would have been different.

Having ruled that option out, Boller knew he had only one other choice, assuming he didn't kill his witnesses: to run away.

He had made plenty of money in his time as a footballer, and, under his father's astute advice, had been siphoning off a large portion of his salary into a private bank account in his homeland. It was a special account that had been set up in his name, with no obvious trace to either of his British bank accounts, and as such, no way that the money could be traced by the Revenue and Customs officials of the country. This also, meant, by chance, that the police would be unable to trace the account. It seemed drastic, but Boller was genuinely considering re-starting his life, in another country, with a new name, and living off the proceeds of his Swiss account. It would mean turning his back on his football career, as there was no way he would ever be able to step back into the limelight again. A life without football or a life behind bars: There was no contest!

His mind made up, he needed to move fast. His Ferrari was parked outside the flat, on the street below. He would need to drive home to collect his passport and some cash. He had ten thousand pounds sat in his safe, for emergencies and this seemed as good a time as any to use it. It would take about twenty minutes to get home, as traffic would be minimal at this time. He had a friend who owned a small, two-person Microlight aircraft. For the right sum, his friend would be able to fly him to France, and from there he would have to call in favours to get himself out of Europe. He was confident he knew enough people in France to obtain a false passport, allowing him to escape to a South American country without an extradition treaty. From there he would just disappear and adopt his new persona.

He paused, as he re-considered what he was about to do. He was going to turn his back on his life, his fans, his friends, his family and his dream of representing his country on the international stage.

Was he really making the right decision?

On the other side of the door, he could hear Sarah slowly coming round. She wasn't coherent yet, but from the sound of her groggy voice, he knew it wouldn't be long until she regained control of her mind. She would have a killer of a headache, but that would pass after a while.

Boller was sat naked, propped up against the door. As he looked down, he could see Sarah's blood drying on him; he looked a mess. That wouldn't matter though, he thought. Once he was safely out of the country and on his way to a new life, he could wash this old life behind then. Boller stood up as quietly as he could, keen not to alert the old man that he was moving around, and therefore, no longer blocking the door. He found his trousers in a heap, in the corner of the room, where he had left them. He quickly pulled them over his legs, and fastened the button and belt. He found his shirt down near the bedroom door, and noticed that it had started to soak up some of the blood from the pool on the floor. It felt wet and sticky as he placed it around his shoulders. It would have to do. He could always put a fresh shirt on, when he arrived home.

Boller figured that the ambulance would be along in the next ten minutes, but the police were unlikely to arrive before twenty minutes. By the time they had taken witness statements from the half-comatose Sarah and her father, he would be home collecting his passport and money. The officers would need to obtain agreement from someone senior before they would head to his house, so he probably had about an hour to be on his way. That would be plenty of time to phone his friend with the Microlight, and get them both to the private air strip, from where they would depart from. The police would undoubtedly watch the airports in Southampton and London for trace of him, as well as the ports in Southampton and Portsmouth. Leaving in the Microlight would avoid possible detention. If his friend landed the plane in a field in France, the French authorities would not even be aware he was there.

Boller looked for his shoes, but they didn't seem to be anywhere in the room. He must have left them in the hallway somewhere, and he grimaced at the thought that he would have to drive with his bare feet.

Boller heard movement outside the door, and sensed that Sarah was trying to sit up, while her father tried to keep her down, resting. Boller looked over at the main bedroom window. It was large enough to fit his body through but as he moved over to it, he was disappointed to find there was no balcony. He had thought there would be one that he could climb over and then drop the shorter distance to the floor below. He looked back at the door and wondered whether he could move quick enough to open the door, jump over the other two and head out of the main door. It was too dangerous to attempt. There was every chance that the old man would get a grip on him, or scream for help, and then he would be trapped. No, he resolved, the window was the only option. He just hoped the drop to the floor would not be too vast.

46

Sarah opened her eyes, and this time managed to keep them open. She felt nauseous, and a pain was starting to form behind her eyes. Her legs ached, in particular her thighs, and she wondered whether she was suffering the effects of a heavy gym session, such was the ache. She was lying on a hard surface; a floor, not her bed. She could now sense that somebody was cradling her head. Was it Erin?

She looked up and was surprised to see the wise, old eyes of her father staring back at her. He appeared to be crying and she wondered why.

Where was she? Why was she in such pain?

Sarah suddenly became aware a cold, sticky liquid between her legs. She moved her hand up so that she could see what the substance was and the deep, crimson stain on her fingers told her it was blood. Oh God, she was bleeding.

Was that why her father was crying?

Sarah's mind continued to try and process the various details of her situation when she heard her father speak.

'It's okay, sweetie. I'm here. Everything will be okay.'

Sarah didn't like being kept in the dark. She had always been the sort of person who needed to know exactly what was going on. She sat upright, and, nearly as quickly, fell back down. The pain behind her eyes was spreading to her temple.

'Easy, there, sweetie,' her father cooed, lovingly.

Sarah attempted to sit up again, this time taking it slower so that she could better manage the pain in her head. Her father adjusted his position, so that he could support her back.

'What are you doing here, dad?' she asked when she realised she was actually in her own flat and not in her father's house. 'What is going on?'

'It's okay, sweetie,' he soothed again. 'There's nothing to worry about. You had an accident, but an ambulance is on its way.'

'An ambulance? What happened?' she asked, unable to hide the alarm in her voice, as her eyes saw the blood trail leading from the front door.

'Don't worry about that for now,' he said eager to keep her calm.

'Dad, tell me what happened,' she said more firmly.

Her father was about to try and pacify her again when they both heard the distinct sound of the window opening in the bedroom.

'Who is in my bedroom, dad? Why are they opening the window?'

47

Boller cursed under his breath, as the hinge of the bedroom window creaked loudly. They were bound to have heard it. As he poked his head out into the night air, he looked down and gulped at the distance between the window and the ground. It must have been a good thirty foot drop. Even if he dangled from the edge of the window sill, he would still drop nearly twenty five feet, and, without anything to protect his feet, the pain would be excruciating. He would be lucky not to break a bone.

A noise behind him caused him to turn. The door handle was rattling. Somebody was coming into the room.

Boller panicked and poked his left leg out of the window, pausing so that he could sit on the lower frame of the window. A cool breeze blew on the toes of the outstretched leg. He heard the door behind him open and it was all the encouragement he needed to swing his right leg up and out into the night air. He was now sat on the window frame with both legs dangling perilously over the edge. For his plan to work, he would need to swivel from his bottom to his waist, before slowly lowering himself until he was only holding onto the ledge by his fingertips.

As he heard footsteps enter the room, he vaulted his body around so that the frame was digging into his belly and he could see Sarah's dad, striding towards him. There was hatred in the old man's eyes that

322

caused Boller's eyes to widen. There was no turning back now. The old man would not be satisfied until he had inflicted pain on him. It was now or never.

The thought of falling through the air, to certain injury was preventing Boller from moving. He knew that if he didn't start to lower himself soon, the old man would be upon him and his chance of escape would be gone.

Boller tried to feel for the brickwork of the outer wall with his toes. He moved from leaning on his belly, to leaning on his elbows and slowly moved his right elbow out so that his right hand held the ledge. All he needed to do now was push his left elbow out and cling on with his left hand.

'Oh no you don't!' came the old man's voice as he gripped hold of Boller's collar.

The surprise forced Boller's elbow out, and now he was clinging to the edge of the window frame with outstretched fingers. The old man's grip was tight on his shirt, but Boller knew that if he let go of the ledge, the old man wouldn't have the strength to keep him from dropping. The fear of letting go, still gripped Boller and so he continued to hang from the ledge, with the old man holding onto him.

Boller could hear Sarah calling out to her father somewhere further back in the room.

'Let go of me, old man!' Boller yelled up into his captor's face.

The old man seemed to consider the demand, and glanced back at his daughter, before releasing his grip on Boller's shirt. Boller grinned as he realised he was now free to drop and hopefully get away. What he didn't expect was for the old man to reach out, grip onto the window's handle and pull it closed.

Boller's eyes widened once more, as he realised his fingers were going to get caught in the closing window and that the decision to let go would be thrust from his hands. Before he could react, he felt the plastic window frame begin to squeeze the fingers of his right hand.

He let out a scream of agony and his left hand shot across to try and protect his right hand, but as it did, he lost his grip on the window, and then he was falling through the air, bottom first, with his hands, arms, legs and feet flailing.

Boller knew he was in a bad way, as soon as he connected with the onrushing ground. He heard a definite snap, as bones broke and the shock of what had happened, kept him flat against the floor, unable to move.

48

Sarah was sat on the end of her bed, when the Paramedics arrived at the flat. She was drinking from a glass of water, still nursing the worst kind of headache she had ever experienced. One of the paramedics remarked how pale she looked, and upon seeing the various trails of blood around the hallway and bedroom, he indicated it would be a good idea to get her to hospital, sooner rather than later. Her father had draped a dressing gown around her shoulders, and the same paramedic asked her if she felt able to walk or whether it would be better to strap her to a stretcher. Sarah attempted to stand to show she was capable of walking but the second paramedic soon ushered her to sit back down, when she noticed the damage to Sarah's pelvic area.

The decision was made and a stretcher was fetched from the nearby-stationed ambulance. Five minutes later, Sarah was in the ambulance, her worried father sat by her side, holding her hand, and trying to hide the concerned look that was visible on his face.

For Alan Jenson, seeing his daughter's assailant falling from the window was an incredibly satisfying image. It wasn't until the ambulance was well on its way that he even decided to mention that there was an injured man back at the flat. The paramedic asked him to describe what happened and Alan told him that his daughter's assailant had fallen from the bedroom window, while trying to make his escape. He neglected to mention the part he had played in the fall.

The first paramedic, who was driving, radioed to control and advised another team would need to return to the flat to check on a possible second casualty. Sarah's condition was deemed too serious for this team to return. Alan tried to fill the second paramedic in on what had happened, but his details were sketchy, and Sarah's memory would not allow her to remember the gruesome details; whether this was because she had repressed the memories, or whether it was a side-effect of the flunitrazepam in the wine, was anyone's guess.

The paramedic attending Sarah, whose name was Maisie, advised them that there was definite evidence of sexual activity, and as they were claiming it had been non-consensual, there would be a requirement to involve the police, make a statement and for various photographs to be taken. Maisie wanted to check that Sarah was prepared for what was to come. Sarah looked the paramedic straight in the eye, and said that she would fight until she saw justice served.

The second team of paramedics arrived at the flat ten minutes later. They found Boller in the same position on the ground, where he had landed. They didn't recognise him at first, as there was limited light, the sun having set. The police arrived at the apartment block minutes later, and based on the brief description of the evening's events that Alan Jenson had provided to Maisie, they began to seal Sarah's home off, in preparation for the SOCOs to arrive and process the scene.

Boller was carefully lifted onto a stretcher and a

neck immobiliser was applied, to prevent any further spinal damage occurring. When he had been discovered, he had been weeping gently. The paramedics had assumed it was because he was in considerable pain. The truth was, Boller could not feel a thing below his waist. His tears came from knowing that his plan to escape had failed, but that also he would never have the opportunity to realise his ambition of representing his country in football. Whether he would ever regain feeling in his legs was unknown at this point, but he knew a convicted rapist and murderer would never be selected to play football, regardless of their talent. Boller wept, because his career and life as he knew it, was over.

Boller was transported to Southampton's General Hospital, as was Sarah, but they were both taken to separate, private rooms for treatment.

*

D.I. Jack Vincent visited Sarah at the hospital the following morning. It was by chance that he had called round to her apartment to break the news about Claude Rêmet's untimely passing and had found officers processing the scene. He was able to find out what had happened to Sarah overnight, and the rumour was that it was local football star Johan Boller, who was guilty of the attack.

Vincent was carrying a bunch of flowers, as he entered Sarah's room. She was sleeping, the doctor having prescribed something to help her rest. Vincent introduced himself to Alan Jenson and explained that he had been Erin's boss. Sarah woke while they were talking and he explained the circumstances in which he had found Claude Rêmet.

'And you're sure he died of natural causes?' Sarah asked, incredulous.

'We are still awaiting the toxicology report, to see if there was anything in his blood. It certainly looked like he had just gotten over excited, mid-passion,' Vincent admitted.

'It just seems a bit convenient,' Sarah remarked.

'In what way?' Vincent asked, not sure why Sarah thought it would be anything else.

'Rêmet told me he had evidence linking Johan Boller with the assault and death of a little girl in Switzerland five years ago. He told me he had a photograph, taken in Switzerland, showing Boller in a compromising position with the little girl. He told me he believed Boller had taken Natalie as well.'

Vincent stood there with his mouth open.

'You told me he hadn't named his suspect!' Vincent spat out.

'That was before he raped and tried to kill me!' Sarah said. 'It was him, Detective Inspector. It was all him.'

'Look, Sarah,' Vincent began, 'I appreciate you've been through a traumatic experience, but there is no evidence to link Mr Boller to the other crimes. I mean, did he confess something to you that you're not telling me?'

'No...I don't know...I can't remember what happened...not properly.'

'We found your Ryan Moss, by the way,' continued Vincent.

'Moss?' spluttered Sarah's father.

'It's okay, dad,' said Sarah. 'Ryan didn't have anything to do with what happened to Natalie. He came and saw me and we talked. I think he was looking for some kind of forgiveness for what happened all those years ago; not that I'm sure I can. He said he was planning to go away somewhere but he didn't say the location. Where did you find him?'

Vincent paused before saying, 'He jumped in front of a passenger train near Southampton yesterday afternoon. At least that's what we've established from the remains we discovered. Nasty business, if you ask me.'

Sarah's head moved to the side as she tried to hide her tears.

'My daughter needs to rest, Detective Inspector,' said her father, stroking her head reassuringly.

'I will personally look into Mr Boller's whereabouts on the dates in question,' said Vincent after a while. 'But without anything concrete to go on, my hands are somewhat tied.'

'Well, you should at least be able to charge him with my daughter's assault,' said Alan Jenson, glaring at Vincent.

'I need to speak to you about that as well,' replied Vincent reluctantly.

'What do you mean?' asked Sarah, uncertain about Vincent's tone of voice.

'Mr Boller is claiming that you invited him around for dinner last night, seduced him into having sex with you and then he was chased from the property when your over-bearing father came in and saw you at it.'

Alan Jenson stood, as if he was going to charge at Vincent. Vincent took two steps backward.

'Look,' Vincent added, 'they're his words, not mine. He has even asked to press charges against you

Mr Jenson for pushing him from the window frame.'

'That's nonsense!' bellowed Alan.

'Mr Boller has been with his solicitor since he arrived at the hospital last night,' Vincent continued. 'He is some fancy-dan from London, by all accounts, although I haven't met him yet.'

'My flat,' said Sarah suddenly sitting up in bed as a thought struck her.

'What about it?' asked Vincent, jumping slightly at Sarah's sudden movement.

'There should be a recording of what happened last night. I had some surveillance equipment installed before he came over. Listen to the recording and then make your own mind up about what happened,' said Sarah triumphantly.

*

Vincent made his way from the hospital directly to Sarah's flat. He had been due to call in on Boller before he left the hospital, but Sarah's claim about a recording of what had happened, had intrigued him. The SOCOs had finished dusting for prints and taking photographs of the flat and most of the crime scene tape had been removed. A single, uniformed officer was stood outside of Sarah's apartment building when he arrived. Vincent flashed his warrant card and was allowed entry. Sarah had told him that the equipment had been installed by a former colleague of Erin's, a chap by the name of Dudley. Vincent had recognised the man's voice as soon as he phoned the electrical shop, where the equipment had been purchased. Dudley had been happy to talk Vincent through what he had installed and where the central recording deck could be located.

Vincent moved through the apartment and headed for the kitchen. In the cupboard, immediately below the sink, he located a small box the size of a matchbox. He disconnected the box from the cable it was attached to and placed it in his pocket. He left the apartment and made his way back to the police station. Once he was in his office and sat comfortably, he plugged the box into his computer via a USB cable and then proceeded to listen to the recording.

By the end of the recording, he was reaching for the bottle of scotch that he had hidden in his desk drawer. He had only replaced the bottle last night, but he felt he needed something, after what he had heard on the recording. Hearing Boller confess to the murders of Natalie, Rêmet, and ultimately Erin made him see red. Boller's claim that the sex had been consensual was clearly a lie, designed to keep him out of prison. Vincent vowed that he would do everything in his power to take Boller down.

The issue he had was that the tape recording would probably be deemed inadmissible in court, and as such it wasn't evidence that they could use against the footballer. That said, it gave Vincent all the evidence he personally needed to launch a full investigation into Johan Boller's movements in the last week. There would be evidence in Boller's house and car of his actions, and so long as he could acquire a search warrant to undertake these checks, he knew he would be able to build a case.

Vincent knocked back the remains of his glass of whiskey and placed the tumbler on his desk. He then reached into his pocket and withdrew a packet of chewing gum, popping two pieces into his mouth. He had an important journey to make and he didn't want to leave the tell-tale smell of booze on his breath when he got there. He opened the door to his office, and switched the light off as he left. He had a broad smile on his face, and it was the first time since he had contemplated taking his own life on Wednesday night, that he felt glad to be alive. His life had a new purpose: he was going to bring Johan Boller to justice for all the crimes he had committed. He even began to whistle, as he headed into the underground car park, towards his squad car. His next stop was Southampton's General Hospital. He was going to visit Johan Boller and laugh in his face when he lied about the previous week's events.

Vincent glanced upwards and offered a silent prayer of thanks to the pair of angels who were clearly watching over; urging him to fight on.

Epilogue

Jack Vincent sat outside Court Room Two at Winchester Crown Court. The jury had withdrawn two hours ago, to consider the facts they had been presented with. He understood why Sarah Jenson didn't want to be here today. The defendant's barrister had grilled her hard when she had been called to the stand to present her version of events, following the abduction of Natalie Barrett, seven months ago. He could appreciate why she had no desire to relive what had happened, through each side's closing statements. He had promised to phone her the moment the verdict was released.

It had taken some time to collate all the facts of the case that the jury had been provided with. As suspected, the recording of Sarah's rape was not permitted to be played in court, as it had been recorded without the permission of the defendant. It had served the unique purpose of giving Vincent the impetus to find as much evidence against Boller as he could. Vincent had developed the habit of listening to the recording of Boller's confession each morning, so that he never lost sight of the end goal.

The forensics team had had a field day examining the inside of Boller's house. They had found a significant volume of congealed blood under the laminate flooring of Boller's kitchen, and the blood had proved a match to that of Natalie Barrett. This, added to the fibres of the girl's skin found in his boot, and even Boller's barrister had told him to cop a plea to kidnap and accidental death.

Proving his involvement in the abduction and murder of Nichole Brunel, had not been so easy. Although that murder had happened on foreign soil, Vincent had argued to hear the case in the U.K. due its similarities to the Barrett case. Despite Sarah's recollections of what Rêmet had told her, they could not discover any evidence to prove that Boller had been in the shed where the assault had occurred, or that he had even been in the vicinity of the camp site. It was another reason why Sarah was not in court today.

The facts that the jury were currently reviewing related to the sexual assault. Boller's discovery outside of the flat, along with Alan Jenson's eye witness testimony, should have been enough to see him convicted and further incarceration being added to his sentence. Boller's barrister was very experienced at getting his clients out of assault charges and was very popular amongst Premiership footballers. Vincent couldn't help but worry that the magician would work his tricks again today.

Since her release from hospital, Vincent had spent a significant amount of time working closely with Sarah Jenson on each of the aspects of the Natalie Barrett case. Where he had originally laughed at some of her outlandish theories, he had grown to respect her insight into the case.

Officer Kyle Davies had continued to look into the whereabouts of Neil Barrett on the day Natalie had gone missing. He had learned that Barrett had been doing some extra jobs for his boss, when business had been quiet: namely delivering small packages to acquaintances, under the guise of repairing vehicles by the road-side. In many ways, it had been the perfect cover: two apparent strangers, meeting in the middle of nowhere, sharing a conversation nobody else would hear or see.

After Boller's arrest and confession, when Barrett had returned to work, Davies had followed him on several call-outs, and had observed the exchanges from a distance. Vincent could not believe his luck; not only had he captured the man responsible for abducting Natalie Barrett, he had also uncovered an international drugs ring, operating in Southampton. Overnight, he became the local media's golden boy, and D.C.I. Young had been quoted in several interviews, praising Vincent's methods of deduction. He had even been described as the 'new Holmes' by one magazine, a quote he had cut out and stuck up on the fridge in his flat.

Neil Barrett had been cautioned for his part in the operation, after turning chief witness and sharing all he knew about the operation. The case against the Stratovsky family was still on-going up in London and Vincent was due to appear in that case any day now. Several witnesses in the case had been threatened already, so Neil, Melanie and Jimmy Barrett had been taken into witness protection and moved to an unknown location, somewhere in the Midlands, for their own safety, until such time as Neil would testify in court.

Cookie's funeral had been incredibly moving, and Vincent had been honoured when Sarah had asked him to read a eulogy at the service. He had spoken with great pride about how well she had worked under him and how he hoped that other existing officers would take a leaf out of her book: to lay it all on the line. There had been tears, of course, but it had been a great way of finding closure. Although he still blamed himself for allowing Cookie and Ali Jacobs to come to harm, he had found solace in the promise that he would fight harder than ever, to see criminals brought to justice, in their memory. He had put Kyle Davies forward for promotion and although he had only recently joined Vincent's team on a permanent basis, the D.C.I. had agreed to Davies' promotion to Detective Sergeant. Vincent saw a bright future for Davies.

Vincent looked up as he heard the Court Usher call for parties to return to Court Two; the verdict was in. Johan Boller rolled by in his wheelchair, flanked by an officer either side of him. The usual protocol for the suspect to be brought up from the holding cell beneath the court had been waved, as there was no wheelchair access. Vincent refused to make eye contact with the young man, as he didn't want to see the look of self-pity. Boller was where he was because of his own actions, and Vincent just hoped that the jury was smart enough to see through the cloud of uncertainty, presented by the defence.

Vincent dialled Sarah's number and held the phone to his ear. It rang twice before he heard her voice answer.

'Is it in?' she asked eagerly.

'Not yet, but I'm heading in now,' he replied.

'What do you think it will be?'

'I'm not sure,' he replied honestly. 'They've only been away for a couple of hours, which either means they have been utterly convinced by the evidence, or utterly unconvinced. I don't know how to call it. I just wanted you to know that the verdict is imminent.'

'Thank you,' she said calmly.

'Where are you now?'

'I've just arrived in Baden. Nichole's parents have a farm on the edge of the town. I hope they are home, as they still don't know I'm coming or why.'

'Do you think they will believe you?' Vincent asked.

'I think they will, yes. I think it is important they know who killed their daughter and I believe they will be relieved to hear that he is going to prison for his crimes, even if it isn't specifically for the murder of their daughter.'

'Is your father still with you?'

'No. I left him and Veronica in Berne, sight-seeing. They have been through enough. I don't need them to hear what I have to say to the Brunel family.'

'Are they enjoying their honeymoon?'

'I'm sure they would rather I wasn't tagging along, but dad said he wouldn't feel comfortable, leaving me in the U.K. while they were away. They have their own room at the opposite end of the hotel we're staying in, so at least they have some privacy.'

Vincent laughed and wished her luck with finding the farm. He finished by telling her he would phone back in five minutes or so. Vincent turned the phone off and placed it back in his pocket, before strolling towards the door and entering the courtroom.

The End

ALSO BY STEPHEN EDGER

Integration

Its 3 a.m. you are alone in bed. A noise wakes you. It is the sound of the front door opening. There is an intruder in your house. What do you do? Confront them or hide?

Mark Baines has been offered one million pounds to carry out a 'favour' for a voice on his answer-phone. What is the 'favour'? Is he prepared to risk everything for the money? Will he actually have a choice?

They will do anything to get what they want.

They won't take 'no' for an answer.

Everyone has their price…

ALSO BY STEPHEN EDGER

Remorse

'I didn't mean to kill her. That is the first thing you need to understand about me...'

So begins the story of John Duggan: locked in a prison cell, his fairytale life in tatters. A week ago he was a happily married father with a four month old daughter and a career on the up. Now he is facing a life behind bars for killing one of them. Where did it all go so wrong?

Discovering that his wife is cheating on him, John Duggan deals with it the only way he knows how; getting his revenge. Hiring a Private Detective with a shady past to spy on her and getting drunk to cope with the relentlessly screaming baby makes him a ticking time bomb ready to explode. As his stress levels reach a dangerous high, he is going to learn a valuable lesson about life.

Not every fairy-tale has a happy ending…

ALSO BY STEPHEN EDGER

Redemption

A year ago, Mark Baines was blackmailed into laundering two hundred and fifty million pounds through the bank he worked for. The same people framed him for murder. Now serving two life sentences in a maximum security prison, the future looks bleak.

On Christmas Day the prison is breached and Mark is abducted by an unknown group. They are after a mysterious package that is locked in a secret vault deep within the foundations of a tower in Canary Wharf and they believe Mark is the key to finding it.

Ali Jacobs is still undercover, trying to infiltrate the Russian mafia. Now based in London, she is shocked when her path brings her into contact with Mark again.

The next seven days will define their lives.

Kidnap, car chases, a botched MI6 operation and an uneasy union with underworld figures mean Mark is in a race against time to prove his innocence and find redemption.